praise for r—

"Expertly blends witty banter, symp[a]... ters, descriptive worldbuilding, and so[me]... crimes with all-too-believable motives. ... creative supernatural elements will hold readers' attention. ... Lively supernatural investigations with humor and heart."

—*Kirkus Reviews*

"A fun, supernatural and historical mystery."

—*Youth Services Book Review*

"Well done, and will help new readers find this series in all its amazingness."

—*YABC*

praise for the jackaby series:

"Sherlock Holmes crossed with Buffy the Vampire Slayer."

—*Chicago Tribune*

"Fast-paced and full of intrigue."

—EW.com

"We honestly couldn't put it down."

—Nerdist.com

"With tension as taut as a high wire, this series blends laugh-out-loud humor and ghastly horror with supernatural skill ... Perfect for fans of Harry Potter, *Grimm*, and Sherlock Holmes."

—*Justine* magazine

★ "Humor, adventure, mystery, gore, and romance all rolled into one well-written package."

—*SLJ*, starred review

rook

Also by William Ritter

The Jackaby Series
Jackaby
Beastly Bones
Ghostly Echoes
The Dire King

The Oddmire Series
Changeling
The Unready Queen
Deepest, Darkest

rook

william ritter

ALGONQUIN YOUNG READERS
WORKMAN PUBLISHING
NEW YORK

This book is a work of fiction. Names, characters, places, and incidents are the product of the author's imagination or are used fictitiously. Any resemblance to actual events, locales, or persons, living or dead, is coincidental.

Copyright © 2024 by William Ritter

Hachette Book Group supports the right to free expression and the value of copyright. The purpose of copyright is to encourage writers and artists to produce the creative works that enrich our culture.

The scanning, uploading, and distribution of this book without permission is a theft of the author's intellectual property. If you would like permission to use material from the book (other than for review purposes), please contact permissions@hbgusa.com. Thank you for your support of the author's rights.

Algonquin Young Readers
Workman Publishing
Hachette Book Group, Inc.
1290 Avenue of the Americas
New York, NY 10104
workman.com

Algonquin Young Readers is an imprint of Workman Publishing, a division of Hachette Book Group, Inc. The Workman name and logo are registered trademarks of Hachette Book Group, Inc.

Design by Joel Tippie

The publisher is not responsible for websites (or their content) that are not owned by the publisher.

The Hachette Speakers Bureau provides a wide range of authors for speaking events. To find out more, go to hachettespeakersbureau.com or email HachetteSpeakers@hbgusa.com.

Workman books may be purchased in bulk for business, educational, or promotional use. For information, please contact your local bookseller or the Hachette Book Group Special Markets Department at special.markets@hbgusa.com.

LIBRARY OF CONGRESS CATALOGING-IN-PUBLICATION DATA
Ritter, William.
Jackaby / William Ritter.—First edition.
pages cm
Summary: Newly arrived in 1892 New England, Abigail Rook becomes assistant to R. F. Jackaby, an investigator of the unexplained with the ability to see supernatural beings, and she helps him delve into a case of serial murder which, Jackaby is convinced, is due to a nonhuman creature. ISBN 9781643752402 (hardcover) | ISBN 9781523526765 (paperback) | ISBN 9781649041371 (ebook) [1. Mystery and detective stories. 2. Serial killers—Fiction. 3. Murder— Fiction. 4. Supernatural—Fiction. 5. Imaginary creatures—Fiction. 6. New England— History 19th century—Fiction.] I. Title. PZ7.R516Jac2014 [Fic]—dc23
First Trade Paperback Edition
Originally published in hardcover by Algonquin Young Readers in August 2023.
Printed in the USA on responsibly sourced paper.

10 9 8 7 6 5 4 3 2 1

This one is for Ashli, Elizaveta, Meghan, Evangeline, and Eddie—and for so many more amazing readers who have breathed life into New Fiddleham and kept the lights glowing, even while I was away.

rook

chapter one

Life goes on—which I have always felt was rude on life's part. It comes crashing into us at full speed, leaves us reeling, and doesn't spare so much as a backward glance as we drag ourselves back to our feet in its dust. It isn't that life doesn't care—although, to be clear, *it doesn't*—it's that life clearly has its own agenda, and no intention of pausing to let the rest of us catch our breath.

I was already out of breath as I crested a hill looking out over the busy streets of New Fiddleham. My mentor had a naturally rapid gait, and it had been too long since I'd had any practice keeping pace. "A moment, if you don't mind, Mr. Jackaby," I called.

"Of course." He paused to stand in what he might have believed was a nonchalant posture, leaning stiffly with his shoulder against a lamppost and his hands in the pockets of his tatty old duster while he waited for me. His restlessness was palpable—it crawled under his lapels and clambered through his messy hair. The man's impatience had little to do with today's hike and everything to do with *me*. I couldn't blame him.

"I'm sorry," I said.

"Don't apologize," he chided, but his aura churned.

Auras, for those who have the good fortune of not being able to see them, look a bit like a glowing light and a bit like wispy smoke and a bit like a dream you tried to hold in your mind after waking up. Auras are slippery. They're also everywhere. *Everything* has its own energy. Sometimes that energy is simple—an average brick's energy is ruddy and brick-shaped; an average pebble's is small and pale. Other times, an aura is a hundred times larger and more complicated than the physical object generating it. A simple silver brooch could fill a room with waves of midnight and sadness, or a strand of hair could burn as bright as a bonfire. That might all sound like a dazzling spectacle, and it is, but one does not wish to be *dazzled* when one is trying to butter a potato. One wishes that a potato would just sit still and be a potato for five blessed minutes. Auras are exhausting. And I had spent my formative months as a Seer sequestered in a building packed with my mentor's paranormal relics and crime scene mementos. They dazzled ceaselessly.

Until recently, Jackaby had been the one to see auras, and he had been good at it. He had made a career out of it, solving impossible mysteries by following invisible clues. The sight should have remained his until the day he died—and technically it had. Fortunately, Jackaby's untimely demise had only been temporary. Less fortunately, his supernatural sight had transferred itself behind my unready eyelids the moment his heart had stopped beating, and there it had remained even after his resuscitation. The power was mine now, whether I wanted it or not.

"Shall we?" Jackaby asked.

I nodded, following him under a narrow brick arch. My eye twitched as we crossed through the tight alleyway. The space was claustrophobic, and the air was thick with the electric grays of anxiety and fear. One wall had been splattered with dull red paint, in which someone had hastily scrawled the words *MUNDUS NOSTER*. Each letter thrummed angrily. It made me feel itchy, like scar tissue forming around a cut.

"What's that?" I asked aloud.

"Hmm?" Jackaby followed my gaze. His lip twisted in a brief sneer. "Don't pay it any mind. Just local gangs demonstrating typical New Fiddleham hospitality. At least they've put some effort into their Latin this time. *Our world.* Not particularly original. I've seen four or five variations in the past week."

I swallowed. "Is that normal?" I asked.

Jackaby didn't answer. He didn't have to. His aura churned faster.

"This is why you wanted me to get back out into the city, isn't it?" I said. "To see things like that for myself?"

"You are *not* responsible for stopping every vandal in New Fiddleham, Miss Rook," Jackaby replied. He kept his eyes fixed forward. "I told you already, this trip is only for practice. No ulterior motives. No pressure. When you are ready, you're ready." A few agitated pinwheels of anxiety spun off his aura, but he kept his expression flat. "You've been cooped up for months. It's good for you to get back into the world, breathe some fresh air." He sniffed. "Or at least some New Fiddleham air. Mind that sticky-looking puddle, there."

He had a point. It had been ages since I had ventured more than a few blocks from home, and on those rare out-ings I tended to keep my attention on the cobblestones. The house had become my safe haven. Granted, it was *also* a safe haven to several species of supernatural wildlife, a handful of temperamental nature spirits, and at least one ghost—but none of those things were as frightening to me as the outside world. As it happens, the resident ghost of 926 Augur Lane had become one of my dearest friends of late. Her name was Jenny Cavanaugh, and she would have given you the coat off her own back, if that coat had not also been a spectral apparition incapable of passing to mortal hands.

I picked up the skirts of my walking dress as I hurried to stay fast on Jackaby's heels. "So this whole exercise isn't even a tiny bit about the commissioner's request?" I asked.

"Hmm? What was that?" Jackaby deflected clumsily.

"For a consultation? I saw the letter in your office."

"Ah. Well. No, this trip is certainly *not* about Commissioner Marlowe. Unless . . ." He raised his eyebrows at me. "Unless you felt like you *were* ready?" A faint hint of bright turquoise formed a hopeful little halo behind his head. "It's only that the police are ill-equipped for a lot of the new cases coming their way. I've been assisting here and there when I can, but the sight would be particularly helpful right about now."

"I don't know." I took a deep breath. "I'm so sorry. I *want* to be ready, truly. Jenny says—"

"It's fine," Jackaby said, hurriedly. "It's fine. His requests can wait."

"Requests?" I asked. "More than one? How many has he sent?"

Jackaby's mouth hung open for a beat. His eyes darted to the left. "Look at that! We're here!" he declared. "Last stop for the day."

We had drawn up along the side of a wide building hewn from broad gray stones.

"Well?" he asked. "What do you think?"

An ordinary tour guide might have been encouraging me to take in the majestic sight of the Romanesque arches above us or perhaps the savory smells of the street vendors half a block ahead. I could tell that this was not my mentor's intention.

"See it?" Jackaby patted the wall beside him. "Should be just about here, yes?"

I nodded. "I see it," I said. "It looks like a stain—only it's not really there, is it?"

Jackaby beamed happily. "Of course it's there. Well. *I* can't see it—not anymore—but I remember it. What does it look like to you?"

I took a deep breath. "It's got layers," I said. "Dark green underneath, but not a proper green. It's a guilty sort of green? Like seaweed and shame. Then it gets lighter and more yellow as it warms up. It's . . . sparkly? It's like there are slivers of diamond mixed up in the bricks. They're good sparkles, I think. Mostly."

"Well, *Detective?*" Jackaby prompted. "You've got all the pieces of the puzzle. Take a guess. What's just on the other side of that wall?"

I bit my lip. For months, I had memorized the unique tints of specific creatures. Elven magic, troll musk, pixie dust—they all gave off distinct energies, like footprints. But the sight didn't stop at species. Every being, human or otherwise, had a history and memories that trailed behind them like swirling eddies, further coloring their energy. Fears and hopes saturated every passerby. Bang any two people together, and you'd find the air thick with a cloud of thoughts and emotions. Reading the residue that people left behind was like trying to tell what had been written on a blackboard based on the chalk dust coming off the erasers.

"Behind this wall is . . . a room?" It was like I had inherited an artist's priceless paints, but I could barely manage to scribble out a finger painting. "It seems like a place where a lot of people have visited."

"Okay," Jackaby said. "Move past the obvious, now. *Why* do people come here?"

"They come here . . . because they feel bad?" I ventured. "Except coming here makes them feel worse, I think. But feeling worse makes them feel . . . *better*, somehow?" My head was beginning to hurt. "Does any of that make sense?"

Jackaby nodded. "Nearly there. What sort of place is it?"

"A . . . pub?"

"So close." Jackaby snapped his fingers. Ripples of disappointment spread along his aura.

"Oh, just tell me."

"We're on the side of St. Mary's," he said. "Behind these bricks is the confessional. Remarkable how those heavy feelings have seeped all the way through solid stone over the years. Beautiful, too, isn't it? I always found it so hard to describe. You should really see the particles of guilt when they catch the light around sunset."

I ran my fingers over the swirling energies that clung to the wall. It *was* oddly pretty. I closed my eyes, but the colors still hung before me in darkness—the sight a stronger force than my own eyelids.

"Ready to head back?" Jackaby asked.

"Why should *guilt* be beautiful?" I asked. "It seems like guilt should be ugly, shouldn't it?"

Jackaby shrugged. "I suppose it's less about the emotion and more about the honesty of confessing." He adjusted the strap on his satchel. "Honesty's rare. Finding a place where you feel safe enough to be open and true—that's something special. I think the sight responds to that." He patted the wall once more, affectionately. "Shall we?"

The walk back toward Augur Lane took us over wide, winding streets, down narrow alleys framed by tall brick buildings, and past the stately grounds of St. Pantaloon's (the latter being a hospital that was supposed to be named for Saint Pantaleon, patron of physicians and mid-wives, but—due to a bit of sloppy cursive on the official documents—had been named, instead, for baggy women's trousers). One of the things I had come to love about living in New Fiddleham was that it refused to abide by the logic of any other town—nor by any logic at all, most days.

Since arriving, I had often mused that the city felt alive—that it hummed in the myriad voices of the people within its walls. In the past, the thought had been merely romantic. Now that I had the sight, the feeling had evolved into less of a metaphor and more of a firm observation. Walking through the city felt like clinging to the back of a great, powerful horse or burying my face in the soft fur of some gigantic bear. Even the cold cobblestones beneath my feet had a life to them, a history. They breathed. The air, perfumed by a mix of wash water and frying meats, carried with it something else as well—an essence that was more than scents on the breeze.

Generations of people had hung their dreams and fears and hopes on this city—I could see them as plainly as I could see the laundry strung between buildings. To countless people, this bulky, bustling beast of a town had meant more than bricks and mortar—it had meant opportunity and second chances. *This* city would be different than the last. *This* city would make manifest the lives they had been waiting for. Faithfully, desperately, countless souls had made the choice to believe in New Fiddleham, and their belief had given the city life. New Fiddleham *was* alive. But it was also aching.

"Is that Anton's bakery up ahead?" I asked.

Jackaby nodded, but his energy soured almost at once. "It might be faster if we cut up along Mason Street."

"Hang on." I furrowed my brow. Something was off. "Why is it all boarded up?"

Jackaby cleared his throat. "Erm. Anton decided it was time to move on," he said. "Packed up shop a month or two ago. A feral brownie swarm nested in the rafters as soon as he was gone, so I don't envy whoever tries to move in next."

My chest felt heavy as we continued past Anton's. Other shops had shuttered as well, and a few of them had broken windows. A cherry tree with a halo of wild magic was growing sideways out of the wall of a used bookstore. The sidewalk beneath it was littered with broken bricks and rotten cherries, as if the thing had simply punched its way out, rather than growing gradually over many years. An axe was buried in the tree trunk, but the bark had swollen around the axe head and trapped it. A soggy newspaper hung in one of the branches. It was tattered from the wind, but the words *The Paranormal Problem* stood out in bold font at the top of an editorial.

New Fiddleham had always been a city with troubles—its shadows had shadows—but I had been under the impression that things had been getting brighter. I eyed my mentor. "Is there something you're not telling me?"

"Loads of things," he confirmed without hesitation. "An octopus has three hearts. Spiderwebs make excellent bandages, provided you take the spiders out first. Let's see—interpreting cheese curds was a popular method of divination in the Middle Ages. It's called tyromancy."

"You know what I meant," I said.

Jackaby's jaw tightened and his pace slowed. "Seven," he said. "Commissioner Marlowe has reached out on seven separate occasions asking when you might be ready to consult again. He needs help. Between you and me, his officers are in way over their heads. And it's only getting worse."

"Why didn't you tell me things had gotten this bad?"

"Jenny felt it was best not to put too much pressure on you before you were ready." He fidgeted with the strap of his satchel. "I promised. And she's right. Besides, there's *always* a bit of bad," he added.

"This is more than a *bit*, though, isn't it?" I asked.

Faded yellow flecks flickered in Jackaby's aura as he wrestled with his answer. In the end, he settled for honesty. "It is concerning," he admitted.

I felt a numb weight in my stomach. "Is this all happening just because the Seer hasn't been around to solve everyone's strange problems?" I asked. "Were you always the secret linchpin holding this city together?"

"Not so secret," Jackaby grumbled. "I told them how important my work was as often as possible—not that anyone used to listen." He must have caught the expression on my face, because his tone quickly shifted. "No. This isn't your fault. Not even tyromancers could have seen things curdling quite like this. It's complicated. The battle at the rift—it exposed a lot of magical beings, some of whom had been living here in secret for years and many more who crossed over for the first time through the new gate. It shook things up, that's all."

"But paranormals stood alongside humans in that battle!" I said. "I was there! It united everyone." The words sounded naive even as I said them.

"Oh, the incident *did* bring people closer together," Jackaby said, heavily. "It turns out people hate being close. Have you ever ridden on a crowded train car? People up close can be deeply unsettling."

We passed a wall from which a wine barrel was protruding at a rakish angle at about head height. The masonry around the thing did not look like it had shifted, nor had the wood been cut or broken. Bricks and barrel simply appeared to be occupying the same space. A scrap of a label was just visible, poking out of the place where they met. It looked scorched, as if melding with the bricks had heated it to burning. I could see residual traces of energy still swirling around it.

"Things like this don't help." Jackaby patted the barrel as we passed. "Supernatural accidents, paranormal crimes, the occasional minor arson—this sort of thing used to come up every week or so, and I could typically handle each one quietly in a single afternoon. Except now they're cropping up with troubling frequency, and I can't . . ." He let the sentence trail off.

"No. You can't. But *I* could have," I said. "And I haven't been. I've been letting it all pile up for months and months."

Jackaby's chest rose and fell. I could see that he wanted to disagree, but his weary aura betrayed him.

"You should have told me," I said.

"Would knowing have made your training any easier? You weren't ready."

I opened my mouth to speak, but then shut it again.

After several paces, Jackaby rallied, willing himself to put on a halfhearted smile. "It's fine. Progress demands discomfort. New Fiddleham is growing to become a better version of itself, just as we all are. Every scuffle in the streets or angry bit of vandalism is merely a growing pain. Throwing yourself at New Fiddleham's problems before you overcome your own isn't going to help anyone—least of all *you*. Although, if you think you might be ready *soon* . . ."

Jackaby's words gradually faded to the back of my mind. My attention had snagged on a blue-black aura in a shady alleyway ahead. Sadness. Fear. Desperation. It was so intense, I could taste the feelings at the back of my mouth. I slowed down and stepped closer.

The figure in the alley was a child, slumped with her back against the bricks, her arms wrapped around her knees and her gaze fixed on the opposite wall. I glanced over to see what she was looking at. Facing her were several official-looking posters. They bore names and rough illustrations of half a dozen people, and each one was topped with the same bold heading: *MISSING*. A smaller, stiff script under each one encouraged citizens to report any information that might lead police to their whereabouts. Two of the posters had red paint splashed across them in crude Xs, and a third had the word *DEMON* scrawled across the drawing's face. Not far off, the wall had been treated to another inscription of the dark red *MUNDUS NOSTER*.

When I turned my eyes back to the girl, she was watching me intently.

"Hello there," I said, softly.

The girl didn't answer. Her eyes, rimmed with red, narrowed as she surveyed me. She had a smudge of soot on her cheek, and the hem of her dress was caked with dirt. Her hair was so black that it almost looked blue in the cool light of the alleyway.

"It's okay," I continued. "My name is Miss Rook. This is my friend Mr. Jackaby. What's your name?"

"Are you with the police?" she asked.

I glanced at Jackaby, who gave me an encouraging nod but remained silent. "Sometimes," I said, turning back to the girl. "Not recently."

"I'm not supposed to speak to police."

"Sound advice," I said. "They're dreary conversationalists, on the whole. You're much better off speaking to me."

"You talk funny," the girl said.

"I'm from England," I said. "I grew up in a town called Portsmouth. Lots of people sound like me in Portsmouth. Would it be all right with you if I sat down for a bit?"

She shrugged gloomily. "It's anyone's sidewalk."

I settled myself gently onto the ground a few feet away from her, our backs pressed against the same cool wall. "Portsmouth is a bit like New Fiddleham," I said. "Ships in the harbor. Church bells on Sunday. But it's different, too. There's nowhere in the world that feels quite like home, is there?"

The kid only watched me, warily.

"I like the ways New Fiddleham is different," I added. "It's good to be different. Different is beautiful."

"Maybe in Portsmouth it is," mumbled the kid.

For several seconds, we sat in silence.

"Do you know any of them?" I asked gently, indicating the posters.

"You ask a lotta questions," said the kid.

"I suppose I do." I nodded. "It's sort of my job to ask questions. I try to help people, if I can."

She sniffed and rolled her eyes. "You're not worried that you'll get your fancy dress all dirty?"

"Dirt's nothing," I told her. "You should have seen my skirts after I fought a whole dragon. I was a right mess."

"You didn't fight a dragon."

"I did," I said. "I've fought a lot of creatures."

She eyed me through narrow lids.

"You don't believe me," I said. "But I can do loads of things. For example, just by looking at you, I can tell that you've got a headstrong aura."

She rolled her eyes.

"And you've spent a good bit of time in a cemetery recently."

Her eyes ceased rolling.

"I'd wager that's where you've been sleeping, yes? Graveyard dirt glows much brighter than garden dirt. I've practiced a lot with dirts. You also ate a cherry tart not long ago—no—raspberry? It was stolen, which I always find makes them taste sweeter, don't you?"

The girl's mouth pursed tightly, her brow furrowed, and she pushed herself up to her feet. "Have you been following me?" she demanded.

"Nothing like that," I said.

"Stay away from me!" she cried, and bolted off down the alleyway.

"Wait!" I climbed to my feet. "I didn't mean—I only . . ."

She was already out of earshot.

"Yeah. You get used to that." Jackaby sighed. "Would you like to give chase?"

I shook my head, watching her vanish around the corner. With a sigh, I crossed the alley to get a closer look at the posters on the wall. The girl's aura hung heavily off one in particular; it was a sketch of a woman by the name of Mary Horne. She had been reported missing two weeks prior. My eyes darted from paper to paper. They were all so recent—none of them older than last month. The ones marred by red paint were known paranormal citizens—their descriptions included species. The others, including Horne, appeared to be human.

I took a slow, deep breath. "So," I said. "You say Commissioner Marlowe could use some help?"

Jackaby's aura bubbled. He failed utterly to conceal a smile. "Welcome back, Detective Rook."

chapter two

The sun was high in the sky as we mounted the steps of New Fiddleham's Mason Street Police Station. My mentor reached the door before I did. "You're *sure* you're ready?" he asked for the dozenth time. I wished he would stop asking.

Obviously, I wasn't ready. I brushed my hands along the pleats of my skirt, hoping no one would notice that my palms were sweating. I had not felt ready once in the past six months. Why should I suddenly be ready now? I would probably never be ready.

"Of course I'm ready," I said.

In we pressed.

The station house felt busier than usual—although everything felt busy lately. Afternoon tea felt busy. The atmosphere as we entered was rife with muddy yellow discomfort and blossoms of crimson anger and frustration. Layers of bureaucratic gray had been packed into every corner, agitated by a fresh, electric tension that rippled from body to body. Ahead of us, a processing officer slapped a stamp onto a set of documents in triplicate before glancing up at our approach.

"Is he in?" my mentor asked.

"He's always in," the officer confirmed.

We made our way through a bustle of uniforms and unprocessed detainees, then down a hallway past the detention cells. I glanced in at the prisoners and instantly regretted it. The waves of energy rolling off the humans and nonhumans packing every bench hit me like a landslide—anxiety, shame, fury, despondency—there were just too many people and too much energy, all of it too intense. I felt dizzy. This had been a bad idea.

I took deep breaths and stared at my mentor's back, trying to ignore my peripheral vision. Jackaby was dressed in his favorite overlong duster, its sleeves scuffed and stained—the badges of a hundred curious cases—and its lining stitched with dozens of pockets that clinked and rattled faintly as he walked. Slung over his shoulder was a battered satchel, the contents of which would require an entire ledger to inventory. Mr. Jackaby was fond of saying that *fortune favored the prepared.* Trailing behind him in the close quarters of the hallway, I couldn't help but notice that his preparation smelled distinctly of sage with accents of garlic.

Several policemen glanced our way as we proceeded, but nobody stopped us. At the end of the last hallway was an inauspicious door marked with a simple brass plaque that read: COMMISSIONER MARLOWE. My mentor rapped twice and did not wait for an invitation before pushing it open.

There had been a time, not too long ago, when the desk of New Fiddleham's police commissioner had been housed in a regal office in city hall. That desk had been a broad, imposing piece of furniture, topped with fine leather and framed by two plaster busts of stately-looking figures who were clearly very important, albeit not important enough to merit full bodies or real marble. That had been a different desk, and the man who had sat behind it a very different commissioner.

In place of gaudy busts, Marlowe's desk was framed by a twin set of wire trays, both overflowing with files and paperwork. Behind the desk was a worn leather chair, and in the chair was Commissioner Marlowe himself. The commissioner was built as if he had been chiseled from an especially square piece of granite. He had a square jaw and square shoulders—even the circles under his eyes looked as if they were trying to square off. His brow rose as we entered.

"Miss Rook." He nodded in my direction, a yellow glint daring to pierce the storm gray of his aura like a timid mouse picking its way through an ash heap. "Good to finally see you out and about." He turned his gaze to my mentor. "Jackaby."

"Marlowe." Jackaby stepped farther into the office and leaned on a cabinet casually as he glanced around the room. "I love what you've done with the space—bleak, yet also dreary. I must admit, it's nice to be back in the old workplace again."

Marlowe rubbed the bridge of his nose. "You don't work here," he grunted. "You were *never* officially employed by the New Fiddleham Police Department."

"Freelance, yes." Jackaby nodded. "Wouldn't have it any other way. All the freedom, flexibility, and financial insecurity of being gainfully unemployed, plus paperwork."

A uniformed woman poked her head through the door behind us, giving the frame a timid knock as she did. "Sorry to interrupt, sir," she said.

"I'm in the middle of meeting with a consultant," Marlowe grunted. His eyes flicked to me. "I *am* meeting with a consultant, yes?"

"I—erm. That's right," I managed, eloquently.

"Very sorry, sir," the woman said. "I just need to know how you want me to write up that MacLir case."

Marlowe closed his eyes and let out a breath. "Call it a four-fifteen. Standard forms are in the basket in processing."

"I thought four-fifteen was for disturbing the peace?"

"Yeah. Shockingly, we don't have a specific code for accidentally transforming a random passerby into a goose." Marlowe grunted. "But if that happened to me, I would find my peace pretty damned disturbed, wouldn't you? Four-fifteen. Basket. Processing."

"Perhaps we've come at a bad time," I said as the officer hurried away. I motioned to the piles on Marlowe's desk.

"This?" Marlowe chuckled. "This is a good day." He leaned back in his chair, his eyes fixing on mine. "Things have gotten messy. I hate messy."

"What sort of messy, exactly?" I asked. "Other than the goose business."

Marlowe plucked a handful of files off the top of one of the baskets. "Petty theft by a vanishing hitchhiker. Caught her twice now, but we can't make it back to the station without her disappearing again. We've lost two pairs of handcuffs already. Some creep has been selling deployable curse pouches to schoolkids. Carriage stolen on Hill Street—fairies implicated. That's a phrase I wasn't prepared to utter when I started on the force. Nature spirits are squatting in an old military training camp on the edge of town. Multiple complaints from neighbors about the noise, but the nasty things have a habit of turning into animals when we try to handcuff them, so that's been fun."

"What sort of animals do they turn into?" Jackaby asked.

"Pointy ones, generally." Marlowe tossed the folders back

on the top of the stack. "It's always something. Last week, three pubs got robbed in one night by a sneaky little thief who could slip through keyholes and make off with entire barrels. Only caught the idiot because he knocked over a sackful of peanuts on his way out and then stuck around to count them all for some reason."

"Got to be a clurichaun," said Jackaby. "Was he drunk? They're usually drunk."

"Drunks I can handle." Marlowe sighed. "I miss drunks. Dealt with drunks my entire career. But drunks who won't stay put behind locked bars? Drunks who can kick down a wall? Drunks who mutter nonsense that turns out to be actual magical curses? Yesterday a little old lady waved a knitting needle at Allan and turned his tie into a live python. Well, mostly live. I think it was made of yarn. Fabric pins for teeth."

"Is Allan all right?" I asked.

"He's fine."

"And the python?" Jackaby said.

Marlowe rolled his eyes. "Allan named it Susan. He's been feeding it balled-up socks. Not every incident wraps up so nicely, though. These ones are just the misdemeanors and minor violations. Violent crimes and missing persons numbers are way up, too. Can't always tell if the perpetrator is paranormal or not. Some cases we just can't explain. That's why I reached out." He looked squarely at me again. "I know you asked for some time, but—"

"It's fine," I said. "I've had time. I'm ready."

Marlowe might not have had my mystical magic eye-balls, but he had been working with criminals his entire career and had developed a talent for knowing when someone was lying. He raised an eyebrow at me, his aura prickling skeptically.

"Really," I insisted. "I can do this."

Marlowe nodded. "I've given Inspector Dupin command of the Paranormal Division. He can get you started. Go see what he's got for you."

Inspector Dupin was just emerging from the evidence locker as we made our way toward his office. His aura sizzled like oil over a high flame.

"Inspector!" Jackaby called. "Just the fellow we're looking for."

Dupin glanced up from the clipboard he was signing. "Didn't you quit?" he said. "Afternoon, Miss Rook. How are the visions?"

I faltered only for a moment. "Unceasing," I answered.

"Fair." He nodded, handing the clipboard back to the evidence clerk. "You here to help or get in the way?"

"Help," I said.

Dupin gestured for us to follow as he made his way back through the hallways. "Let me know as soon as Thompson is back," he said, tapping the duty sergeant's desk. "I want him to take lead on the Humans First mess. We're going to need statements. And could we get someone to clean out

interrogation room one? It still smells like wet dog in there."
He continued moving through the station. "I thought you
were broken," he said, glancing at me as we walked. "I
could use help, but the last thing I need is a project."

"I'm not broken," I said. "And I'm nobody's project."

He turned to Jackaby. "She ready?"

"Ask her that."

Dupin turned back to me. "Well?"

"I—I think so," I said. The inspector's aura did not reso-
nate with confidence at my reply.

"She's ready," Jackaby declared.

"I was thinking I might be of use on a recent missing per-
sons case," I said, trying to sound more confident this time.
"There's a woman—her name is Horne. I was wondering if
I could see her file?"

"Mary Horne?"

"That's the one. You know the case?"

"Sure." Dupin shrugged. "Witch. She got caught peddling illegal substances and split before we could arrest her.
Nothing exciting—some otherworld herbs and powders
and things. We were looking for her suppliers more than for
her, but I guess she got spooked. Neighbors filed the report
when she didn't turn up for a few days, but she's most likely
just gone into hiding somewhere. Not a high priority."

I scowled. "Did she have any family?" I asked. "Children?
There was a girl."

"I don't know. If she did, they ran when she ran. Look,

they're probably holed up in someone's basement right now playing checkers. I'm not worried about her. All the petty Mary Hornes of this city are just symptoms of a bigger problem. We're focused higher up the chain. Come here."

He walked us just around the corner to the detainment wing.

"See that cell?" He nodded toward the lockup on the corner. I tried not to let my stomach get woozy as I peered in. "I've got a whole crew of tough guys in there right now who know more about a smuggling network than they're saying. With any luck, those are the guys who are gonna lead us to the top of this thing. Mary Horne was just one of their many shady customers."

"I sec. Would you like me to interrogate them?" I asked.

"What? No." Dupin shook his head. "I'd like you to stay out of the case entirely. It took us a month and a half to arrange the raid, and cracking these guys for information is delicate work."

"You don't think I can do it?"

Dupin raised an eyebrow. "Not exactly what I said." His aura spun a hazy, dubious orange as he surveyed me. "You want a case? Great. I'm sure we can find something for you that's not flagged for oversight and liable to start a riot if it goes south." He waved over a constable from across the detainment hall.

"I *can* do this," I said. *Not if you can't even look at a handful of suspects without their auras making you woozy*, my thoughts added, but I kept that to myself.

"No," Dupin said flatly. "We'll find you something . . . *smaller*." His lack of confidence in me resonated uncomfortably well with my own self-doubt. I took a deep breath, trying not to let my anxious thoughts spin out of control entirely and prove the inspector right. What would Jackaby have done?

I stepped past Dupin into the miasma of auras that was the detainment area.

"Miss Rook, please—" Dupin began.

"They're chock-full of interesting clues, this lot," I said, trying to channel my inner Jackaby. The prisoners glanced up as I approached. There were goblins, trolls, elves, and humans all tucked into the cell together. Some of the paranormals maintained glamours to hide their inhuman features, their magical masks overlapping their true faces, like dizzying double exposures. It made me appreciate the ones who didn't bother. My head was already aching, but I did my best to keep a confident tone as I glanced from face to face.

"Let's see. That one there has a pinkish, sparkly energy ground into his shirt cuffs. He's been working with pixie dust. Lots of it. And the one on the end has been to the Annwyn recently—I can see the soil caking his boots."

"Already documented all of that," Dupin said. "We have samples in evidence. If you please . . ."

I swallowed. "What about *secrets*?" I said. "I can see them bubbling with secrets; can you? Those two on the bench together are sharing a secret—something about money, I think. And the fellow in the corner. He's keeping an especially big secret. It's dangerous—positively fizzing."

"That's enough, Miss Rook," Dupin said, but I was finally feeling the rhythm of it.

I focused hard on the man in the corner of the cell. He had a stubbly chin and a mop of dusty brown hair, and his aura was swimming with nerves. He tensed under my gaze, his energy humming like a piano string about to snap.

"He's draped himself in lies," I said. "But there's one secret in particular that's pushing all the others aside. He's desperate to keep it hidden. It's something about who he is—no, who he works for. That's what you're looking for, isn't it, Inspector?"

Dupin said something else, but his voice suddenly sounded far away. I was focused entirely on the twinkling light of the prisoner's deep, dark secret, everything else fading into the background. This was it. I was doing it.

"The man's loyalties," I mumbled, "I can feel them. They're . . . well, they're . . . *here*. How bizarre. It's almost as if he actually works for . . . well, for *you*." I blinked, and the police station gradually came back into focus all around me.

"Did she just say Mick's a *cop*?" one of the other inmates

hissed. I could feel every eye in the room suddenly fixed like arrows on the man in the corner.

"*Oh*," I said. "Oh."

"Get him out of there," Dupin grunted.

The room erupted in a flurry of shouts, threats, snarled curses, and a clattering of keys. My head spun as I was ushered back around the corner and shoved into an empty briefing room. It was several minutes before Inspector Dupin joined me. His lips were pursed. His aura was a tight, white-hot knot.

"Sorry," I whispered, meekly.

"Two months," he said. "He's been undercover for two months, building up that identity, establishing trust."

"Yes." I nodded. "That makes a lot of sense now."

Dupin pinched the bridge of his nose in very much the same way Marlowe tended to when Jackaby was speaking.

"Right," I said. "So maybe I should just work on that missing persons case I mentioned? Yes?"

"He said *no*?" Jackaby asked as we stepped out into the sunlight together.

"Emphatically," I confirmed. "He doesn't want me poking around anything that even brushes shoulders with his ongoing investigations."

"Not the most auspicious start." Jackaby's feet scuffed the cobbles as he led the way along Mason Street.

"Not a complete loss, though," I added. "He said that if I can manage to arrive tomorrow morning without starting another riot, he would still find me a nice petty crime to sort out. So that's something."

"A step in the right direction," said Jackaby. "You'll be back up to monsters and murderers in no time."

"Hooray," I managed, unenthusiastically.

Perhaps starting simple was for the best. It was pressure enough to get my gift to work on demand; it would be another thing entirely to have matters of life and death resting on my abilities. And yet, my mind kept drifting back to that sketch of Mary Horne . . . and to the soot-streaked face of the girl who was missing her.

chapter three

The trouble with the truth is that it sticks around, even when you've had enough of it. This is why good parents, as a rule, lie to their children early and often. Not cruel lies—quite the opposite. Lies can be kind. They can be soft and comfortable. They can weave into existence a world that makes sense and follows rules. *There are no monsters*, the lies coo. *Everything is going to be okay*, they purr. *The grown-ups know exactly what they're doing.* The lies are a warm blanket.

Inevitably, however, those lies begin to dry and peel away. They itch. Like frantic lizards shedding their skins, we scramble to free ourselves from the discomfort of the lies that no longer fit, not knowing that there are few torments in this world more harrowing than the naked truth.

"Miss Rook?" my mentor called. He shifted the strap of his satchel, which cut across his chest. The midmorning sun beat down on the weathered flagstones as we walked. "Are you all right?" he asked.

I swallowed. A million disconcerting images and wild apparitions danced in front of my eyes at all hours of the day and night. If they had simply been hallucinations, I might have had the slim comfort of being able to tell myself they weren't real, but my visions were something much more insidious: they were the absolute, unrelenting truth.

"I'm fine," I lied.

"Good." He nodded. "Because we've arrived. It's time to go to work, Detective."

New Fiddleham was a city that wore many faces. There was the stern, sober face of the Business District uptown, and the scarred, aging face of the Inkling District on the other side of the river. The one staring back at us as we rounded the last turn was clean-shaven and respectable, as metropolitan faces go. Shops lined either side of a broad lane, and the men and women making their way up and down the sidewalks were clad in fine hats, fitted waistcoats, and bright, clean dresses. Neighborhoods such as this one tended to wear their pedestrians like posh jewelry, showing them off proudly in the light of day. I had been down my share of another sort of street, the kind that wore its pedestrians more like knuckle-dusters, tucked away just out of sight, but always waiting and ready.

When Jackaby had been the lead detective and I merely his assistant, our services had typically been requested in those shadier corners of town. I was silently grateful that this case, our first case in months—my first *ever* since inheriting his unique gifts—would begin in sunnier environs.

The case that Inspector Dupin had plucked off the top of his inbox that morning had brought us to the stately storefront of Talman's Timepieces & Fine Jewelry. A policeman held the door for us as we approached. His aura was a soft orange.

"Officer . . . Schmitz," said Jackaby, reading his badge. "Nice to meet you."

The man raised an eyebrow. "We've met, Mr. Jackaby," he said. "On several occasions."

"Have we?" Jackaby looked him up and down. "Sorry. New eyes. Well—old eyes. Still getting used to them again. Hold on—I think I do remember you. Pumpkin-colored aura, right?"

"I'm afraid I wouldn't know about that," Schmitz said. "Miss Rook." He tipped his cap to me as I approached. "Thank you both for coming."

I nodded and took a deep breath before crossing the threshold.

The door clicked shut behind us with the tinkling of

a bell. "The manager should be out again in a moment," Officer Schmitz informed us. "Feel free to have a look around, though."

The narrow shop was alive with the gentle, steady ticking of clocks and watches. Display cases lined the walls, proudly housing ornate necklaces and brooches set with fine diamonds. The sun had let itself in through the broad front window and was leaning lazily on glass countertops, carelessly smattering the walls with tiny splashes of color.

At least rainbows hadn't changed. Everything else in the world had gained a magical aura since I had inherited the sight—people, rooms, doorknobs—but rainbows were still just rainbows. This was probably because rainbows were mere tricks of the light. But a part of me wondered if perhaps rainbows had *always* been magic that common people could see. Rainbows did look like auras. Maybe they were auras that slipped through the cracks to dazzle average folks, allowing humans a peek at the magic we were missing.

I let my gaze drift across the shop again. Catching only the tiniest colorful glimpse of magic in a mundane world sounded marvelous. Of course, auras weren't even truly *colors*, not exactly. It was as if the sight had so much magic to feed into my unprepared brain that it just processed it all in whatever manner it could, rubber-stamping parcels of input with whatever labels my mind could accept. Sometimes, the ethereal colors of an aura would spill into smells and tastes, but somehow they still *felt* the same to me. It was like when you see a certain shade of blue and something inside of you just knows that it smells of peppermint and sounds like plucking violin strings.

Jackaby was watching me intently, his head cocked like he was observing a science experiment. "What are you seeing right now?" he asked.

I straightened up and focused. The shop was tidy. Nothing appeared to be physically amiss. The tile floor was recently swept—not strewn with broken glass. The door frame was prim and white—not splintered to bits from a forced entry. There was a faint charred odor in the air, a hint of something like cigarette smoke mingling with glass cleaner and metal polish. There was nothing concrete to indicate that a crime had taken place . . . except an inescapable cloud of *wrongness*. It lingered about the room like a tactless party guest. When I opened my mouth, the air tasted like turnips and turpitude, and it made my tongue feel prickly.

Marlowe had been right to request a consultation. Something sinister and supernatural had definitely taken place in this room, and fairly recently, too.

"There." I pointed to the spot that felt most saturated by the foggy aura.

"Describe it," Jackaby prompted.

"Please don't make me," I said.

"Come on, Miss Rook. You need to get used to putting this sort of thing into words."

I took a deep breath. No paint made by mortal hands could commit to canvas the hues that hung before me. "It looks . . . almost purple?" I tried.

"What sort of purple? Violet? Indigo? Be as specific as you can."

"Sort of a . . . *villainous* purple?" I swallowed. "It feels crooked, like a loose tooth. And it's sparkly, like . . . like malted pickles." They were the right words, but even as they fell from my mouth, I knew they were nonsense. My head hurt. "Also it smells of avarice and yellow mustard."

"Huh." Jackaby gave a satisfied bob of his head.

"Did that make any sense to you?" I asked. If there was anyone in the world who might help me understand the knotted jumble that was my senses, it was Jackaby. All of this would have been a lot easier if the sight had stayed in *his* head instead of hopping to mine.

"Of course not," he said, cheerily. "But you're getting more willing to sound like an absolute loon in public, and I'd say that's progress. Confidence first, Miss Rook—competence to follow."

"That's less than reassuring, sir."

"Let's try another approach. Does the room smell

like anything? Not actual smells . . . but beneath those. Supernatural smells. Clandestine carrots, by chance?" Jackaby asked. "Or electric raisins?"

"A bit like turnips?" I admitted.

"Root vegetable." Jackaby nodded. "I suspected as much. That fits."

"But what does it *mean*?" I implored.

"You tell me." He grinned. "You're the expert now. Monet and Renoir don't paint over each other's canvases. You've got to form your own impressions."

I drew in a slow breath and let it out with a sigh. Jackaby was rocking back and forth on the balls of his feet, waiting patiently for me to take the lead. I had not seen him look so content in all the time that I had known him. The sight had always weighed heavily on Jackaby's shoulders. It had been a burden and a responsibility from which he had never dreamed of escaping. But now it was mine, and he looked so light he might float to the ceiling at any moment.

"You could at least pretend not to be so tickled about this whole situation," I said.

"I could," he agreed. "But then you would be forced to see that I was lying, so what good would that do for either of us?"

The door to the back of the shop swung open, and the owner emerged. His aura was a deep emerald, rimmed with a halo of anxiety. It pressed outward in front of him, inflating like a balloon as he drew nearer, taking up more space than it needed to. I blinked, willing myself to see the man and not merely the energy. He was tall and broad-shouldered with silver hair and a pair of round spectacles. He nudged these up on his nose with one finger as he closed the door behind himself.

"Mr. Talman," the policeman greeted him. "These are the consultants I told you about."

"You're the . . . the specialist?" the man asked.

There followed a brief pause as I waited for Jackaby to answer. He did not. His eyes flicked, instead, to me. "Oh. Erm. Yes," I replied. "Yes, we are the specialists. My name is Detective Rook, and this is my—my *associate*, Mr. R. F. Jackaby. I understand you've reported a crime of a paranormal nature?"

"That's right," the man said. "The police couldn't find anything, but one of them mentioned that you might be able to help." He swallowed. "Well?"

Jackaby turned to me. "Yes, well?" he echoed.

I flashed my mentor a glare, but rallied quickly. "I believe you, Mr. Talman," I said. A cool blue ripple of relief ran over the man. "Could you explain precisely what happened in here? It might help to have some context for what I'm observing."

The shopkeeper took a deep breath. "Like I told the police earlier, it all started when that unscrupulous-looking fellow came into the shop."

"That would be Squiffy Rick," Officer Schmitz added.

"Squiffy?" I said.

"That's right. Squiffy Rick has a bit of a reputation," said the officer. "Quick fingers. He's in and out of lockup every few weeks—never anything major. Mostly haunts the Inkling District. I interviewed the neighbors, and one of them confirmed seeing him lingering about, looking like— well—looking like Squiffy Rick. It's an aesthetic that tends to make people double-check their purses and pocket watches."

"Indeed," said Mr. Talman. "So, this Rick fellow came in around noon, just after my security man usually takes his lunch break. I suspect the timing was not coincidental. He strolled up and down for a few minutes, looking at the displays. He seemed to take a particular interest in the Casella necklace. Needless to say, I politely asked that he vacate the premises at once."

"How did you know he wasn't a legitimate customer?" I asked.

Mr. Talman shook his head. "The Casella necklace is a collection of one hundred and seventeen exquisitely cut diamonds surrounding baroque pearls in a setting of fourteen-karat gold and silver. The gentleman in question was wearing a belt made out of rope."

I shrugged. "Appearances can be deceiving."

"That necklace is conservatively worth more than three thousand dollars."

"Good lord, you could buy a house for that!" said Jackaby. "You really sell bits of shiny rock for that much?"

"I do not if the bits of shiny rock are stolen before I have a chance," Mr. Talman replied, coldly.

"What happened after you asked Squiffy Rick to leave?" I pressed.

"The man cautioned me not to get my undergarments in a twist and informed me that he would leave when he was good and ready. I informed him in return that I would be summoning security, and that's when I foolishly turned my back on him—only for a moment—to pull the cord behind the counter. It's just there. It rings a bell in the back room."

"And when you turned to face him again, the necklace was already gone?"

"Not just the necklace," Mr. Talman replied, "the entire display case! Glass, frame, contents and all."

"Bold move," said Jackaby. "But I suppose with a posh piece like that, you would want somewhere to put it once you got it home. Not the sort of thing you toss into the sock drawer. Thoughts, Miss Rook?"

"I think one would need to be both extraordinarily strong and extraordinarily fast to accomplish a feat such as that," I said. "Did you happen to see which way he ran?" I turned again to Mr. Talman.

"No, no," Mr. Talman continued. "You don't understand. He didn't take the case *with* him. That degenerate was *still here*, feigning ignorance. Only the case had vanished. He acted as surprised as I was, but I could tell he was lying, of course. My security man searched him head to toe, but he didn't have anything on him other than a fistful of crumpled banknotes and a few loose cigarettes."

I ran my foot along the ground where Mr. Talman had indicated the case used to be. The fog of residual magic was, indeed, heaviest here, but there was no sign of a trapdoor or scuff marks or anything else helpful.

"Is Squiffy Rick a known magical creature?" I asked.

"Not that I'm aware of," answered Officer Schmitz.

A year ago, the question would have at least raised an eyebrow, if not gotten us kicked off the crime scene for flagrant disrespect. New Fiddleham had seen a few things since then.

"His previous arrests have never involved anything so . . . so strange," the officer continued. "Lots of incidents these days seem to have a bit of—well—of your kind of thing mixed in. It's getting weird out here. Nine out of ten reports that I file don't even get any follow-up. Inspector Dupin says we just don't have the resources. That's why I was so surprised to get word back on this one. I thought, in the past, you usually handled the big stuff. Murders and apocalypses and things."

"Oh, you know how it is," Jackaby said. "Nice to have a quaint heist or two between murders, just to shake things up. Anyway, I assure you, your case is in good hands," said Jackaby. "Dupin's entire Paranormal Division has nothing on Miss Rook."

My throat felt dry. I had mastered walking in a straight line while auras spun around me; I had practiced differentiating between the energy of one person and another for countless hours. I had trained for weeks until I could accurately recognize traces of a hundred unique creatures—but none of that was the same as really doing the job. Identifying bizarre clues and turning those clues into answers were completely different things.

I took a deep breath. How had I done this before gaining the sight? I had always just begun with what I did know and then asked a lot of questions until something clicked. "Okay," I said. "There's definitely magic in the air, so let's assume that our suspect *is* nonhuman. What sort of magical being can make objects vanish in a puff of smoke?"

Jackaby's eyes narrowed as he considered. "Fairy magic could certainly do the trick. Some imps can cause a temporary evanescence. All manner of brownies and pixies have been known to pilfer small items and then dissipate. Nothing as big as this, usually."

"Okay—lots of potential culprits to pick from," I said. "We just need to narrow it down."

"*We* don't," said Jackaby. "*You* do."

I sighed.

When I was a little girl, my parents had hardly let me

do anything for myself. I couldn't so much as pick out my own clothes without Mother bustling in to demand that I change into something more suitable. My entire life had been spent leaning my temple against the rear window of our family carriage, watching as the world rolled past while someone else drove the horses. I had dreamed of taking those reins and finding my own way down wild and winding roads.

My parents were thousands of miles away now. The reins were firmly in my hands, and the horses were straining at the bit.

I could do this. I had been practicing aura identification for months. It was like trying to pick out the individual ingredients in a stew just by sniffing, but it was possible.

Once again I focused on the swirling energy in front of me. Who—or what—had been here before us? The clouds of residual magic spun around the room in swirls and eddies, gradually thinning and fading. The only clear trails within the haze were mundane, beige wisps. Humans. The strongest of the bunch matched the shopkeeper's. Like ripples in a lake, I could see the echoes of him pacing the shop. I tried to focus on the others. Fainter, more blurred, they trod up and down the tiles. There was at least one nonhuman aura as well—but it was paper-thin. Try as hard as I could, I couldn't single it out. Every time I thought I had it, it slipped away.

I shook my head and blinked. The supernatural haze was

beginning to make my head spin. My eyes were watering. Jackaby would have been able to identify something more clearly, I was sure of it.

I heard Jackaby's voice beside me, but he sounded distant and muffled. "You're quite certain that it was Squiffy Rick who made the necklace disappear?" he asked.

"Of course it was," said Mr. Talman. "There wasn't anyone else here."

I closed my eyes, trying to focus on their words. The gears in my mind felt like they were spinning through molasses. There was just too much to take in, too many senses, and all of them wanted to be felt at once.

"But did you actually *see* him do it?" Jackaby was asking. "How did he pull it off? Did he wave his hands about before it vanished? Draw a circle around it with some sort of powder?"

"I told you, my back was turned," Talman reiterated. "But if you have any doubt of his guilt, he gave my guard the slip as soon as I went to summon a policeman. Innocent people do not run from the police."

"I've found it advantageous to run from the police on a number of occasions," Jackaby said. "And I was definitely innocent on at least a few of them."

I turned my gaze out the window, trying to escape the dazzling fog of auras clouding the shop. Something shifted in the alleyway across the street. Was there someone out there? My vision swam.

"I just want the necklace back," Mr. Talman was saying. "So if you could please look into your crystal ball or whatever it is that you do and tell me where that vagrant has stashed it away, I would be most grateful."

"I'm afraid it doesn't work that way," I managed, shaking my head.

"Well, how does it work?"

"Not very well, just yet," I admitted. "I'm still figuring it out."

"Miss Rook?" Jackaby's voice was edged with concern.

"I'm . . ."

Mr. Talman put his hands on his hips. "They said you were the best at this sort of thing. Well? Can you tell me where my stolen property is or not?"

"I can tell you . . ." I hesitated. The room was pulsing. "I can tell . . ."

"What? What can you tell me?"

"I don't know!" I screwed my eyes shut out of habit—not that my eyelids blocked out any of the visions. "Nothing! Too many things! Useless things! I can tell that there have been people through here. Just ordinary people. People who were proud and people who were in love and people who felt small and sad and broken. I can see echoes of their nerves and their greed and their eagerness and their stubborn, willful hope. I can see your frustration, even now, and I can see your confidence in us—in me—fading. And I can't blame you. The truth is, I have no idea where to find your necklace, Mr. Talman. I can barely find myself in the mess, most days."

The wall of clocks and watches ticked meekly in the ensuing silence.

I heaved a heavy breath and turned to go.

"But she will," Jackaby added, behind me. "She's hot on the trail. We'll be in touch when we have more information for you."

chapter four

The city around me was too bright as I strode out of
Talman's shop. The glare made my head throb even
more. My eyes found themselves seeking the respite of the
darkness, and there they landed on a familiar dirty face
watching from the shady alleyway across the street. The
girl must have seen me looking, but she didn't drop her
gaze. We stared at each other wordlessly for several seconds. The sound of hooves clopped away in the distance.

"What's your name?" I asked.

She bit her lip and did not answer. Threads of sharp
distrust and yearning hope competed for purchase at the
edges of her aura.

"Who is she?" I tried.

Her eyes narrowed.

"Mary Horne? I saw her picture on that poster. You know something about her. Do you know where she went?"

The girl's aura twisted around her in a tight knot of fear and anger and loyalty. She was hungry and achingly alone. Her emotions squeezed her so tightly that the sight made *my* lungs hurt. For a moment, all of the surplus energies of New Fiddleham faded into the background.

"Please," I breathed. "I want to help you."

"*Can* you?" she finally said.

I opened my mouth and shut it again.

Behind me, a bell tinkled and a door latch clicked. The girl ducked and vanished back into the shadows of the alleyway.

"I don't know," I whispered to the empty place where she had been.

"Don't know what?" Jackaby asked.

"Nothing. Never mind." My throat felt tight, and I turned and stalked across the street before he could look me in the face.

He caught up with me just as I reached the mouth of the alley.

"I'm sorry," I mumbled.

"Really? Why?" he said. He glanced back toward Talman's, confused, and then at the street around us. "Oh, wait. Are you apologizing to a ghost? Did we just walk through a ghost? Sorry, ghost! That *is* awkward."

"Stop. No. There's no ghost," I sighed. "I'm sorry about *the case*. I can't do this. *You* knew how to be the Seer. I just make a mess of everything."

"You think I didn't make messes?" he said. "My life has been one long series of messes, strung together like sausages. The trick, as far as I've been able to tell, is to *clean up* slightly more messes than you *cause*. Keeps the scales tipped in your favor."

As I pressed through the alleyway and out the other side, I was met with a now-familiar cloud of angst and panic splashed across a dirty brick wall. Half a dozen posters of missing people had been hung in an uneven line, and every one of them had been marred by angry streaks of red paint. The words *HUMANS FIRST* and *MUNDUS NOSTER* were largest of all, with dribbles of paint bleeding all the way down to the sidewalk. I spotted Mary Horne's face among them yet again. Someone had scrawled the word *WITCH* across her eyes.

"I've got a *lot* of cleaning up to do to catch up on messes," I breathed.

Jackaby pursed his lips, scowling at the vandalism.

I could see the paint clearly in front of me—but soaked deep within each letter, I could also see the fear and fury that had written them. The hate in each brushstroke hissed like a cornered animal, small and wretched. The people of New Fiddleham were terrified. I could taste it in the dusty air. And worse, they wanted desperately for *their* terror to be anyone else's.

"This nonsense is not your mess," said Jackaby. "Remember that." He rummaged in his bag until he produced a small vial with a nozzle, like a perfume bottle. "Mostly I try to ignore petty vandalism. Can't stop a kettle from venting its steam, after all—unless you're aiming to turn that kettle into a pressure bomb. But some unkind messages have a way of turning up the heat rather than releasing it." He slipped the cap off the bottle and gave the wall several wide sprays. "I hardly have time to scrub every alleyway by hand, so Jenny and I have been working on a formula for quick and effective removal."

The paint was already beginning to bubble and blister under Jackaby's cleaning solution, curling and flaking away from the bricks. He gave a satisfied nod as the words melted away in front of us—although the emotions that had spawned them remained firmly in place, hanging in the air. "There, that's better. See? So, things have gotten worse. It doesn't matter. You're back now. We'll have the worst of it cleaned up in no time."

For a moment, the alleyway looked almost respectable, but then the bricks themselves began to blister and crack, chips of stone flaking away with a series of angry pops and snaps. Where the drips of paint had run, the cobblestones hissed. The poster of Mary Horne burst into flames. "Whoops," Jackaby muttered. "Not again."

"Oh lord!" I gasped. The smell was tangible. It was as if the liquid that collects at the bottom of the bin had joined forces with spoiled eggs and old fish in an all-out assault against decency.

"Ugh. Yes. That. We're considering adding a bit of lemon zest for future batches," Jackaby said, coughing. "Try not to breathe through your nose. Or your mouth. Maybe just take a step or two back?"

"How is it both wet *and* burning?" I managed, edging away as a flaming ball of brick-colored sludge dripped to the sidewalk. Jackaby shuffled hastily back, as well.

"We're still tinkering with the concentration."

"I didn't even know brick could melt." The mess continued to fizz and crackle. A second poster caught fire, spiraling to the cobblestones, where it smoldered.

"It'll be fine," Jackaby said. "Probably. It's a good, thick wall, anyway. Should we be going? Yes, let's be going. Try not to breathe too deeply."

Once we were a few blocks away, I cleared my throat. "Dupin might be right about me."

"Dupin is rarely right," Jackaby said. "Certainly not when it counts."

"I'm serious. How am I supposed to clean up more messes than I cause," I said, "if everything I try to clean up only becomes a bigger mess?"

Jackaby took a deep breath. He held up his cleaning solution and gave it a wiggle. "You readjust the formula," he said. "And you have patience." He tucked the bottle carefully back into his satchel. "Come on. Jenny and I were planning on doing some tinkering, anyway. You can help. We'll hunt for necklaces tomorrow."

I shook my head. "I told Charlie that I would meet him for lunch after the investigation."

"You're still feeling up for it?" Jackaby asked.

It wasn't yet noon and I was exhausted. The world was awful, and I wanted to collapse on my bed and cry into a pillow until I fell asleep, but if I did that every time I felt this way, I would scarcely leave the house at all. "Of course I'm up for it," I said.

The sun was warm on my neck as I sat alone at a café table about an hour later. I had arrived much too early, but I didn't mind the wait. I stared deep into the cup of Assam in front of me, shutting out the rest of the world, just as I had practiced. It was only me and the tea. I took a deep breath, feeling my heartbeat gradually calming.

My fingers found themselves absently rubbing the ring I wore on my left hand. Charlie's ring. My heartbeat quickened again. I had watched him die.

So many people had died that day, but no loss had weighed as heavily on my heart as Charlie's. I had seen his body, seen it both with my own eyes and then with the merciless clarity of the sight. I had been there at Rosemary's Green when they placed his coffin on display for the service. I had held this ring—my ring—the ring that he would never be able to give to me himself, and I had cried.

And then the universe, in its own inscrutable way, had given him back. His life had been the final, benevolent gift of an unfathomably powerful creature. One minute, Charlie's body had been an empty husk, and the next, he had been whole and real and healthy once again.

Charlie had recovered more quickly from his own death than I did. Of course he had—he'd enjoyed the good fortune of being peacefully dead for the heavy emotional lifting.

I took a sip of tea.

The café was not far from Charlie's apartment. We had already discussed finding a place of our own someday. We would, we had decided, but only after the wedding. The wedding, of course, was a whole different discussion, and one we'd not yet had in earnest. With everything I had gone through—was still going through—planning a grand, life-changing event involving both of our families was not on the table. How would I even begin to tell my parents?

Dearest Mother and Father. Do you remember when I took the tuition money you gave me and ran away to find dinosaur bones and then ended up in New England helping a mad detective solve grisly murders? Well, guess what?

I've decided to marry the nice policeman I met standing over my first dead body. Also, you should probably know that my fiancé and his family are shape-shifters who can turn into dogs, and they are charged with guarding the gateway between universes. We've selected a lovely venue. Please wear blue.

The wedding could wait.

In the meantime, the upside to living apart was the quiet thrill of meeting again each day. Auras could be overwhelming, but the one vision I would never tire of was the sight of Charlie seeing *me* all over again. A warm light danced in his chest all the time, fluttering like a hinkypunk's flame, and when he locked eyes with me after a night away, it swelled so hot it made his ears turn red and sent a blush across his cheeks. It never failed to make me smile.

There was a horrible voice in the back of my head that worried the flame would fade with time. It wouldn't be his fault, of course—we cannot control what we feel on the inside—and it was already unfair that I could see into him in a way he would never be able to see into me. Still, it would break my heart to pieces the day there was no fire at all. I took another sip of tea and tried not to think about it.

A carriage rolled by noisily, and when it had passed, he was there, stalking up the sidewalk. Charlie looked handsome in his pressed shirt and his new suit. The rich browns suited him, even if he did have a habit of retreating into his collar and fidgeting with the cuffs when he was nervous. Charlie had always been more comfortable in a standard uniform, blending in as one of the pack. He had accepted new responsibilities, though—addressing otherworldly dignitaries and hosting meetings with everyone from civil servants to royalty—and he had to dress the part.

He spotted me as he was brushing a curl of hair behind his ears, and he flashed me a warm smile. And there it was. That fire. The joy that rippled through his aura washed over me, and I felt my own cheeks flush. But there was a dark cloud hovering over him today, as well. It retreated as he neared, but did not fully dissipate.

"Is something the matter?" I asked.

"Nothing pressing," he said. His voice was gentle and tempered with that faint Slavic accent, and his smile was so earnest. He closed the gap between us, cupped my cheek with his hand, and gave me a kiss on the forehead. I leaned into his touch, but his arm slid away too quickly. "Well?" he said. "Your first new case in months? Tell me all about it!" He slid into the chair opposite mine.

"I wish there were more to tell," I answered. "Jewelry theft. Not much progress yet. What about you? Don't you have a big meeting of some sort coming up—when was that happening?"

The dark cloud behind his head burbled dyspeptically and darkened. "Wednesday."

"Oh my. You're nervous," I said.

"It's just . . . very public," Charlie said. His fingers worried the cuffs of his suit. "Part of the job. It had to happen eventually. Mayor Spade informed me this morning that they have shifted the venue to allow for a larger crowd. Apparently there will also be a few federal agents overseeing the briefing. It seems the capital has taken an interest in New Fiddleham."

"Well, you're going to be splendid, as always," I said. "And you still have tomorrow to prepare. I'll help."

Charlie brightened a fraction. "Are you sure? I don't want to take you away from your own work."

"Those fancy jewels aren't getting any more stolen." I reached over and gave his hand a squeeze. "We'll spend all afternoon together. I promise. We'll talk through the issues together like we used to. If we end up with any extra time, maybe you could even help me with my case. I could use the best nose in New Fiddleham."

"I would love that, actually," he said. His shoulders relaxed a fraction, and he gave me an earnest smile, holding my hand across the table.

"But there won't be any extra time." Alina Cane's footfalls were as soft as feathers, but she tugged a chair over from a neighboring table with a loud screech and plopped down beside us. "Big brother is an important cultural concierge these days. No time left for the ladies in his life. Have we ordered yet? I want coffee. And maybe one of those flaky bread things."

"It's *cultural liaison*," said Charlie.

"No, I'm pretty sure it's *croissant*," Alina replied.

"What are you doing here?" Charlie asked.

"Detective Girlfriend said she needed my help," Alina said. "Good morning, Abigail. How are your eyeballs?"

"Crazy and obnoxious," I answered. "How are things at the veil-gate?"

"About the same, actually."

Alina's energy was much like Charlie's in many ways. Their personalities were very different, and yet their auras balanced each other like a pair of finely composed counter-melodies. It stood to reason—they had grown up together. They were also both Om Caini—able to transform into noble hounds at will—but the hound inside Alina kept itself much closer to the surface than the one in Charlie. It pawed at her from the inside, pacing its human kennel.

"You invited my sister?" said Charlie.

"I'm fairly certain that I didn't," I said.

"Of course you did. I believe your precise words were *I could use the best nose in New Fiddleham*," Alina said. "And here I am. Like magic. Best nose. What's the job?"

"She clearly meant *me*," Charlie said.

"Don't be silly," Alina scoffed. "If she had meant you, she would have said she needed the *third* best nose in New Fiddleham. Probably fourth by now, if we're being honest. Little Fane has been making excellent progress. He takes after his auntie."

"Alina—" Charlie began.

"Just being honest." Alina shrugged. "I promised I always would be. Just ask Detective Girlfriend if I'm not."

I chose silence.

"See?" Alina smirked. "Fourth best."

Charlie shook his head. "Did you leave your solemn post just to harass me?"

Alina waved him away. "Don't flatter yourself. I have business in the city today."

"Something amiss?" I asked.

"Not certain," she said. "By the way, Kazimir, I borrowed the nightstick from your apartment, just in case. People in town make such a fuss when I let out the hound in public."

"What? No," said Charlie. "Stop taking my things. And you can't just walk around with a truncheon—people are already looking for a reason to distrust us. Please. Do not cause an incident two days before I have to give a public briefing about how you're *not* a threat."

"I would be exceedingly bad at my job if I were *not a threat*," said Alina. "And if you didn't want me to take it, why was it just sitting around invitingly in an unlocked cabinet?"

"Because you broke that lock the *last* time you came to *borrow* something," Charlie said.

"And whose fault is that?" Alina countered. "Locks are rude. Siblings should not keep secrets."

"Soră." Charlie shook his head. "You need to stop. There will always be things in my life that I do without you."

"The last time you decided to *do without me*, you didn't come home," she snapped. Her brow furrowed and her lips tightened. "*I* had to come find *you*, remember? And by the time I did, you had already been run out of town by an angry mob, cut to ribbons by a redcap, nearly roasted by a dragon, and even hunted by a strigoi."

"He was a vampire," corrected Charlie, weakly.

"I don't care. Me staying out of your life while you run off to help Detective Girlfriend has put you in danger countless times and gotten you *killed* at least once. I don't intend to stand by and wait for it to happen again."

"Are we going to get into that?" Charlie raised an eyebrow. "I seem to recall the man who killed me being assisted by someone I trusted. Who was that, again?"

Alina sniffed and leaned back in her chair sullenly. "I did apologize," she said. "And that only goes to prove that siblings should not keep secrets." She turned to me. "So, Detective, who are you tracking? Murderer? Kidnapper?"

"Just a thief," I said. "He stole a necklace."

"That's it?"

"Well. Yes. He did take it in a rather peculiar way," I said. "Probably. Or maybe someone else did."

Her brow crinkled. "And if you do not find this necklace . . . bad things will happen?"

"Erm. No. A rather huffy shopkeeper will probably need to file a lot of insurance paperwork."

"Freci menta. Then why are you being wasted on this?" said Alina.

"It's . . . important?"

"It's important? *You're* important. How many people in this town have your magic eyes and your weird brain? Kazimir, tell your stupid Detective Girlfriend she's important."

"Of course she's important," Charlie said. He wrapped a hand around mine and gave it a squeeze. "If the police asked for her help on this case, then I'm sure it's of some deeper significance."

I winced.

Charlie must have caught the expression, because he altered course. "Or . . . it's the case she *wants* to investigate," he said, "because her instincts are pulling her toward . . ."

He trailed off as I sighed, heavily.

"No?" Charlie said.

"Honestly?" I said. "I'm starting to think it's a nothing case about an unimportant crime—which is almost certainly the point, because if I botch it utterly, nobody will be fussed. Inspector Dupin certainly doesn't care. But it's important to *me*, because if I can't even solve a simple problem that *doesn't* matter, then how can I hope to solve a messy one that *does*?" I flopped my face into my hands.

"Ugh. Mr. Jackaby would have had this whole thing sorted in an hour and we could have long since moved on."

Charlie scowled. "You need to stop comparing yourself to him. I seem to recall a clever, tenacious woman solving more than a few problems he never could crack on his own. And that was before she got the sight."

"But I'm not that person anymore," I breathed. "I wish that I were, but it's like I'm stuck somewhere between her and me, and I don't know how to be either."

"Ugh." Alina rolled her eyes. "*Oh, heavens. I'm not somebody else. I'm not who I used to be,*" she whinged in a mock English accent. "What you *are* is exhausting."

"Alina," Charlie growled.

"What? Of course she's not who she *used* to be." Alina threw her hands up in the air. "*Nobody* is who they *used* to be. That's not how time works."

"You, for example," said Charlie, "used to be *nice.*"

"And thank god that changed. If I were still a nice, obedient little pup, I wouldn't make a very good Suverana, would I? Controlling the veil-gate, enforcing the balance between realms, holding the responsibility of two entire worlds squarely on my shoulders—these are not tasks for someone nice. *You* could stand to be less nice, brother. Maybe if you were, people would stop wiping their boots on your head."

"That's uncalled for," I said.

"You have no idea what's called for." Alina flashed me a stern glare. "You're so obsessed with who you're *not*, you don't even know how to be who you *are*. It's sad. And you wonder why you fail."

Charlie planted his palms on the table and stood up, his chair scraping angrily on the paving stones.

Alina kept her eyes on me, willfully ignoring her brother. When she spoke, her voice was quieter. "Imagine for a moment that you could just be who you are instead of constantly wishing to be something else."

The intensity of our little chat had begun to attract the attention of a few passersby. A pair of women in high-necked dresses crossed to the far side of the street, whispering and darting glances our way.

"Or don't." Alina pushed herself to her feet and turned to go. "What do I know? Go waste your talents on petty thefts. The *fourth* best nose in New Fiddleham should be more than sufficient. Ai grijă, Kazimir."

"Stay out of trouble," Charlie called after her.

"We'll see!" she called back.

He shook his head as she vanished into the bustle of the sidewalk traffic. His stormy aura had only grown darker.

chapter five

Alina's voice echoed in my head as I stared at my ceiling that night. *Be who you are.*

In my dream, I stood on the deck of a wide steamer ship, caught in the middle of a storm. The ocean churned all around me, and beneath the angry waves I spied the sweeping tendrils of some eldritch horror. As I glanced down, a gleam caught my eye. Diamonds glittered on the surface of the deck as the craft heaved up and down. The missing necklace slipped along the watery boards, sliding toward the bow of the ship.

I was too slow to catch the thing, but before it could be

washed overboard, it snagged against the feet of a figure standing at the prow—a young girl. The crashing waves reached up on either side of her like greedy hands. I called out, but the child's eyes never turned from the tumultuous sea ahead. Somehow, I knew that this was the girl I had seen in the alleyway.

The boat lurched, and bloodred tentacles crept up over the railing, encircling the ship. The wood beneath our feet buckled and split under the pressure of the terrible sea monster's grip. I was thrown to my back. The necklace spun to port and the girl to starboard—and as I scrambled to regain my footing, I could see that there wasn't time to catch them both. I leapt for the girl. The crimson tentacles came barreling down toward us, and I threw my body around the child to protect her.

And then there was light. A bright shape burst into my vision. It raced from my shoulder down my arm, then hopped to the boards at my feet. I knew the shape. This was a domovyk—my domovyk. The little house spirit screeched and chirruped like an angry squirrel, dancing around my legs and gnashing its little teeth until the tendrils withdrew.

I felt my chest rise and fall with slow breaths. Gradually, the girl in my arms melted into a mass of soft linens. The dream ship faded away into the velvet darkness of my eyelids. The domovyk, however, its aura a pale violet and bursting with loyalty and concern, did not fade. It remained alert and vigilant as I opened my eyes. Only when it noted my stirring did the wee valiant thing dart away, its nightly watch concluded.

"Thank you," I whispered into the soft gloom of my bedroom. I would leave a slice of fresh bread out for the dear in the evening. My tiny sentinel had been with me since before I had arrived in New Fiddleham, and he was probably the only reason I ever managed to secure what little sleep I did get lately. With visions that crept through even closed eyes, it was often difficult to find the line where dream ended and consciousness began.

I stretched and rubbed my arms where I had felt them wrapping around the child. It was still quite early, but I dressed hastily in one of my favorite outfits. Jenny had helped me stitch pockets all along the waist of the dress—I could never have enough pockets. I paused in the hallway outside my room, hesitating in front of the tall Elizabethan mirror. Its heavy frame barely fit between the floor and ceiling, and the silver behind the glass was slightly warped and scratched. I could barely make out my own reflection behind the densely woven magical field that saturated the entire surface of glass.

The mirror had been Jackaby's idea. It was, in truth, a portal, a magical gateway between Charlie's apartment and the house on Augur Lane. It should have been impossibly expensive to commission such an artifact, but it turned out saving the world—two worlds—from cataclysmic disaster had earned us more than a few favors. The thing was far from perfect. Crossing through it always made me dizzy for several minutes after, and the trip left a funny, coppery taste in my mouth. According to Jackaby, all teleportation magic has its kinks—but at least this one worked, and it was reasonably stable. I considered for just a moment zipping across to greet Charlie before he went out for the morning—but he would be coming to me soon enough. In the meantime, there was something else I needed to do.

The morning sun was barely peeking over the roof of the Mason Street Police Station as I hurried up the steps and into the building.

Inspector Dupin seemed baffled to find me waiting for him outside the door to interrogation room two. "Can I help you?" he asked. "I'm sort of in the middle of something here."

"I need the missing persons file for Mary Horne," I informed him. "And any other files you think might possibly be connected. I know you don't think I'm ready, but I am."

Dupin blinked. "You solved that burglary I gave you already?"

I swallowed. "No."

He raised an eyebrow.

"I'm ready."

"You're really not," he said. "What you are is overconfident, and overconfidence is going to get you killed. I've got a repeat offender behind this door right now with a reputation for ripping the arms off people he doesn't like. Is losing an arm something you're *ready* for?"

I peeked over his shoulder into the interrogation room. My vision swam slightly as I took in the creature's aura. Decidedly not human.

"Quarry troll," Dupin explained. "Stubborn, too. And now, if you don't mind, I need to get back to interrogating that antisocial mountain before he starts growing lichen."

I nodded. "Of course."

Dupin opened the door and stepped back inside, but before he could close it behind him, I slipped in. Dupin spun. "What do you think you're—"

"I've never seen a quarry troll up close," I said, directing my attention to the prisoner. "Hello. I'm curious by nature, I guess. I was under the impression that you lot didn't often brave the big city."

"Troll not have to be brave in big city," the creature grunted from the other side of a sturdy table. "Big city has to be brave around troll."

"You're not intimidating anyone, Rock-Jaw," Dupin said, giving me an angry glance. He dropped his notebook on the table across from the detainee.

"No?" said Rock-Jaw. "How about now?" And without any further warning, he lurched forward in his chair, his fist rocketing toward Dupin's head.

Dupin reacted with lightning reflexes by stumbling

sideways over his own feet and landing on the floor of the interrogation room.

Rock-Jaw's booming laugh echoed painfully in the tight space.

"Not funny," Dupin grumbled.

The prisoner smirked as he settled back into his seat. The chair creaked in protest, but it held. "Rock-Jaw very funny. Stupid human not get joke."

"Precisely what I was talking about." Dupin dusted himself off as he stood up.

"Is that what Mr. Jaw is in for?" I asked. "Attacking people?" I cocked my head, taking in the creature's unique aura. Magic spun around him in crisscrossing wisps, weaving in and out like loose braids.

Dupin eyed me. For a moment, I was sure he was going to order me back outside, but instead he let his gaze roll back to the prisoner and shook his head. "Not if they paid up," he said. "Dozens of victims. If you're going to observe, Miss Rook, please stay back and remain silent. Our guest here was just about to disclose to me where he stashed his cache."

"Don't think he was," the creature said. "That don't sound like Rock-Jaw." He scratched the back of his neck. "All those shiny coins was given to Rock-Jaw. Gifts is gifts. Rude to give gifts back. Bad luck. That's old magic."

"They weren't gifts," Dupin replied, flatly. "It was extortion money—paid monthly—after you explicitly threatened their homes and businesses."

"Gifts," the creature grunted. "In exchange for Rock-Jaw's gift: protection. Everyone want Rock-Jaw's protection. Dangerous town these days. Rock-Jaw very good at protecting."

"Really? Very good at protecting? Is that why at least four of the properties under your supposed protection have been robbed and vandalized in the past two weeks?"

"Like Rock-Jaw said, dangerous town."

Dupin flipped a few pages in the notebook. "And when you came to collect more money from the people you'd failed to protect, you told them, and I quote: *Current service not cover that. Too bad. Pay up.* Do I have that right?"

"Terms and conditions is old magic, too."

"I'm sure you don't love being stuck in cramped spaces any more than I love being stuck in here with you," Dupin pressed. "If you would just pay back the money, we could talk about shorter sentencing. Play nice, and we might even be able to avoid jail time entirely."

The creature let out a chuckle that sounded like a volcano burbling. "Rock-Jaw could give humans all the shiny coins he worked so hard for, and then Rock-Jaw have no monies at all," he said. "Or . . . Rock-Jaw could *keep* monies and go to human jail. Rock-Jaw not stupid. Time in jail give Rock-Jaw even better reputation as tough guy. Humans feed Rock-Jaw in jail. And Rock-Jaw back on the street in few days anyway, because humans not have enough evidence for to hold Rock-Jaw—and even if humans did, they not have enough room to keep Rock-Jaw. No. Rock-Jaw will keep monies for himself. Rock-Jaw choose jail."

Dupin ground his teeth.

"He makes a fair point," I said, helpfully.

Dupin shot me another glare. Before he could resume, the door opened behind us and Commissioner Marlowe leaned his head inside. The commissioner's aura always draped over his shoulders like a weary weight, but something was different today. His heart rate had quickened and his nerves were humming.

He caught sight of me with mild surprise but turned quickly to Dupin. "Inspector," he grunted. "I need a word with you in the hallway when you have a moment. Something's come up."

"Now is fine." Dupin shot the prisoner one more scowl. "This hardheaded lump can wait."

Rock-Jaw propped his feet up on the interrogation table with a thud and waggled his fingers at Dupin in a mock goodbye as we cleared the room.

"Detective Rook," Marlowe said once we were all in the hallway and the door had clicked shut. "I wasn't aware you were involved with this case."

"She's not," Dupin said.

"Not yet," I said. "But I could close it for you."

Dupin's eyebrows rose incredulously. His aura, dull and gray-blue as he surveyed me, was without a fleck of confidence.

"Tell you what—I'll make you a deal," I said. "Let me speak to your intractable inmate for five minutes. If I can convince him to give up the information you're after, you let me have the file on Mary Horne."

"And when you can't?"

"Then I won't bring the matter up again."

Dupin rubbed his chin contemplatively.

"Never hurts to approach a problem with a fresh perspective," I added. "And he was right. It's not as though you have room for a troll in your detainment center right now anyway, and you can't transfer paranormal prisoners anywhere else at present. How many seats on a standard bench do you suppose Mr. Rock-Jaw would occupy?"

Dupin glanced to the commissioner. Marlowe gave a curt nod. "Two minutes," he grunted.

"Sir. This guy has a rough reputation even among the nastiest street crews," Dupin cautioned. "There's a reason all those people paid up when he came calling."

"I'll be fine," I said, not certain if I was assuring Dupin or myself. "You can wait for me just outside the door, if you like. It will give the commissioner time to share that bad news he has for you in private."

Dupin shot a concerned glance at Marlowe, but then whipped his eyes back to me. "Wait—you want to speak to him *alone*?" He shook his head. "No. No way."

"*You* were in there alone with him before I arrived," I said.

"Yes, but you're . . ." I tried not to take offense as Dupin sized me up. I might not have been all that physically imposing, but I had made an effort to at least dress for the part. My skirts were pressed, and I had tied my hair up in a bun as neatly as I could manage without a proper mirror. Even mirrors that weren't magical portals had been giving me headaches lately, so I didn't like to linger. But I looked *very* professional. Probably.

I straightened and cleared my throat. "Two minutes," I said. "I promise not to be too rough on him."

Dupin looked as if he was ready to object, but Marlowe cut him off. "We'll be watching," he said.

Rock-Jaw raised a lumpy eyebrow as I slipped back into the room and closed the door behind me. I breathed in and out, steadying myself.

"Other humans must not like you much," he rumbled, amusement coloring his deep voice, "if they willing to lock you in room with Rock-Jaw."

"That's quite good," I said. "You sound thoroughly intimidating. I'm sure you've rehearsed even more threats, but in the interest of time, do you mind if we forgo all that? It's just that we only have about two minutes before those men open up the door and you come to the prudent realization that it's in your best interest to make a full confession. Powerful thing, confession. I was talking to a friend about it, just the other day."

The creature's brow furrowed. "Rock-Jaw not confess."

"You will," I said. "And you'll also disclose the location of your ill-gotten bounty. I wouldn't mind if you apologized to that nice policeman, either, for giving him such an unnecessary fright earlier."

"Why would Rock-Jaw do this?"

"Out of fear," I said, simply. "Of me."

Rock-Jaw's eyelids clicked faintly as he blinked.

"I'd rather you did it simply to be nice, of course. But as I said, we're running out of time. Ninety seconds left."

Rock-Jaw forced a chuckle and slid his feet off the table. "Foolish human not know Rock-Jaw's reputation?"

"Oh, it's an impressive reputation," I assured him. "And it's clever, too. One does not need to engage in any actual brutish violence so long as everyone *believes* that you engage in brutish violence. Quick piece of advice, though: *real* monsters don't try so hard to keep up appearances. I think the department would have caught on eventually— Marlowe's not a fool. You're fortunate they've been preoccupied. Fifty seconds."

Confidence was rapidly draining from Rock-Jaw's face. "You . . . you threatening Rock-Jaw?"

"Not threatening," I said. "Worse. I am *seeing* you."

Rock-Jaw paled.

"The *real* you," I continued. "The *you* that you've got wrapped up in all that trollish glamour. The voice is a nice touch, by the way. Top-notch magical augmentation. You're not a troll at all. You're a . . . a hob? Did I get that right? I can see you much more clearly now that everyone else is out of the room, but I've always been better with faces than I am with names. Twenty seconds, Mr. Rock-Jaw. We are nearly out of time."

His eyes darted from me to the door and back again. And there he was, under all those layers of magic. Hobs were unassuming creatures—no taller than a primary school child, with bodies like pudgy, overgrown turtles but without the shells. The glamour he was wearing hovered above him, well constructed but immaterial.

"Please." The creature leaned in, its booming voice suddenly reduced to a desperate whisper. "Rock-Jaw owes powerful people many shiny coins. If lady takes Rock-Jaw's secret away, Rock-Jaw has nothing. Rock-Jaw is dead hob walking."

"Hmm. It sounds to me as if Rock-Jaw is about to come to a *prudent realization*," I whispered back, "in three—two—"

With a click, the door opened and Dupin stepped back inside. His eyes darted from me to the visibly rattled Rock-Jaw.

"Hello again, Inspector," I said. "I believe your guest has something he would like to tell you."

Dupin raised an eyebrow.

"There is knotty old willow tree," Rock-Jaw mumbled. "It grow at end of low fence, just off road humans call Tanner Lane. Rock-Jaw bury his money in box between roots. It all there. Rock-Jaw promise."

Dupin blinked.

"And?" I prompted.

Rock-Jaw sighed. "And Rock-Jaw is . . . sorry," he mumbled, "that he made policeman look like frightened baby man. Even though it very funny."

I smiled. "Now, then, was that so hard?"

From the doorway, Commissioner Marlowe let out a huff that might have been a chuckle.

"I think you'll find him more amenable moving forward," I said, standing up and tucking the chair in behind me. "Have a lovely day, Mr. Rock-Jaw. I do look forward to seeing you again sometime."

The commissioner held the door for me, and I stepped back into the hall. "So," he said, "you're ready to assist on bigger cases?"

"I am," I said. "The Horne file?"

Marlowe shook his head. "Bigger than Horne." He took a deep breath. "Step into my office. We need to talk."

chapter six

Marlowe's office felt even more crowded than last time. The pressure of responsibility inside the tiny room made my ears ache. The commissioner shut the door behind me gently before speaking.

"I need to preface this by telling you that you're not here, Miss Rook. I did not invite you into my office today. We're not talking right now."

"Understood," I said. "Might I ask *why* I am not here, not in your office, not talking to you?"

"Because bringing you in on this matter is a terrible option." Marlowe trudged behind his desk and slid into his chair heavily. "But frankly, I can't afford to not use an asset with the ability to spot paranormal prints at a glance. We need a highly sensitive matter resolved as quickly and quietly as possible in a manner you're uniquely qualified to achieve."

"I'm listening," I said. "Or I'm *not*—whichever is the right response presently."

Marlowe nodded. "Uniforms brought a high-profile case this morning," he said. "Juliette D'Aulaire. Heiress. Prominent socialite. Highly connected to a lot of influential people. Dead."

"Murder?" I asked.

"Almost certainly."

"Supernatural?"

"Looks that way."

I considered. "I must admit, I don't especially approve of money and influence moving a victim to the head of the line for justice."

"It's not the money or influence that flagged this one," Marlowe grunted. "D'Aulaire was a vocal advocate of some extreme political initiatives. Creating a registry of all inhumans. Reduced rights. Relocation. That sort of thing. *Humans First* and *Mundus Noster* seem to be the favorite rallying cries."

"I've seen the paintwork."

Marlowe nodded solemnly. "D'Aulaire has a lot of followers. Avid ones. She gave their movement a respectable face. But every time a new column prints, a gaggle of excitable idiots vandalize the city or assault the elderly and call it heroism. Putting out fires is exhausting enough without those buffoons finding excuses to throw fuel on any ember they can find."

"The sort of followers who would happily turn her death into a martyrdom for their cause?" I said. "I think I'm beginning to grasp the weight of the thing."

"It's a political powder keg," said Marlowe.

I swallowed. A scandal on this scale was more than a few steps above stolen frippery. "Has Charlie been apprised of the situation yet?" I asked.

Marlowe winced, and I could see trepidation crackle across his aura. "I'd rather not engage Mr. Barker on this one," Marlowe answered. "In fact, I think it best he stay well away from the whole affair."

"Why?" I asked. "You were the one who recommended him for the liaison position in the first place. Wouldn't this be the perfect time for him to *liaise*? People *like* Charlie. He's good at de-escalating situations."

"Not this one, he's not," grunted Marlowe. He gestured at a newspaper lying open on his desk. "D'Aulaire's last editorial is all about the Om Caini. It ran yesterday."

I felt a cold weight in my stomach. The Om Caini had claimed jurisdiction over the veil-gate, with Charlie's sister, Alina, heading the operation, as sovereign of the pack. It fell to them to control who came and went between worlds, which meant they also received the brunt of the blame whenever anything otherworldly went wrong.

"Charlie is mentioned by name," added Marlowe. "Twice. It is . . . unflattering."

I scanned the dead woman's scathing prose and felt my face growing hot. *Unflattering* was an understatement.

"I don't need to tell you that the situation is tense," Marlowe continued. "Ever since that rift opened, everyone seems to think *they* should get to make the rules, and nobody's happy. We've gotten demands from religious leaders, covens, occultists. Federal agents are now overseeing our operations, threatening to seize control entirely if we can't keep this mess tethered down. We can't afford a flashy public scandal. The last thing we need is the same newspapers that printed D'Aulaire's hogwash in the first place getting wind that a key person of interest was involved in her murder investigation."

"Yes, I can see the conflict of interest." I gritted my teeth. That D'Aulaire woman had used her last words to paint a target on Charlie's back—but there was no reason to paint it even brighter. "Why tell me all this, then?" I asked. "Charlie's relationship with me is no secret. "Would I not be seen as having just as much of a conflict?"

"Which is why it's convenient that you're not here," grunted Marlowe. "It's why this conversation never took place. It is most decidedly why I am not writing an address on this piece of paper, along with a very specific window of time during which one could expect all of the supervising officers at the crime scene to be otherwise occupied." He scribbled a few words on a piece of paper and folded them into a crisp square.

"Wait." I blinked. "You . . . you *want* me to insert myself into an ongoing investigation and trespass onto an active crime scene without official clearance?"

Marlowe sighed. "For the record, I obviously want no such thing." He slid the paper across the desk. "*Off* the record, I'm sure Mr. Jackaby can give you a few pointers about trespassing onto a crime scene. There's a window on the first floor, rear," he added. "I definitely would *not* know anything about the latch being left unlocked."

My hand was shaky as I picked up the paper.

"Time is a luxury we don't have, and you are an asset we can't waste." Marlowe's eyes fixed on mine. "You don't need to tell me that it's too much to ask," he acknowledged. "But I'm asking it anyway, because you're the only *you* we've got. Are you up to it?"

I met his gaze. I could say no. I should say no. My throat felt dry.

"Of course," I managed. "I'm up to it."

chapter seven

The walk back across the city is a blur in my memory. I felt dizzy. Peace in New Fiddleham was apparently balanced on a knife's edge—and *I* was somehow supposed to tip the scales? And what about Charlie? I was finding it difficult to draw full breaths. The auras all around me felt like they were darkening, churning around and around into a foreboding tunnel. This was bad.

"This is wonderful!" Jackaby slapped his hands together, jarring me back to the present and to the cluttered office on Augur Lane. "I'll pack the usual charms and wards, of course." He was already beginning to bustle around, opening drawers and pulling out little bundles and beads as he spoke. "Do you think you'd use the new scrying stones if I brought them? Oh, I'll bring them just in case. Did Marlowe happen to mention if there was any dismemberment involved? Bodily mutilation? No details? That's fine—the surprise is part of the fun."

"Fun? Mr. Jackaby—the woman is *dead*!"

"Obviously." He lifted his head up from the bottom drawer of a cabinet. "I was, however, under the impression she was also awful. Awful first and then dead?"

"Yes. Sure, fine," I said. "But awful or not, her death makes things complicated. Did you know those Humans First people have been targeting Charlie? By name? *My* Charlie?"

"First I'm hearing of it," Jackaby mumbled. His aura flushed a muddy pink.

"Jackaby!" I gaped. "You do know that I can see you're lying."

"Yes, but I was hoping that in the heat of the moment you wouldn't notice," he said. "You caught it straightaway, though. Very keen! Good job. An excellent sign that you're ready to tackle this case. I'm packing ankhs and rosaries." I had not seen the insufferable man so excited in months.

The window of time written on Marlowe's clandestine note was not for several hours, which gave me at least a brief period in which I could try to settle my nerves.

I took a deep breath as I stepped off the spiral staircase onto the third-story landing. There were several upsides to remaining a tenant at 926 Augur Lane—the protective wards around the perimeter, the enviable library—but none of these compared to the oasis that was the third floor. If one looked hard enough, one could pick out the telltale signs of the stately study and sensible office space that had once occupied the floor—a filing cabinet stood against that wall, a weathered davenport under that window—but these had all been given freely to the vines and wildflowers. The work had been completed by supernatural contractors in exchange for assistance Jackaby had provided years ago, and the result was well and truly magical. The wood of the floor extended only a few feet from the landing before melting into soft peat. Where once there had been carpets, lush meadows of moss and clover now covered the floor. A butterfly flitted by as I made my way down the worn path toward the pond.

I eased myself onto the bench at the water's edge just as a stately mallard paddled up to the shore to meet me.

"Good morning, Douglas," I said.

Douglas quacked a polite greeting in response.

I tore off several chunks of soft bread and tossed them into the grass in front of him. He bobbed his head in my direction before tucking in. Douglas had not always been a mallard. Before I had ever stepped off the boat in New Fiddleham, Douglas had been Jackaby's assistant. Jackaby insisted that the spell was reversible, but that by the time he had acquired the necessary resources, Douglas had settled in. He could change back at any time—at least my mentor believed that he could—but he had to *want* to. His human features were almost visible in the halo of his aura, but they were like an impression left in the sand, an imprint of humanity in a body that was now entirely waterfowl.

I watched as Douglas rooted for bread crumbs, his tail feathers wiggling contentedly.

"Do you still remember it?" I asked. "Being a person?"

He lifted his head to look me in the eyes for several seconds. He did not respond, but his aura betrayed comprehension. He understood perfectly well.

"Do you ever miss it?" I asked.

With a noncommittal shrug of his wings, he returned his attention to the grass.

I leaned back against the bench and looked out across the rippling water. "Between the two of us, confidentially, I'm beginning to think you got the better curse."

Douglas waddled closer, flapped his wings, and hopped up onto the bench beside me. His eyes shimmered with the reflection of the morning light catching the water.

"It's not that being the Seer isn't a great privilege," I amended. "It is, I know, and I suppose I should be more appreciative. I've been given a power some people would kill for. *Have* killed for." I took a deep breath. Douglas watched me intently. "I just keep feeling unequal to it. What if it's wasted on me? Maybe I find a clue at that house that nobody else could find, but I don't know what to do with it, and so a killer goes free. Or maybe I do uncover a killer, but that truth sets off a war, and countless more are killed." I sighed. "And maybe I just mope about, staring at the water and feeling sorry for myself while the world burns."

Douglas bobbed back and forth, straightening up. He was every bit a duck, but the humanity in his aura pressed right to the surface. The feathers that hung around his chest looked like a prim vest, and the ring around his neck was like a starched shirt collar. It was not difficult to imagine him tallying expenses and updating ledgers. After a pregnant pause, he opened his bill as if to speak, then hesitated.

"Yes?" I prompted.

Decisively, Douglas snatched the other half of the baguette from my lap and flew off over the pond. His feet skimmed the water as he made his landing.

"You used to be a better listener," I called after him.

He replied with a hearty and unapologetic *quack* from the comfort of the mossy armchair that occupied his island in the center of the lake.

I pushed myself up to standing and shook my head. Well, if Douglas could seize the opportunities that felt right to him, then I supposed I could, too—I just had to sort out for myself what they were.

As I headed back down the stairwell, a dull *thunk* made me pause on the second floor. I peeked out at the landing and saw Charlie, rubbing his head and righting himself in the hallway.

The mirror portal, convenient though it was, had a habit of tilting midway through. This made crossing feel a bit like stepping from a moving train onto a platform—if the platform was also on a hill and obeyed a different gravity than the train's.

Charlie dusted himself off. He spotted me watching as he was brushing a curl of hair behind his ears, and he flashed me a warm smile. There it was again, that ripple of joy as he looked at me. All of my stresses did not exactly vanish in that instant—but for just a moment, they ebbed.

Sheepishly, he nodded at the mirror. "Overcorrected. Every time."

"Oh, poor dear," I said. "If only I'd been here faster, I would have caught you."

Charlie's aura pulsed. "I certainly would have preferred if my landing had been in your arms."

My ears felt hot. I opened my mouth to say something clever and flirtatious in return, but found speaking more than impossible.

"I really appreciate this," Charlie said.

"Mm?" I tried to find my way back to solid ground.

"It's good to have someone to talk to before the briefing," he said. "I'm probably overthinking it, but I've been nervous about it all week."

I blinked. "Right," I managed, at last. "Your big meeting. Tomorrow." The warm, pleasant haze began to slip away, letting the cold breeze of reality creep back in.

"It's just that there are going to be a lot of people there."

"Wait," I said. And all at once an icy lump formed in my gut as all the stresses that had been patiently holding back began jockeying for position in the front of my brain again. "Are there going to be reporters there? Like from the newspapers?"

"Well, it *is* a press briefing," he said. "But it's also for the public—an open forum. The mayor felt the community should be kept informed about evolving policy matters and given a chance to voice their feelings on the—"

"It's a terrible idea," I interjected. "Couldn't you just write it all down and send them a report?"

"That's not how it works, I'm afraid." He shrugged. "I've got to be there in person."

"But anyone could attend! Aren't you the least bit concerned that people will blame you for all the things they don't like? That they might take their frustration out on you? That they might become an unruly mob?"

"Of course I have my concerns," Charlie answered. He swallowed and fidgeted with the cuff on his jacket. "But showing up is the job. And letting people be angry at me if they feel they must—well, that is also the job."

"Then it's a terrible job," I said.

Charlie let out a sigh and nodded, his brows crinkling. I could see lightning flashes of anxiety piercing the storm cloud around him now. I had not made things better.

"Have you considered," I asked, "running away with me and avoiding all of our responsibilities forever and ever as a mature and reasonable alternative?"

He smiled weakly and stepped closer. "Daily," he said.

My head slipped under his chin as his arms wrapped around me. He smelled of sandalwood and mint, and for another fleeting moment the chaotic world melted away into the background.

And then the moment was pierced by a crash and the clatter of porcelain downstairs. Charlie straightened, and I reluctantly pulled away.

"Charlie, I don't mean to make you more anxious than you already are. I'm sorry. It's just . . ." I hesitated. What was I planning to say, exactly? *It's just that you have every reason to be afraid? It's just that loads of total strangers have, indeed, decided to hate you personally and quite possibly accuse you of a murder you don't know anything about?* Maybe I would have something more reassuring to say *after* solving the case and clearing Charlie's name. "It's just that there's this small errand I need to run before I can really give you my full attention."

Charlie raised an eyebrow. "Something to do with the robbery case?" he asked. "I could come with you."

"No! No, I—" I searched for a way to tell him about D'Aulaire. Did he already know about all the libelous articles she'd penned? Of her final scathing indictment? The poor man was buzzing with nerves already—it made my heart ache to make it worse.

From the floor below came another muffled crash.

"We should probably go see if Jackaby hasn't managed to set fire to water or something," I demurred.

Charlie followed me down the stairs. I had to tell him. He was putting on a brave face, but the clouds hanging over him were still heavy and thick. "I'm sorry," I said. "I want to help. I do. It's just . . ."

"You have a lot on your plate right now," he offered. "I'll be fine." His assurances only made me feel more wretched as I watched the anxiety circle his head. My throat felt tight. I was making everything worse.

We reached the ground floor, where we were met by the sound of raised voices in the kitchen.

"She is not a *child*!" Jackaby was saying.

"But she *is* a human being," Jenny's voice countered, hotly. "You would do well to remember that adults experience emotions, too, and have need of empathy from time to time."

"She says she's *fine*," Jackaby was saying as I opened the door. Both of them turned. Jenny looked embarrassed. Jackaby did not. "She can speak for herself," said Jackaby. "Are you fine, Miss Rook?"

"Of course I'm not fine," I sighed.

"See?" Jackaby spun back to Jenny. "A highly self-aware and reflective response, indicative of a healthy state of emotional awareness. She's fine."

Jenny threw up her hands in exasperation. "Charlie, tell me you've at least tried to talk some sense into her?"

Charlie looked confused.

"Charlie clearly appreciates the magnitude of the situation," Jackaby said, jabbing a finger in Charlie's direction. "Tell her."

"I'm not sure that I—" Charlie began.

"Actually, I had not yet gotten around to fully explaining the situation to Charlie." I shot him an apologetic glance. "I was . . . getting to it."

"The situation," Jenny announced, "is that Abigail has been through a monumental trauma and transformation. She should be taking the time to discover herself, not discover some horrid murderer."

"Murderer?" Charlie asked.

The emotions in the room were beginning to collect like smoke pouring off a grease fire. I could feel the muscle just under my right eye beginning to twitch. In the back of my head I could hear a sort of tapping.

"She has spent the past six months cooped up in this house," Jackaby yelled. "If she was going to discover herself here, she would have found herself already! Maybe she's looking in the wrong place. Who's to say she won't turn up on the trail? Somewhere around the corpse of that awful woman?"

"Come again?" Charlie said. "What woman?"

"The dead woman!" Jackaby snapped. "Keep up, man!"

"Don't look at me," said Jenny. "Different dead woman."

"Stop!" I finally burst. "Would everyone cease shouting on my behalf, please? Yes, I am feeling rather overwhelmed at present—but I am tired of telling you all that I can handle it. The truth is that I have no idea whether or not I can handle it, but I have made the decision to handle it anyway, so you can all kindly stop arguing about it!"

In the silence that followed, the tapping was clearer. It was coming from the front door.

Charlie cleared his throat. "I can answer that," he said, "if you all would like a moment?"

"I am perfectly capable of answering a door," I said, a bit more sternly than I had intended.

I took several steadying breaths as I made my way to the front room.

I could see two auras on the other side of the door. The first was prim and stiff, a halo of rich amber marbled with proud violets. The second, taller and softer, was a coppery brown with sunny wisps of curiosity. They were familiar, but I could not quite place them. I threw the door open and froze.

"Well?" said my mother. "You've forced your father and me to come all this way—are you going to force us to stand outside in the cold, as well?"

chapter eight

In classic tales, there are several means by which a person might retain youthfulness. The ancient Greeks believed in a restorative ambrosia, the ancient Norse consumed golden apples, and the ancient Chinese had peaches of immortality. The poet Oscar Wilde published a novel in which the feat was achieved by means of an enchanted painting and the sale of one's soul—although that story did not end well for the titular Dorian Gray. There is, of course, a much less miraculous method of becoming a child again. Should one feel the budding onset of adulthood and wish to stave off any pesky sense of maturity or autonomy, one need only spend the day with one's overbearing parents.

"Well of course we came to rescue you," my mother said, straightening the collar on my blouse. "You didn't think your mother and father would leave you helpless and alone, stranded on this brutish continent all by yourself, did you?"

My eye twitched. "I am not alone, Mother," I said. "And I am not in need of rescuing."

"Of course you're not," said my father, setting a pair of traveling bags down just inside the door. He exchanged a knowing look with my mother. "And bully for you! Really. Good show, making it this far."

My mother rolled her eyes. "Don't encourage her, Daniel. It's all right, dear. You've had your great big, grown-up adventure. There's no need to stay in this dreadful place any longer just to prove some silly point." Her eyes scanned the room disapprovingly, drifting from one eclectic keepsake to the next, ultimately landing on Ogden's terrarium.

"I am not proving a silly point," I said, wishing that my voice did not sound exactly as it had when I tried to stay up for two days straight when I was fourteen just to show them that I could. I had awoken in my father's arms as he was carrying me to bed. "And don't stare at the frog," I added.

"Don't rush the girl," my father said. "We only just arrived. Besides, she set out to pursue her passion, and we didn't raise our little Abisaurus to give up too easily. We're very proud of you, dear. How is the excavation going?"

"Excavation?" I said. "Oh. I mean, yes—I did set out for a dig . . . at first. But the thing about that is that I took a slightly different path when I arrived in New Fiddleham. It's a perfectly normal path, though. Normal and safe. Nothing to fret about."

"Don't be modest!" my father insisted. "Tell me about Gad's Valley. What a beast that must have been!"

My heart dropped into my stomach—that particular caper had involved a dragon towering over the treetops and blasting fire across the landscape. "How—how do you know about Gad's Valley?"

"They devoted half a page to the dig in the *Modern Scientist* a few months ago. Great stuff. I made contact with the paleontologist—Owen Horner. He spoke very highly of you. Rather cagey about the details, though. I gather there was a bit of trouble toward the end?"

"You could call it that," I said. It had been a bit of trouble that had taken several lives and burned down acres of pristine wilderness. "It all got rather out of hand."

"No reason to be embarrassed just because a dig went south. I've had my share of those. Every keen scientific mind has the occasional setback."

"That's really not—" I began.

"Couldn't agree more!" came a voice from over my shoulder.

"Oh, Mr. Jackaby," I said. "I thought you were in the kitchen."

My mother's eyebrows rose. "And who is this man?" she asked.

"He must be the gentleman Mr. Horner told me about," said my father. "The one Abigail's been working for."

"Mr. Jackaby," I said, "I would like you to meet"—I took a deep breath—"my parents."

"I must admit," said my mother, "that I cannot approve of your living unescorted with a strange man. People will talk."

"I'm sure he's not a strange man," my father said.

"No, that does seem to be the general consensus," Jackaby confirmed. "But you needn't worry about your daughter taking up residence in my abode. I have laid very clear boundaries—and am happily spoken for anyway."

"Ah." My mother seemed somewhat mollified. "Is the lady of the house at home?"

"Nearly always." Jackaby nodded. "She is, however, rather shy around new faces. And also she is deceased."

My mother was uncharacteristically at a loss for words.

"A widower?" said my father. "You have my condolences."

"Mm? Oh, no—nothing like that," Jackaby said with an amiable chuckle. "She was already dead when we met."

"Ha, ha," I said, urgently. "Very droll, sir. Mr. Jackaby has a singular sense of humor." I shot him a cutting glance. "It takes some getting used to."

"I see," my mother said, in a tone that clearly meant the opposite. "And he is your employer?"

"Yes," I said. "Well, no. He *was*. It's different now."

"Is that so?" My father raised a bushy eyebrow.

Jackaby gave him a cheerful, if oblivious, nod.

"Not like that," I told my parents. "Nothing romantic. We're strictly business."

"Well, I don't mind admitting, that's a tremendous relief," said my mother. "He's much too old for you. But speaking of your romantic life—"

"I'd really rather we wouldn't."

My mother ignored me and plowed on. "If we don't dally too long in this . . . *hmm* . . . charming city, then we should make it home just in time for the Autumn Ball. Won't that be nice? You love the Autumn Ball. Of course, we'll need to stop somewhere along the way to have you fitted for some suitable clothing. You have gained weight, obviously, but not so much we can't make you look presentable."

The air felt heavy in my lungs. I was fifteen again and still painfully awkward in my own skin; I was eleven and fidgeting with my itchy Sunday dress; I was six with mud all over my new white stockings. I took a deep breath.

"Mother!" I said. "Stop."

"What?" she asked, innocently.

"All of it," I said. "Firstly, I have not enjoyed the Autumn Ball since I was a child—and secondly, I am not simply going to pick up and leave. I have obligations here."

"Don't be contrary," my mother chided. "It's unbecoming. That foolish bone business is over, and you no longer work for this . . . *hmm* . . . gentleman. Your father and I have agreed to forgive you for the way you left, so the important thing now is to put the whole business behind us. Besides, I'm sure you will find something to see in the young men today that you did not see in them when you were seven."

"You're not listening, Mother."

"Give them a chance," my father said. "There's a certain young fellow who likes research as much as you do who was asking about you right before we left."

"Tell me," I managed, "that you did not travel four thousand miles just to try to set me up with Tommy bloody Bellows again."

"Language!" my mother gasped. "The Bellows family is well respected, Abigail, and Thomas is set to inherit a sizable estate. You could do a lot worse."

"I could do a lot better!" I countered. Out of the corner of my eye, I could see Charlie's aura where he was hesitating at the doorway, just behind Jackaby. "In fact, I *have* done a lot better." I held out my left hand. My mother gaped at the ring, looking as if she might topple at any moment. "Mother, Father, I would like to introduce Charlie Barker. My fiancé."

Charlie slid into the room in the midst of a silence so intensely uncomfortable it warped time around it. "Hi," he managed hoarsely, pushing his words past the wall of awkwardness. "A pleasure to meet you both."

He stepped forward and shook hands with both of my parents, the silence still clinging to him like molasses.

"Barker, was it?" my mother finally said. "Are you related to the Totton Barkers, by chance?"

Charlie cleared his throat. His fingers were fidgeting absently with the cuff of his suit again. "I don't believe so," he said. He conveniently left out the fact that *Barker* was a pseudonym, one which he had adopted only recently, while hiding out from the torches and pitchforks of one of New Fiddleham's less tolerant days.

"Shame," said my mother. "Good family."

"Charlie comes from a perfectly good family," I said.

"Royalty, even," said Jackaby.

This caught my mother's attention. "Really?"

Charlie looked as if he had swallowed Ogden.

"Yes, indeed," said Jackaby. "A remarkable lineage. What do you know about therianthropy?"

"That's quite enough about Charlie," I said. "Look, it's really lovely to see you both. I should have written more often. But I'm afraid your timing is not ideal. Mr. Jackaby and I have a pressing appointment this afternoon. Perhaps you could check in wherever you're staying tonight and then tomorrow we can—"

"Nonsense," my mother said. "You have not seen your dear parents for more than a year. I'm sure you and your friends can reschedule."

I could sense Charlie's discontent beginning to shift from an uncomfortable, muddy brown to a steely silver.

"This is not the sort of thing that we can reschedule," I said.

"Poppycock." My mother waved her hand dismissively. "She's always been like this. Nearly made us miss a dinner engagement with the honorable Lord Tennyson once."

"You do not give your daughter enough credit," Charlie said, his voice suddenly firm.

"I think I know my daughter better than some—"

"I think you don't." His aura was hot, but his voice remained measured and even. My mother put an affronted hand to her chest. "If you did," he continued, "you would show her more respect. It is clear you do not appreciate how important your daughter is to this city. You should know that she is the most highly sought after consultant in all matters of—"

"Nothing," I interrupted, "that can't wait until later to discuss." I gave Charlie a pleading look, hoping he would understand. Every aspect of the life I had built in New Fiddleham was a nesting doll of explanations, and I was not ready to open them all.

Dissatisfaction colored Charlie's expression, but he let it rest for the time being. His aura was swimming with frustration.

"As I was saying," I continued, "why don't you two get

settled at your hotel—or wherever you're staying—and we can meet back for lunch tomorrow?"

"That's no good," said Jackaby.

I glared at him.

"Charlie will be delivering his briefing about lunchtime," he clarified.

I blinked. How could I have forgotten? Oh, good lord. If Jackaby was more considerate than I was, then the world really was topsy-turvy.

"It's fine," Charlie said. "Perhaps it is best that I'm away. I'm sure your parents would not mind a moment alone with you. Time for you to fill them in on . . . everything."

"No," I said. "No, I said I would be there to support you, and I meant it. Perhaps after my parents check into their room—"

"A shame you don't have a spare room right here in the house," my mother said.

"Well, I mean, we do, technically—" Jackaby began. I cleared my throat pointedly, and he attempted to correct his trajectory midleap. "That is—erm—we do not?"

"You *don't* have a spare room?" my father said.

"We *do* have a room," Jackaby said, "but not to spare. Or rather, it's a spare, but there's no room. It's a mess. It would take some work to get it all tidied up."

"Oh, that's very generous of you," my mother said. "Are you sure?"

"Am I?" said Jackaby, confused. "Not at all."

"Well, that's settled, then." Mother clapped. "We're most happy to accept your invitation, Mr. Jackaby."

"Oh." Jackaby nodded. "Is that what just happened? Great." His aura looked a tad dizzy. The man was better with monsters than he was with mothers. He glanced at me. "If that's all right with you, of course, Miss Rook?"

I pursed my lips. "Of course it's all right," I managed. "Lovely. Grand."

"Right. Well, then." Jackaby edged toward the hallway door. "I'll just go move a few odds and ends into the attic before we go. Do you two mind sharing your room with a taxidermied cow? It's a smallish cow, although—full disclosure—it *is* slightly cursed. You know what, never mind. I'll tuck it upstairs."

My mother's mouth opened, but words failed her.

"Ha, ha!" My father jabbed a finger at Jackaby and nodded his head, smiling. "Abigail's right! You have a cracking sense of humor. Now, we really don't wish to be a nuisance."

"Oh. Yes," my mother agreed, rallying. "Please don't ask your cook to prepare anything fancy."

"We don't have a cook," I said, wearily. "Mother, *most* people do not have personal cooks."

"Then who does your cooking?" she asked. "Certainly not *you*?"

I could feel my cheeks flush.

"I'll handle dinner this evening, as well," Jackaby cut in. "It's no trouble. That should give the Rook family more time to catch up. We'll have the place feeling like home in no time. A proper rookery!"

I tried not to think about the last time Jackaby cooked a three-course meal—and the number of people who had been injured in the process—but that was somehow the least concerning part of the whole arrangement.

"I suppose it's settled, then," said my father. "We'll stay here, and Mr. Barker and I can get acquainted while we await your return from your errand. I'll just go and fetch the rest of our bags from the coach."

The noise that escaped Charlie sounded a bit like steam escaping a kettle just before it properly boils.

"Won't this be—erm—fun," said Jackaby. "You may actually find the decor quite diverting. Some of the artifacts we've stored in there are genuinely one of a kind. Out of curiosity, do either of you have an allergy to cats?"

"No," said my mother. "Have you got a cat?"

"Not a whole one," answered Jackaby. "This way."

They bustled away, Jackaby's voice fading into a murmur as he gave my mother a whirlwind tour of the house. For a brief moment, Charlie and I were alone in the drawing room.

"I'm so sorry," I said. "I'll explain everything to them, I promise. Eventually. It's just that my mother can be rather—and I just wasn't ready for—"

"It's all right," Charlie said. I would not have needed supernatural sight to spot the lie—Charlie's nerves were so taut I could hear them strumming—but I nodded gratefully. He gave me a kiss on the cheek and the heartiest smile he could muster. "I'll do my best to keep them entertained until you get back. Don't worry, I will avoid . . . *atypical* topics as best I can. Then we just have to worry about surviving dinner."

"I do not deserve you," I said.

"Tell me that *after* we've survived dinner," he said.

chapter nine

O ur carriage slowed as we neared the scene of the crime. I did my best not to feel guilty about leaving poor Charlie stuck in a house with my parents while we investigated, but it had been a necessary sacrifice. He would be much safer in there, making uncomfortable small talk, than he would be out here anyway. To the best of anyone's knowledge, the victim's final words had been a public condemnation of Charlie and his whole family. Until I had seen the whole matter well and fully resolved, I would be listening for the sound of an angry mob sharpening their pitchforks and lighting their torches.

The wheels ground to a stop, and I peered out the window. Our driver, Miss Lee, rapped on the roof, and we stepped out into the sunny street. Miss Lee had stopped the horses on a narrow lane about two blocks away from the D'Aulaire mansion. We would make a more inconspicuous approach from here.

"Thank you, Miss Lee," I said.

"Anytime," she answered. "Nice to finally have a reason to get out and about. I did notice several uniforms and a barricade a few streets down. If you don't mind my inquiring, will you two be preserving the law today or breaking it? Not judging, mind. Just nice to have a guess at how fast I should get the horses moving upon your return."

"Preserving?" I said without confidence. "Mostly preserving. Definitely not breaking. Well. Maybe bending, but only the smaller ones."

"Bending's good for laws," Jackaby added. "Keeps them flexible."

Miss Lee nodded. "I've missed this."

Jackaby and I soon found ourselves slipping along a narrow alley and onto the back road that would take us to D'Aulaire's property. As we neared, my anxiety about my parents finally ebbed, leaving room for my anxiety about the case to surge. I just needed to find something—anything—to make it crystal clear that Charlie and his family had nothing to do with the woman's death. Sadly, crystal clarity had not been my strong suit lately.

"What if I'm not able to find anything?" I whispered.

"Then there was never anything for you to find," Jackaby replied simply. "That would be a small blessing. If the murder turned out to be nothing more than a common burglary gone wrong, it would certainly take a lot of pressure off the matter."

I swallowed. "That does make me feel slightly better, I suppose."

"Of course, if the investigation turns up nothing at all, the anti-magic zealots will almost certainly claim that as proof of some grand conspiracy, which will simply postpone the pressure as it builds. Still. That would be a best-case scenario."

"That doesn't say much for the *other* potential scenarios," I said. "What do you suppose will happen if I *do* turn up evidence of a paranormal perpetrator?" The Humans First crowd would turn *any* supernatural criminal into proof that they were right about people like Charlie.

Jackaby shrugged. "Then we follow the trail and bring them to justice. Unless it turns out to be a non-sentient creature—and then I suppose we bring whoever is responsible for *that* creature to justice. That's presuming it's not some wild beast who just slipped over on its own from the other side of the veil. Not sure if that would be better or worse. The mob is so rarely satisfied without someone to blame."

"But there *would* be someone to blame." I sighed. "The Om Caini control the veil-gate." If the killer was just some mindless monster who slipped through, it would still be blamed on them. Every outcome led back to Charlie and his family. I swallowed.

I could see Jackaby considering a response, but ultimately he gestured forward. "Speaking of gates, this one appears to be open. We can make our way along those bushes to the back of the house."

The D'Aulaire mansion occupied half a city block of real estate. We crept behind the shrubberies as we neared, but we needn't have bothered. I could see plainly that there were no watchmen posted at the back of the house. There had been, and fairly recently, judging by the freshness of their auras, but as he'd promised, Marlowe had cleared our approach.

"What would we even do with it?" I asked. "With a wild creature from the other side, I mean. If we caught one, would we take it to the police? Animal control? It's not as though New Fiddleham is prepared to handle magical beasts."

"I suppose we would turn it over to Alina and her guards," Jackaby answered. "As you say, it would be their responsibility to put it back where it belongs."

I considered. An idea was steeping in the back of my mind. "How far does their jurisdiction reach?" I asked. "I mean—I know they're in charge of the gate, but if someone did cross over from the Annwyn and slip past the sentinels, how far could the Om Caini pursue them before turning matters over to Marlowe?"

"Depends on the heat of the pursuit."

"Heat?"

"When an officer is in hot pursuit, their jurisdiction follows them. If it runs cold, then they report the matter to the New Fiddleham authorities."

"I've got it," I said. Jackaby raised an eyebrow at me. "This whole situation is bad, no matter what we find, right?" I said.

"You seem much happier about that realization than I would expect."

"No, listen. If we find out that this was a run-of-the-mill *human* murder, then the zealots call foul and make trouble for Charlie's family. If we find out that it was a supernatural culprit, they blame *all* nonhumans and make trouble for Charlie's family. If we find out it was just some random creature, they *still* make trouble for Charlie's family . . . so what's the common factor in all those scenarios?"

"Trouble?"

"The common factor is *we*. No matter how *we* bring justice in this case, it makes things worse—but what if the Om

Caini get credit? Think about it—we're not officially working with the police, so we don't have any official obligation to give the police our findings first. Maybe this is what Marlowe intended."

"I'm pretty sure it's not."

"Maybe it should be. We could use D'Aulaire's own notoriety to publicize the heroic efforts of her supernatural neighbors."

Jackaby's head bobbed left and right as he weighed the idea.

We reached the window, just where Marlowe had said we would, and slipped quietly inside.

The house was only slightly less silent than the grave. Flies buzzed incessantly. The smell was an almost tangible thing, and an overwhelming energy poured down the corridor, seeping like ink, curling and twisting as it spread. I did not need Jackaby to define this aura. There was no question that we were in the presence of death.

Glistening notes of brutality and violence ran through the creeping tendrils. Whatever had happened to Miss D'Aulaire, it had not been gentle.

"This way." I nodded to a door on the left, and Jackaby and I tiptoed into the crime scene.

The sight within was roughly as grisly as I had anticipated. A blanket had been laid over the body, but there was blood all around it. With a pencil, Jackaby carefully lifted one corner of the shroud, and I had to look away.

"Claw marks," Jackaby observed. "And a torn jugular. If this wasn't the cause of death, it certainly cinched the deal."

I knew that I needed to go in for a closer look, but I allowed myself a minute to scan the room first. Underneath the stain of death, several auras crisscrossed the chamber. Most of them were human. No surprises there—Juliette D'Aulaire was not the sort to keep company with elves and trolls. There was another trail, however. A tingle ran up my neck and a cold lump dropped into the pit of my stomach. "No."

"I've spotted some scratches along the floor. Signs of a scuffle. It appears the victim put up some degree of resistance. I wonder . . ."

Jackaby peeled the blanket back farther and knelt to examine the woman's hands.

My limbs felt leaden as I finally turned to face the body. The aura all over her, saturating the woman's injuries, was all too familiar. It was unmistakable.

"Aha!" Jackaby declared. He straightened, a few coarse hairs clutched in his tweezers. "It doesn't look human to me. Werewolf? Come have a look, Miss Rook. We trace who this fur belongs to, we find our killer. Miss Rook?"

But I did not need a closer look. I could read that aura from across the room. For the first time in weeks, I wished that my sight could be *less* precise.

"Not a wolf," I managed. "A dog." I felt as if I might throw up. "It's Om Caini."

Jackaby swallowed. "One of Alina's own kinsmen gone rogue? That's not a conversation I'm looking forward to having."

"It's worse than that," I said. "That fur *is* Alina's."

chapter ten

All the evidence pointed squarely at Charlie's sister. I felt ill. I had seen Alina only yesterday, and everything had been fine. She was Alina—flippant, a bit brash, perhaps—but not a murderer. Surely I would have seen *murderer* in her aura. Wouldn't I? What *did* a murderer's aura look like pre-murder?

"One more look," said Jackaby, his voice hushed. "Just in case we've missed something?"

I peered around the room, willing the sight to latch onto any trace that wasn't Alina's—even the faintest aura of some other creature. The heady presence of death overwhelmed my senses, but I pushed past it. Something lingered in the air near Alina's trail. It was almost an absence of details. There was an acrid smell, like burning lime, but every time I found its trail again, it wriggled away.

"What is it?" Jackaby asked.

I shook my head, blinking. Without realizing it, I had wound up on the other side of the room, tracking the elusive energy. I tried to recall any specific description of the trail, but even the memory of it shied away from me. It was difficult to be sure I had even been following an aura at all and not simply chasing my own desire to find a clue that pointed anywhere other than to the obvious. Alina's trail, I had to accept, was anything but elusive. It was impossible to ignore.

"It's nothing," I sighed. If Alina, the sovereign leader of an already unpopular group of paranormals, had killed her most vocal critic, there would be rioting in the streets. The Om Caini would be painted as public enemies—Charlie included.

"Then we should go," he said. "Our window of opportunity is rapidly closing."

I furrowed my brow. It felt as if we had only just arrived, but I nodded and followed Jackaby back through the open door and down the hall. From the front of the house, I could hear voices. One of them sounded like Dupin's.

I ducked my head under the window as I slipped back out into the open air. Two things struck me as I straightened up. The first was how clean and fresh the world felt beyond the saturated stink of the mansion. The second was that we were not alone.

"You can go ahead and stop right there," said a man with a pencil mustache and a black fedora. Ever the pragmatist, I stopped right there. The gentleman wore a three-piece suit with an impeccably straight, black necktie. His outfit was a matched set to that of the fellow standing next to him, although the latter looked at least thirty years older, his chin dusted in peppery stubble and gray sideburns emerging from the brim of his hat. "Come on out, you," the first man said, peering into the window behind me. "We can see you inside there, still."

"Which is it?" I asked. "*Stop right there* or *come on out*?"

"You don't want to play games with me." The man pulled open his jacket to reveal a holstered pistol on his hip. "Unless you're prepared to win the prizes."

The older man behind him watched the proceedings dispassionately.

"All right, all right." Jackaby clambered out through the window. "You needn't threaten me with heavy-handed metaphors."

"What are you two doing back here?" Pencil Mustache demanded. "Who let you onto the property?"

"We could ask you the same question," I said.

His eyes narrowed, and he adopted the sort of stance I had only seen on the cover of Western magazines when two men duel at high noon. "I asked you first. I want names and occupations, now."

"Go get your own, then," said Jackaby. "We're still using ours."

The man's face reddened, and his hand slid back to hover just over the holster. "I'm real close to being done asking nicely."

"That's enough of that." The older man finally spoke, his voice deep, gravelly. He took an unhurried step closer and produced a slim leather wallet from his jacket pocket. Without any particular pomp or pageantry, he flashed a badge. It bore a triangular seal with an eye in the center and an eagle spreading its wings over the top. "We're from the Bureau of Curiosities," he said. "I'm Agent Garabrand, and the firecracker with the short fuse is Agent Kit. I'd appreciate it if you would stop trying to make him pop, please and thank you."

"Bureau of Curiosities?" I said. "Are you the ones who investigate counterfeit currency?"

"That would be the Secret Service," Agent Kit responded hotly. "We were established four years before they were."

"Secret Service got the better name," I said. "Nice alliteration to it. Easy to remember."

Kit bristled. "The Bureau of Curiosities doesn't *need* to be easy to remember. That's the point. We operate discreetly."

"Well, then—Secret Service still got the better name, didn't they?"

Agent Kit just glowered.

The men's auras were inscrutable. There was an austere frankness to the older one and a sincere ferocity to the younger, but they were both saturated with a silvery tinge of secrecy and manipulation.

"Don't trust them," I said to Jackaby. "They've got something they're keeping hidden."

"A whole lot of somethings," agreed Garabrand, looking amused as he tucked the wallet back into his jacket. "Wouldn't be very good at our job if we couldn't keep juicy secrets, now would we, Mr. Kit?"

"No, sir, we would not," Kit said, not taking his eyes off us.

"Some of them are so juicy, you wouldn't believe them even if we told you," continued Garabrand. "Go ahead. Ask me about the last city we assessed for the bureau."

I glanced at Jackaby and then back to the men. "What was the last city that you assessed?" I asked.

"That's classified," he answered with a contented smile.

"What do you mean, *assessed*?" asked Jackaby.

"Classified," he said. "I never get tired of saying that. You see, secrets are ninety percent of the job. Go ahead. Ask me about the other ten percent."

"You're just going to say that's classified, too, aren't you?" I said.

"Well, not if you go taking the fun out of it." Garabrand scratched his stubbled chin. "Here's the thing. A couple of government officers keeping secrets isn't particularly special. But a young lady who can see those secrets hovering around us like ghosts? Well, now. That's enough to give a fellow pause."

"She's very intuitive," Jackaby said.

"I'd say she's a bit more than that," Garabrand countered.

"Should I check their pockets for identification?" Mr. Kit asked, his eyes still narrow with suspicion.

"That won't be necessary," Garabrand answered. "Unless I am very much mistaken, we have just had the good fortune to make the acquaintance of one Miss Abigail Rook, occasional asset to the New Fiddleham Police and known extrasensory diviner. That would make her associate Mr. R. F. Jackaby, yes? What does the R. F. stand for, Mr. Jackaby? Your file didn't say."

"If you already know who we are," said Jackaby, "then you already know that we have saved this town and the people in it from countless threats, both natural and supernatural. You turn up just as a woman has been murdered, and all that we know about you is that we don't know much."

Garabrand nodded. "That is our preferred state of affairs. How about this, though." He turned his attention to me. "Your . . . whatever you call them—*special visions*—they could spot a lie if I told you one, yeah?"

I nodded.

"We're the good guys," Garabrand said, plainly. "We do

the same as you do: we find monsters and we protect innocent people. Any lies so far?"

I swallowed. Garabrand was cagey. He was a one-man dam holding back an ocean of information, but he was telling the truth. I shook my head no.

Garabrand nodded. "Agent Kit." He glanced at his partner. "Tell the nice detective what we had to do with the untimely death of Juliette D'Aulaire."

"Nothing," Kit spat. "We don't kill innocent people. But we will find the culprit, whoever he ... or *she*"—he eyed me accusingly—"might be." And although his aura was dripping with suspicion, it was clear of guilt. He was speaking in earnest.

"Satisfied?" Agent Garabrand asked. "Good. That's a handy party trick. Using a paranormal to track paranormals is a more adept move than I would have given the average normie police force credit for. But then again, the details in your file are brief. Took some time off, right? Bit of a hiatus?"

I stiffened. "I don't see how that's any of your business."

"Hmm. Your file also mentioned a stubborn streak and a willful curiosity."

"And?" I said.

"My kind of résumé." He smiled, and in spite of myself, I found it oddly reassuring. Agent Garabrand's aura was perplexing, but not antagonistic. "We could've used someone with your skill set out in Oregon last summer," he said.

"Why? What's in Oregon? Wait—classified?"

Garabrand tapped the side of his nose. "Afraid so. I'll tell you what we *could* talk about, though. We could talk about that woman in there. You two find anything . . . *interesting* while you were having your private tour?"

My mouth went dry.

"Are we being detained?" Jackaby asked from over my shoulder. "Or are we free to go?"

"You're not going anywhere," said Mr. Kit. His gaze was still acidic. If Garabrand's aura bespoke an earnest interest in the two of us, Kit's was about as friendly as a hornet.

"Stand down, cowboy. We don't need to detain these two." Garabrand chuckled. "You'll have to excuse my partner. He's a lively one. Love that energy, though."

Mr. Kit sneered.

Garabrand patted his vest and drew from the pocket a slim card. "I'm sure if you think of anything that might assist in the resolution of this case, you'll be sure to bring it to our attention."

I took the card from him. It was embossed with the same logo as his badge. Beneath, it read simply: *F. GARABRAND. BUREAU OF CURIOSITIES.*

"You're welcome to report your findings directly to your own local law enforcement, if you're more comfortable with that arrangement," Garabrand added. "It all reaches us in the end, either way. It would save us all some time if you report directly to us, though—and saving time saves innocent lives. You can have messages delivered to the address I've written on the back. Do be careful out there, now."

"Just like that?" I asked. "We're free to go? No menacing interrogation or vague threats? No checking our pockets?"

"That's a good point," said Jackaby. "I put a lot of interesting stuff in my pockets before we left—vials of holy water, witching knots, a shiny rock I found yesterday."

"Do you *want* us to check your pockets?" Garabrand asked.

"Of course we don't," I said. "But it seems rude not to ask."

"That won't be necessary," Garabrand said. "I trust we can rely on the two of you to be as helpful as possible in this sensitive matter."

"Not that I don't appreciate a vote of confidence," I said, "but what makes you so certain that we will be reporting our findings to you? Or to anyone? That is—*if* we find anything to report."

Garabrand's eyes crinkled in a half smile. "Because every time I say the word *classified* it makes your eye twitch," he said. "Because you hate not knowing, and you know for darn sure that there are a *lot* of things I know that you don't. Knowing things is a bureau perk. And because it could be your perk. Bureau assets are privy to more secrets—more funding—more resources. You could do a lot worse."

I blinked. "Sorry, am I being threatened or offered a job?"

"I guess we'll both find out, won't we?" Garabrand chuckled. "Good day, Miss Rook." He tipped his fedora. "Mr. Jackaby."

Miss Lee had the carriage waiting for us just where she had dropped us off.

"Miss Rook. Mr. Jackaby." She opened the door as we approached. "I notice you're not in handcuffs or running to beat the devil, so I take it everything went to your satisfaction?"

"*Satisfaction* might not be the right word for it." I glanced at Jackaby before climbing in.

"Deeply unsatisfied," agreed Jackaby.

Miss Lee nodded. "What's next, then?"

"Next we need to go accuse a friend of ours of murder," I sighed.

"Making a full day of it, then, are we?" Miss Lee clicked the door shut. Jackaby gave her the address, and she hoisted herself back up into the driver's seat.

"We don't really think Alina is guilty, though," I said as the carriage began to move. "Do we?"

"You're the one with the magic eyeballs," said Jackaby. "Do you think it could have been someone else's aura?"

"No," I admitted. "But—it just doesn't seem like something Alina could be capable of."

"Right," said Jackaby, throwing me a sidelong glance. "Because her track record is so clean. It's not as if she's double-crossed us once already and threatened to sell out the entire world to an evil king for a taste of power."

"That was only one time," I said, weakly. "All right—I'm not ruling out the possibility that she is guilty, but we don't *know* that. Not yet. Not with certainty."

"Only two people know with certainty," said Jackaby, "and one of them is currently collecting flies."

"Just allow me to broach the subject," I said. "No offense, but you have the tact of a battering ram."

The approach to the veil-gate was a bumpy trip up a packed dirt road. The Om Caini had been granted roughly half a dozen acres of land, providing them with a wide berth around the gate in every direction and room to construct their own homes, workshops, and other facilities. The last time I had been here had been months ago. Most of the area had still been makeshift tents and bare wooden frames, but Alina and her people had worked fast. A miniature village of strong, sturdy buildings had risen up, the sturdiest of which stood right in the center of the property.

The rift itself was situated squarely on the ruins of an old church. Pieces of stonework from the former building had been repurposed into watch towers. An iron gate encircled the pavilion, and I spotted several guards on either side.

The opening within was called a gate, but in truth it was more of a jagged, tattered hole in the fabric of reality. Through it lay the intense emerald greens and ruby reds of the Annwyn, the lands beyond this earth where magic was everywhere and nature as we know it obeyed different rules. All around it were the usual earthly auras, but trying to focus too hard on the rift itself hurt my eyes. The thin separation between the two worlds was the only place that I could see *nothing*. It was neither dark nor light, it simply *wasn't*, and the last time I had tried to focus on it I had given myself a headache that lasted for days.

A curly-haired boy called Fane—one of Charlie's younger cousins—came down the hill to greet us as we climbed out of the carriage. He walked us up a flagged path toward the new building beside the pavilion. It was even nicer on the inside. The foyer was neatly furnished and bordered by Romanesque arches with elegant trim. Ahead, there was a wide processing center with benches for waiting and space to queue in front of a long desk, not unlike a post office or train station. To the left was a hallway that led to a series of closed doors.

"Remember," I whispered to Jackaby as the boy trotted off down the hall to fetch Alina, "let me broach the subject. Tactfully."

"Alina doesn't strike me as the sort to enjoy beating about the bush," said Jackaby, shrugging. "If she's capable of murder, she's capable of handling a direct question."

"We don't *know* that she's capable of murder," I hissed.

A door ahead opened and Alina herself emerged, scowling. She trod down the hallway toward us, her shoes tapping a steady rhythm in the silence. Her aura looked no different than it had yesterday—pragmatic, earthy tones dappled with sharp sparks of orange and gold. I don't know precisely what I had been expecting, but there was no lurking shadow of evil or bloodred guilt stain spreading across her halo. Alina looked like Alina. I simply could not imagine her committing so violent a crime. She drew to a stop a few feet from where we stood.

"Hello—" I began.

"I'm assuming you're here because I've killed someone?" she asked. "Yes. That makes sense. Would you like to step into my office to talk about it?"

chapter eleven

"So, is this an interrogation, then?" Alina asked, shutting the door to her office behind her.

"Not exactly," I said.

"Yes," said Jackaby at the same time.

"Fine. Maybe," I amended. "Look, it doesn't matter what it is. Did you really do it?"

"Apparently," said Alina. "It would explain my blood-soaked clothing this morning. Was it anyone I know? Or just some unlucky stranger in the street?"

"Juliette D'Aulaire," answered Jackaby. "In the privacy of her own home. You left fur behind."

"Hmm. Vile woman." Alina's voice was tight. D'Aulaire's

name had sent a sour ripple through her aura—but I still could not detect any true malice or wrath. She was eerily detached about the whole affair. "How did I do it?"

"Hold on," I said. "This isn't just you being coy and cagey—you really don't know?"

"Was it a knife?" Alina continued. "Not poison, I hope. I like to think I'm better than poison."

"She was mauled," said Jackaby. "Severed jugular. Well—*severed* might be the wrong word. There wasn't much jugular left."

"I thought I tasted blood this morning," Alina said, numbly. Her energy was lead gray and grim, but without remorse. "I tried to convince myself it was pig's."

"How are you so calm right now?" I demanded. "And how can you not know if you've brutally murdered someone?"

"Because I have no memory of the act," she answered. "Last night I returned home late and slept fitfully—a night of unpleasant dreams. In the morning, I found myself covered in dried blood. When I cleaned it off, I found that none of it was my own. Whatever happened before that, I could not tell you."

"Well, where were you going?" I asked. "When Charlie and I last saw you, you said you had to attend to something in town. What was it? Oh, lord. Did you take his baton with you?"

She shook her head. "I don't remember seeing you

yesterday. Or Kazimir. I'm sorry, but it's the truth." Her aura confirmed it.

I pursed my lips and nodded. "Well, what's the last thing you *do* remember?" I asked.

Alina closed her eyes as she cast her memory back. "There was an old elven man," she said. "He came through the veil from the Annwyn because he had lost contact with someone. A grandson."

"Did the old man seem . . . evil?" Jackaby asked.

Alina shrugged. "I think we both know I'm not the one to make that judgment. The charms at the entry activated, so he was detained. Happens several times a day. There's a waiting list. We took his statement, but there was little we could do for him. His grandson was under no obligation to maintain communication. Some otherworldly immigrants simply choose to cut ties with their kin. This is their right. The old man did not like that answer. That—that's all I can remember."

"Is it possible the fellow put some form of curse on you?" Jackaby asked. "Rook, have you checked Alina for elven magic?"

I looked Alina over again. The stain of D'Aulaire's death clung to her like tree sap. Beneath it, her own magic hummed, grounded, cool, and very similar to Charlie's. If I really focused, I could sense a third presence hovering all around her head like perfume clinging to her hair. It was weak and washed-out, but I could tell that it wasn't elven. It felt like burning lime, but the moment I looked away it tried to slip from my mind. A nagging feeling at the back of my skull told me I had seen the residue somewhere before. I scowled. If memories were library shelves, that particular volume had been stolen from the stacks. I shook my head and refocused.

"Did he touch you in any way?" I asked. "Speak in strange tongues? Do you know if he was a trained mage or enchanter or anything like that?"

"I don't think so. Wait." Alina crossed to her desk and flipped open a wide book bound in red leather. "The logs from last night should have—ah, yes. Here he is. He gave his name as Arnar Odengaard. He is an accountant."

"Elves have accountants?" I asked.

Alina rolled her eyes. "Who did you think handled their accounting? The gnomes?"

"I guess I never really gave much thought to elven economics," I admitted.

"What about the grandson?" said Jackaby.

Alina ran her finger down the entry. "He's called Einar," she said. "Hold on; I can check the register." She slid open a cabinet and shuffled through files. "Here we are. The grandson requested an alternate name on his paperwork."

"That seems a bit suspicious," I said.

"Not really." Alina shrugged. "Many newcomers opt to

take on less conspicuous names that they feel will help them blend in more easily with their new community. Einar's New Fiddleham name is . . . Terwilliger Highcourt."

"Excellent choice," said Jackaby. "I'm sure he blended in seamlessly."

"I've heard that name before," I said. "Or seen it. Where have I seen that name?"

Alina read farther. "The boy applied for an extension to his residency permit two weeks ago. It was granted. He seemed to be settling in. That's all his file says. Like I told his grandfather, this sort of thing happens."

"And that was when he grew angry?" I asked.

"He did not wish to be turned away," Alina recalled.

"How did you calm him down?"

Alina shook her head. "I don't remember. It's all fuzzy. But the logbook states that he crossed back over to the Annwyn."

"Does it say what *you* did after that?" I asked.

"No. Oddly enough, it seems I did not feel that murdering a woman merited an entry. I made no further record of my own actions that evening."

"Does this sort of thing happen to you often?" Jackaby asked.

Alina raised an eyebrow. "Do I often awaken drenched in the blood of my enemies?" she said. "I would have far fewer enemies, if that were the case."

"Not that part—do you often lose track of long periods

of time?" Jackaby clarified. "Forget doing the things that you've done?"

Alina looked down as she answered. "Not since I was a pup." She glanced at me. "How much has Kazimir—*Charlie*—told you about our people's relationship with the hound?"

I took a breath. The rare occasions when Charlie had spoken about his canine transformations with me had been intimate and solemn. The whole process was deeply personal—and I had felt honored to have been allowed into a world that was not my own. "He told me that hound and human coexist inside him—and that they have nothing to hide from each other," I said. "My understanding is that all Om Caini are taught to accept and celebrate both sides of their nature, and not to allow one side or the other to go neglected or shunned. It's a balance based on love. It sounds better the way he explains it—but is that about right?"

Alina nodded. "*Love.* He would phrase it that way," she said. "You grasp it well enough. But this relationship—this love—it must be nurtured. As young ones, it is often difficult to recall our humanity when we are in animal form, and difficult to channel the hound when we are human. The two halves must be taught to share one mind rather than taking turns. Om Caini who deny their true nature have also been known to fragment, losing themselves entirely when their other half takes over. This breeds internal bitterness and hate and goes against everything we strive for.

It is not our way. We are not werewolves, Detective. We are not wild. We have pride and self-respect. To lose this balance . . ." She bit her lip. Her aura tightened painfully, like a knot in a sore muscle. "To lose this balance is to lose ourselves." I could see her fingers clenching and releasing as she composed herself. "And to lose ourselves is an unspeakable shame."

A pregnant silence settled over the room for several seconds.

"But you've always seemed to have a healthy respect for your hound aspect," I said. "And you're not trying to hide who you are. Charlie has often said—"

"My brother does not know me like he thinks he knows me," Alina said. "And it is not the *hound* who deserves to be shunned. It was not the *hound's* blind ambition that nearly cost Kazimir his life. It was not the *hound* who took his place as sovereign. It is not the *hound* whose every decision continues to bring more discontent to this town. I may not be hiding who I am, Miss Rook, but I have been pretending to be what I am not. *Suverana. Noble Sentinel. Keeper of the Veil.* These titles were never mine. I suppose it was only a matter of time before the great lie collapsed in on itself."

"No." I shook my head. "You're just overwhelmed. That's understandable."

"I have made many poor choices," she said. Her eyes were focused somewhere in the distance behind me. "Perhaps the worst was accepting a responsibility to which

I was not equal. Now I must accept the consequences of failing that responsibility."

"Stop," I said. "We don't know that you've failed anything yet. We don't know what happened at all. We need to retrace your steps last night and—"

A knock sounded against the door, and the curly-haired boy from earlier poked his head into the room. "A thousand apologies, Suverana," he said.

"Now is not a good time, Fane," said Alina.

"But I thought you should know," Fane said, "that there are men in the receiving room. They are most insistent."

"What men?" Alina stiffened.

"Men with badges," said Fane. "A lot of them, too. There are even more outside."

Alina took a deep breath. "Thank you, Fane. Tell them I will be with them momentarily."

Fane bowed and shut the door.

"They know," said Alina, flatly. "It is fine. I will allow you to turn me in to your local authorities."

"But we don't—" I began.

"I will not resist." She looked me in the eyes, her gaze intense. I could feel her aura trembling with a fear her physical body dared not show. There was a blanket of shame and resignation draping itself over her—but with all of this, I sensed a cool air of relief, as well. "Will you do me one favor," she added, "after you have remanded me into their custody?"

"A favor?" I managed.

"I accept that I have done this thing," she said. "Will you discover for me *why* I did it?"

"You want me to find your motive?" I asked. "Your motive for killing a woman you openly hate? A woman who regularly insulted and threatened your family?"

"I don't mourn her death," Alina admitted. "Frankly, I would not be unhappy to hear that she suffered. She was awful. But I have never been to her home—neither as a human nor as a hound. I would not even know the way, and I certainly do not know what brought me there last night. I can accept that I killed her. I am more than capable of violence—but not without cause. I am no wild beast. So what was the cause? I do not mean to excuse my actions. I only wish to understand them."

I nodded. "I think we all do."

chapter twelve

Inspector Dupin was jotting something down in his note-book when I strode up in front of him.

"You're making a mistake," I said.

The inspector did not acknowledge me right away. He finished his note with a firm stab of his pencil before finally looking up. Two of his officers were already escorting Alina toward an armored police wagon. I couldn't help but notice that the more experienced of the pair seemed to be allowing the other to do the bulk of the actual escorting. "No mistake. She confessed," Dupin said.

"Well, she's obviously making a mistake, too!" I insisted.

"She doesn't know what happened last night any more than we do."

"We know enough." Dupin glanced over my shoulder at the uniforms behind me. "McIntosh, Schmitz. Do a sweep of her office for anything of interest. Where is my support team?"

"How did you piece it together?" asked Jackaby. "Just out of professional curiosity. I mean, I know how *we* pieced it together, but I'm used to your being several steps behind."

Dupin gave him a sour look. "We didn't," he said. "*They* did." He nodded toward the front entrance, where two men in matching suits were just stepping inside. Agents Kit and Garabrand.

"Inspector Dupin," said Agent Kit as he approached, his pencil mustache twitching on the final syllable. "I've just had to tell four of your uniforms to join that prisoner transport detail. In the future, I'd advise you not to underestimate a paranormal. That's how you get officers killed."

"You did what?" Dupin's expression tightened. "I already assessed the threat," he said, keeping his voice even. "The suspect surrendered willingly, and she has a history of cooperation with my department. In the future, I'll thank you to avoid giving my officers orders without my approval. I have accommodated all of your requests thus far, but this is still my division."

"For now," said Kit. The mustache twitched again.

"What did we say about antagonizing local law enforcement?" Agent Garabrand came strolling up behind his partner. Unlike Kit, his aura was awash with the cool, confident tones that spoke to his experience.

Kit bristled. "More flies with honey," he grumbled.

Garabrand nodded, drawing to a stop in front of Dupin. "Of *course* this is still your division, Inspector, and you're doing a fine job with it. I mean that. You keep learning this fast, it might even keep you alive. Forgive my associate, but I hope you'll take a piece of advice from someone who's rooting for you. If a paranormal is violent, you double the guard. If the limits of their abilities are unknown—particularly if those abilities include any form of transformation magic— you double it again. I've learned the hard way just how important that is." His gaze drifted upward for a moment as a painful memory danced across his aura.

"And just how much experience do *you* have?" I asked.

Garabrand turned his eyes toward me. "Enough."

"Not enough to get here before we did," Jackaby said.

Garabrand only looked amused.

"What was the clue that tipped you off?" I asked. "Stray hair? Paw print?"

"A few things," said Garabrand. "Witness testimony. Evidence at the scene of the crime. Lunar cycles. The police detail we assigned to follow your coach was helpful, as well." He winked. "You certainly didn't waste any time making your way here to tip off your friend after you left the scene of the crime. I can respect the alacrity."

I planted my fists on my hips. "You had us followed!"

"Of course we did," said Garabrand, frankly. "You have phenomenal powers, Miss Rook, but a convincing poker face is not one of them."

"You're lucky we stepped in," Kit chimed in. "This soon after a full moon, their kind can get ornery as anything. Strong, too. We hit a werewolf den in Georgia a few summers back. Wasn't pretty."

"Alina is not a werewolf! And she isn't some wild thing, neither as a human nor as a hound."

"You are personally familiar with the perpetrator, is that right?" Agent Garabrand asked.

"I know her, yes."

"And you are fully aware of her affliction?" he added.

"It's not an affliction—it's who she is," I said. "And yes. I know about the Om Caini. More than you, I would wager. They aren't mindless monsters."

"I agree." Garabrand spoke gently, but there was grit to his voice. "Were*wolves* are one thing. Their actions are not intentional. They are victims themselves, in a way. I believe a were*hound's* choices, on the other hand, should be considered willful and conscious. Would you agree?"

"Yes—wait, no. It's not like that."

"Hmm. I'm always eager to learn how it is." He tilted his head slightly as he looked at me. "Didn't get where

I am by assuming I already have all the answers. Care to elaborate as to how you came to know so much about their kind?"

"That's none of your business," I said, trying not to let him get me flustered. "But I know without a doubt that they are perfectly decent people."

"Decent or not," Agent Kit grumbled, "this city never should have given paranormals so much control. Now *we* have to do all the work to fix *your* mistakes."

"What do you mean by that?" Jackaby asked, his eyes narrowing.

"Mr. Kit lacks tact, but he is not wrong," said Garabrand. "Your friends seem like reasonable folk—but it was a gross oversight to grant them sovereignty over the access point in the first place. A port of entry of this magnitude represents an unfathomable threat. It's not personal. If anything, it's unfair to put that responsibility on their shoulders. The matter should always have been under our purview, not theirs. Juliette D'Aulaire's death was a tragedy, obviously, but perhaps auspicious in the long run for a smoother transition of power."

"The Om Caini were chosen as sentinels precisely because they are a neutral party," I said. "Not strictly human, but not of the Annwyn, either. Unbiased guardians prevent either side from abusing the power of the gate."

"The leader of your so-called unbiased group just murdered the first person who questioned her right to lead," said Agent Garabrand. "That doesn't strike you as an abuse of power?"

"Technically not the *first* person to question her," I mumbled.

Agent Garabrand raised an eyebrow.

"So you want to order New Fiddleham's finest to seize control of the veil-gate?" said Jackaby. "With all due respect, police officers can barely keep control of Mason Street. They aren't equipped to manage interdimensional security."

"Good point," said Kit. "All the more reason to man the outpost with fully armed and armored bureau operatives rather than leaving matters in the hands of untrained locals."

"What?" Jackaby and I both blurted together.

"That's not decided yet," Garabrand cut in. "But this is what we do. The Bureau of Curiosities was formed to look into supernatural incidents all over the country and quietly turn problems into solutions."

"We can find our own solutions," I said.

Garabrand nodded contemplatively. "I wouldn't be surprised if you did," he conceded. "Most cities aren't even aware of the presence of paranormals in their midst. Frankly, it's a breath of fresh air to find a town whose leadership is open to an earnest dialogue on the topic at all, and I do love to root for the home team. But that doesn't make the chaos here in New Fiddleham any less dangerous. If

Commissioner Marlowe and his existing structures of governance prove inadequate in maintaining the safety and stability of this city—then we *will* be forced to step in and take control. That's just the way it is."

"You can't simply take over a city!" I said.

"We can, and we have, many times. Sometimes we just insert our own operatives in key governing positions to ensure effective management. Other times the situation calls for a more drastic approach. Ever heard of Brigginsburg?"

"No."

"And you never will." Garabrand let the information hang in the air without elaboration. I could tell with certainty that the agent was neither lying nor exaggerating. I swallowed.

"What if she didn't do it?" I asked. Garabrand's brow rose, curiously. "What if we can prove that the murder was not her fault? Would that make you trust the Om Caini?"

"That," said Garabrand, "would be quite a feat."

"Your friend is guilty," Kit said, bluntly. "And we're done here." His attention turned to Officers McIntosh and Schmitz, who were emerging from Alina's office with a small stack of books and ledgers in their arms. "You—what do you two think you're doing in there?"

"Collecting evidence?" Schmitz answered.

"As their commanding officer instructed," Dupin added, pointedly.

"It's fine," Garabrand said. "Inspector Dupin has the

situation here well in hand, Mr. Kit. And we have a suspect to interrogate. Good day, folks."

Dupin scowled at their backs as they exited the building.

"We should probably be going as well," said Jackaby.

"One more thing, Inspector," I said. "I don't suppose the name Terwilliger Highcourt means anything to you?"

Dupin shook his head. "Should it?"

"Just something Alina mentioned before you arrived. It might be unrelated, but I only wondered."

"Excuse me, miss?" Officer Schmitz stepped over, his arms still laden with Alina's paperwork. I could see the red logbook about halfway down the stack. "Didn't mean to overhear, but I don't expect the inspector would have anything to do with that, on account of it's not the sort of case he oversees."

"You know the name?"

"Pretty sure. Not a lot of Terwilligers. I helped process the paperwork before I was transferred to the Paranormal Division. It's a standard missing persons case. Friend of his from work came and filled out the report when he didn't show up for a few days. They were under the impression he was human, or else I'd have stamped it for paranormal earlier."

"Hmm. Reported missing from both sides of the veil, it seems," said Jackaby.

"That's where I've seen that name!" I said. "It was on one

of those posters in the street. Sounds like his grandfather was right to worry about him."

"Not that that helps Alina," Jackaby said. "Ignoring a concerned grandparent when it turns out he was right to worry? That story won't exactly make her appear likable to the public."

Dupin shook his head. "Things aren't looking very good for your friend," he said.

A thought was bubbling in the back of my head. "What if she didn't ignore him?" I said. "The last thing Alina remembers is talking to the old man—what if she listened to him and went looking for Terwilliger Highcourt after all? What if her investigation somehow brought her into conflict with Juliette D'Aulaire?"

"That would be stepping well outside of her jurisdiction," said Dupin. "They're supposed to turn cases like that over to our division to handle."

"Which she would have known would be as good as doing nothing at all," Jackaby mused. "No offense, Inspector."

"How is that *not* offensive?" Dupin asked.

"Stepping outside her jurisdiction," I said, "and pursuing a not-strictly-legitimate investigation would be a good reason not to write her plans down in the logs or tell anyone where she was going."

Jackaby nodded. "It's a better lead than anything else

we've got. Shall we look into it tomorrow morning? I did promise your parents dinner."

"Don't remind me," I said. "Oh, lord—Charlie is stuck with them right now. How am I supposed to come home and tell him—in front of my parents—that we just arrested his sister for murder and that his entire clan is on the cusp of being labeled public enemies and dishonorably stripped of their posts?" I closed my eyes and pressed my fingers to my temples. "No. No, I can't do it. We need more answers first. He might not be enjoying the company, but an evening of sitting with my parents is better than a morning of running from an angry mob."

"I can pull the missing persons report for Highcourt," said Dupin. "But if we're looking into this, we're looking into it together. You report directly to me. No ducking away and hiding evidence, got it?"

"And no going over your head to the despotic duo?" Jackaby added.

Dupin's nostrils flared.

"We're with you," I assured Dupin. "Take us to Highcourt's home so I can have a look around. If there's something there that can explain all of this, then at least I can give Charlie that much."

"And what if what you find is only more proof that his sister is a cold-blooded killer?" said Dupin.

"Then tonight's dinner conversation is going to be rough," I said.

chapter thirteen

The contents of chapter thirteen have been omitted. To assuage any fears eager readers might experience that these missing pages are the result of a villainous theft or that they imply some worrying memory loss—rest assured that I recall every step we took that chilly afternoon in vivid detail. I'm just not telling you.

chapter fourteen

Terwilliger Highcourt's home was spacious for a walk-in closet with plumbing and brown drapes. For any reasonably sized person, it left one with the sensation of being hugged by muted floral wallpaper. The windows rattled as a train thundered past, and the front door bumped into a steamer trunk when Inspector Dupin attempted to push it farther open than it wanted to go. The main room of the apartment was a living room right up until it was a dining room and also a slim kitchen, and there were crates and empty canning jars and books stacked against every wall. The countertops, too, were cluttered with balls of twine, tinned beans, and all sorts of odds and ends. A door to the left was open, revealing an unmade bed and more clutter.

"Anything?" Jackaby asked, almost as soon as I had set foot inside.

I let my gaze roll over the scene. The aura was distinctly elven, but it was stale and old. Terwilliger Highcourt hadn't been home for weeks. Alina's aura, on the other hand, was fresh.

"She was here," I said quietly. "She must have been looking for Highcourt." I followed the aura as it wove in and out. Lying on the floor in the corner of the room was the baton she had borrowed from Charlie. His aura still clung to it. I bit my lip, grateful the investigating officers could not see what I could. Alina incriminating herself was bad enough without getting her brother mixed up in it all.

I narrowed my eyes, peering around. There were other auras littering the place—old and new, earthly and unearthly—but floating over it all like a fine layer of dust was the same energy I had sensed in the jewelry shop.

"What is it?" Jackaby whispered.

"Turnips," I said. "And turpitude."

"You're sure?"

"Rarely." I stood up straight. "But I think so. The air tastes the same as it did in Talman's."

"Squiffy Rick is getting pretty ambitious if he's gone from snatching necklaces to kidnapping interdimensional immigrants," said Jackaby. "Any idea what Alina was looking for?"

I peered once more around the cluttered room. In the mystery stories I used to smuggle into my book bag, the crime scenes detectives had to investigate were always conveniently neat and tidy, save for some muddy shoe print or a single hairpin on the carpet. Anything and everything in this room could be a clue. Was the bottle of hair tonic a clue? The unidentifiable canned fruit? The stack of old newspapers?

"What sorts of energies would *you* look for?" I asked.

Jackaby shrugged. "I never really knew until I found one. I just looked around and went wherever things seemed most oddish. What seems oddish?"

"I don't know. What color is oddish?"

Jackaby shook his head. "If you're going to insist on trying to be *me*, then perhaps what you need is a *you* to do your side of the job. Actually, that's not half-bad. Maybe all you need is a handy Rook to point you in the right direction. Let's see. What would you do if you were me being you? Oh! Wastebaskets. You do love rooting through garbage."

He crossed the floor and picked up a rubbish bin, rummaging around inside it eagerly.

"I never said that," I protested. "It's just the sort of thing that detectives check, isn't it?" I let my eyes wander around the room. Dupin was poking at jars in a cupboard.

Highcourt's aura was, unsurprisingly, everywhere in the cramped apartment, but it was a slightly different tone in different places. It carried fatigue with it to the bedroom, and it glimmered with hope by the windowsill. The trunk beside the door, on the other hand, was alight with nervous importance. I could almost feel the elf's heart beating faster as I approached it.

"There's a broken tobacco pipe in here," said Jackaby, behind me. "And spent matches. Banana peel. Piece of string."

I ignored him and knelt to open the chest. Within it was a pile of innocuous knit sweaters and scarves—but the heap practically glowed from the light of something magical beneath them. Gingerly, I moved the winter wear aside. Beneath them rested scores of smooth, polished stones, each about as wide across as my palm and glowing a pale green. The light was so intensely elven, it hurt my eyes to stare at them for too long.

"I've got something!" Jackaby declared triumphantly. "This matchstick is made out of cardboard!"

I stood and turned. "Erm. Mr. Jackaby."

"Look! The rest of the ones in there were wooden matches. But this one's different. That's something, I think."

"Mr. Jackaby." I nodded toward the open steamer trunk and the hidden cache of stones.

Jackaby leaned in to have a better look. "Ah. Those are also something." He glanced a little dejectedly at the spent match in his hands, but rallied quickly and tucked it into a pocket. "Right. I haven't seen these with plain eyes before, but I'd wager these are elven dwimmerstans. They glow, yes? Pastel green? That's them, then. They're a bit like chemical batteries, but instead of storing electricity, they store magical energy. Not generally very strong, but handy for the modern elf on the go—especially on this side of the veil. Just enough kick in each one to boost a simple spell or two. I knew a sailor who liked to keep a dwimmerstan in his pocket when he was out to sea. Didn't even tap into it. Said just holding it made his joints feel better on the cold nights."

"So—these are commonplace? They're not . . . *oddish*?"

"Well . . ." Jackaby hedged.

"They're illegal," said Dupin, peeking over my shoulder. "At least in that quantity. One or two would be a reasonable allowance—but with this many, he's probably selling them."

"That's not a real law," Jackaby said.

"It *is* the law," Dupin said.

"It's a *regulation*," Jackaby corrected. "Barely."

Dupin shook his head. "It could have landed Highcourt some serious fines or jail time. Devices that store or generate magical energy can't be stockpiled or distributed in New Fiddleham. Too dangerous and too much of a liability." He shook his head. "Of course, it's almost impossible to enforce from our end. The Om Caini are supposed to screen for this sort of thing. We're still trying to work out which artifacts will blow up in our evidence locker and which ones won't."

"Oh, dwimmerstans are harmless," Jackaby scoffed. "This is why the magical community doesn't like you."

"It might explain his disappearance," I said. "If Highcourt got mixed up with a criminal element out of necessity to distribute his stones, that could have landed him in some dangerous circles."

"I'll have an officer circle back to collect the evidence." Dupin nodded at the trunk. "He wouldn't be the first contraband trader who's gone missing recently. You ever meet Alfie Scather?"

"I know Alfie," Jackaby said.

"Alfie's been in and out of lockup for the past few months for peddling hex bags and single-use spells. His auntie reported him missing last week. I had him pegged for skipping town, but it's possible Scather and Highcourt both crossed paths with the wrong bad guy."

"Ooh. A mysterious criminal kingpin? That's good." Jackaby closed his eyes, his hands hovering in front of his face as if preparing to conduct an invisible orchestra. "Maybe Alina went to check on Highcourt and stumbled onto his admittedly shady but ultimately harmless underground business." Dupin rolled his eyes, but Jackaby continued. "One thing leads to another, and the trail takes Alina into the lair of this mysterious unknown kingpin, who, in turn, gets her mixed up with D'Aulaire. Oh, wait!" Jackaby's eyes popped open. "Maybe D'Aulaire *is* the nefarious king-pin. It's the perfect cover. Denounce magic by day, deal in magic by night."

"Except that Juliette D'Aulaire was doing more than denouncing," Dupin cut in. "She's put pressure on the mayor from day one to close the gate entirely. She spear-headed the anti-magic campaign for increased restrictions. She's half the reason the laws have become as tight as they are."

I shook my head. "Dupin's right. D'Aulaire wasn't work-ing with magic. I'm pretty sure Alina was the only paranor-mal to pass through her house in a long time. If our victim had anything to do with a supernatural underground, it would have left traces. We're not going to get anywhere with a lot of wild conjecture. We need more pieces to this puzzle. Who else has been taken, Inspector? Anyone who lived nearby?"

Dupin leafed through his notes for a moment. "A tailor. Three blocks from here. Next closest is a greengrocer about a mile away, a pipe fitter uptown, and a midwife and her daughter a little north of that."

"Then I guess we have a lot of ground to cover before the sun goes down," I said.

chapter fifteen

The nearest site to Highcourt's apartment was the home of the tailor, a gnome by the name of Pip Townsend. He was the most recent victim on Dupin's list to have gone missing—the report had been filed only a few days prior. A white-haired neighbor peered over her fence at us as we stepped into Townsend's house to have a look around.

"There's that same turnippy aura in here, as well," I announced as we entered. "I'm starting to recognize it more clearly."

"What exactly does that tell us?" Dupin asked.

"Not enough," I admitted. "But it proves the crimes are related. Probably. Maybe."

"That's an excellent start!" Jackaby said. "You're finding your stride. Just watch, Inspector. She's about to crack this case wide open."

After several minutes of searching, I had cracked open precisely nothing. A thorough tour of the house had turned up only a pair of charmed reading glasses, a few magically reinforced spools of thread, and a loaf of uneaten zucchini bread. The bread wasn't even supernatural; it just smelled pleasantly like nutmeg and cloves. What it did not smell like was a clue.

"I found another spent match!" Jackaby called merrily, pulling his head out of the tailor's garbage can.

"Everybody uses matches," Dupin said.

"This is no use," I sighed. "Let's try the next site."

Townsend's neighbor was still watching as we filed out of the house sullenly. "You find anything about our Pip?" she asked.

"The investigation is ongoing," Dupin replied automatically.

"Did you know him?" I asked, pausing. Something about the woman felt off. She seemed pleasant enough, and her question was steeped in earnest concern, but there was a hazy mist hanging around her. It was barely visible, but it looked the way burning smells, with just a hint of lime. I scowled. I had seen that energy somewhere before, I was sure of it. I strained to remember, but I felt as though my mind had magnets in it repelling my thoughts every time they came too close. The aura had something to do with D'Aulaire, didn't it? Or possibly Alina? The memory hid itself away like an awkward child at a fancy party.

"He's a sweet young man," the woman said. "A bit lonely. I tried to set him up with my niece once, but they were both too shy. Anyway, I always make an extra portion for him whenever I'm baking, and he helps mend my Harold's work clothes when they get too worn out. Harold's always wearing out his trousers."

"I take it that was your zucchini bread, then?" I asked.

The woman looked confused. "How'd you know about that? Never did get around to bringing it over to him. I did my baking a few days ago, but I think someone must have run off with it while it was cooling on the windowsill."

I glanced at Jackaby and back to the woman. "It seems to have made it into his house," I said. "It smelled nice."

"Oh." The woman shrugged. "My memory's not what it used to be. You'll find him, though, won't you? Harold and I are worried sick."

"We'll do our best, ma'am," Dupin assured her.

As we left, I tried to place where I had sensed that tint on the woman's aura before, but the thought slipped around in my mind like a marble in a drawer full of odds and ends. Soon it was gone entirely.

Our next stop was the home of the greengrocer—a half goblin called Dibb.

"I examined this one myself, two weeks back," Dupin said. "Neighbors seem to think he's an upstanding citizen. We searched the property. He's been growing a handful of otherworldly plants in a makeshift greenhouse, but none of them appeared valuable or dangerous. Maybe you can see something I missed."

Dupin opened the door, and we were immediately hit by a noxious odor. Inky black clouds rolled down the staircase to spill out the open front door. Jackaby coughed.

"Death," I whispered.

Dupin covered his nose with his sleeve. "Didn't smell like this two weeks ago."

I followed the aura up to the second-floor landing, where it was pouring like a waterfall down the steep attic stairs. Jackaby nodded toward a large crack and a dark crimson patch on the ceiling where the plaster had been stained from above. The drips had long since dried, but the smell was horrible. My head was starting to spin again, and I bit my lip to keep myself grounded. I could do this. I had seen bodies before, and if I was going to be of any use, I couldn't be squeamish.

I ascended, steeling myself as I reached the top step.

"I should be the first to investigate," Dupin began, mounting the stairs behind me, but I was already pushing open the narrow door.

The sight that awaited us was a nightmarish mess. A rough hole in the roof about three feet around provided a beam of light, which shone like an unforgiving spotlight on the remains of Mr. Dibb. Flies buzzed all around him. I stepped off the top stair and out of the way, but couldn't bring myself any closer.

"Good lord," Dupin choked as he climbed up the stairs behind me. He inched past, his back hunched under the low ceiling. "He must have fallen through the roof."

"At considerable speed," I agreed, trying not to breathe through my nose. "Watch your step. The impact cracked the supports beneath him."

I looked up at the hole in the ceiling and followed a dim trail down to the corpse. The aura must have been painfully vivid once, but it was two weeks faded now. "For what it's worth," I managed, "I don't think he felt the impact. I'm pretty sure he died on the way down—half a mile up from here, maybe more. I would guess heart attack."

Dupin leaned forward to peer up through the hole. "*How?* Where did he fall from?"

I shrugged. "No idea. That's where he came from, though."

Jackaby poked his head into the attic behind us. "Oof." He grimaced. He turned toward me. "Turnips?"

I swallowed, glancing back at the body. The odd, tur-nippy aura was a darker shade than it had been in the other crime scenes, stained no doubt by the gruesome nature of Mr. Dibb's demise, but the tint was definitely there. I nodded.

It was longer than I would have liked before we were out of the attic and back in the fresh air in front of Dibb's house. Dupin left Jackaby and me to wait while he flagged down a patrolman and instructed him to summon officers who would attend to the remains of Mr. Dibb.

"Good work so far," said Jackaby. "We're making stellar progress."

"Are we, though?" I asked. "Because missing people seems preferable to dead people." I sighed. "It seems like every step we take makes this whole thing less clear than it was before."

"That's how you know you're doing it right," he assured me. "Got to get the whole knot out into the open before you can untangle it all. Let's review. We've got our bodies, D'Aulaire and Dibb. Wildly different causes of death. No obvious connection between the two. Yes?"

I nodded.

"Then we've got Townsend and Highcourt—both missing. Totally different lives. No obvious connection between those two, either."

I nodded again.

"And then we've got Alina—in custody and linked to just *one* of the missing people and *one* of the dead ones. No memory of either and no obvious motives. Oh, and a stolen necklace—you noticed turnips there, too—that's somehow also connected to the whole thing. Am I forgetting anything?"

"The mystery auras," I said. "There have been two

distinct traces at multiple crime scenes, tying all of the cases together."

"Right." Jackaby raised an eyebrow. "Wait. Two?"

"Yes," I said. "The turnippy one and the . . . the other one." I scowled. What had the other aura felt like? Where had I noticed it? My head hurt. What was missing? And what was the thread that tied it all together?

"I'll have uniforms here within the hour to secure the site," Dupin announced, striding back toward us.

"In the meantime, who's next on our list?" Jackaby asked.

The inspector flipped through his pad. "Two not far from here. Both have been missing about a week and a half. There's a pipe fitter several blocks uptown by the name of Bo Thurse. Quarter troll. Or, in the opposite direction, we've got a midwife named . . . Mary Horne." His eyes flicked to me.

An image of the child in the alleyway, alone and afraid, flashed in my mind. "Horne," I said. "Let's finally look into Mary Horne."

My feet were aching as we stepped up the walk to the next house, but I pushed the pain to the back of my mind. The sun was already beginning to hide behind the buildings to the west, but it was not too dark for me to catch a glimmer of movement between the leaves of a tree across the street. I chalked it up to neighborhood pixies and followed the inspector into the midwife's house.

The house smelled of sage and lemongrass, and jars filled with all manner of herbs and powders lined the shelves. They were labeled in swooping cursive—things like witch hazel and mugwort and rose hips—and they shared their space with crystals and books and bundles of dried sticks.

"You were right, Inspector. This is definitely the home of a practicing witch," I observed.

"Always nice to have one of those around," Jackaby added. "Practical magic has a way of lifting up a neighborhood. It's the subtle things."

"What did you say was her line of work?" I asked the inspector.

"Midwife," said Dupin.

"Mm. Good career for a witch," said Jackaby.

"Anything magical pop out to you?" Dupin asked me. "We gave this one a once-over, but most of her ingredients are things you can buy at a corner shop. Just plants and things."

"Just because you can get something from a shop doesn't mean it isn't magical," said Jackaby. "Besides, all plants have a little magic to them, and putting the right plants together can make their magic even stronger. The right ingredients blend together and become something special. There's a jinni who runs a delicatessen on Market Street, and his roasted red pepper hummus is positively enchanting."

"I'll look around," I told Dupin.

"I'll check the garbage!" Jackaby called merrily.

There were two bedrooms off the main hall. One of them housed a wide bed with books piled high on the nightstand. The other had a small, humble bed with a thick quilt and a well-worn stuffed elephant beside the pillow.

The magic in this house was not flashy or bright—it felt solid, grounded. It carried its energy the way a sensible basket carried books home from the lending library. That faint trace of turnip-tinted energy hung in the air, just as it had in the other homes, but in this one, the energy of the rest of the house seemed to bristle against it.

"Aha!" Jackaby's voice drew me back into the front room. He marched toward me, holding something triumphantly between his fingers.

"A spent match?" I asked.

"A third one!" Jackaby confirmed. "The question is—are they matches? Matches to the other matches, I mean."

"I'm sure lots of people use matches," I said, but Jackaby was already digging the first two matches out of his jacket. He held them up side by side.

"They're just ordinary old—" I hesitated. I blinked. "Hang on. They *do* match." I took them from Jackaby, who grinned proudly.

"I'm pretty good at being you, as it turns out," he observed, smugly. "That's something."

"All three of these came from the same matchbook," I said. "Or at least, they were handled by the same person. And that aura—the turnippy-colored something—it's heavy on their tips. I can see it as clearly as the charred black. Okay. So this *is* something. But *what* is it?"

"It's odd," said Jackaby. "Odd is good."

"It's not odd *enough*," I countered. I don't know what I had expected. I'd been holding Mary Horne in the back of my mind for so many days—I suppose I had imagined that coming here would somehow unlock it all. "We need more. What's next, Inspector?"

"Next," said Dupin, "is a nice roast beef and potatoes with my wife, and then bedtime stories with the kids. We've been across half of New Fiddleham, Miss Rook. The night shift will look after Mr. Dibb's body, and whatever is behind this, it will wait until tomorrow for us to track it down."

"Right," I consented, miserably. "I suppose it will have to. We have a dinner of our own, and we're already late for it."

We bade Dupin good night, and he hailed a hansom cab outside of the midwife's house. The bushes ahead trembled in the cool evening air.

"It's not so late yet," Jackaby said. "We can still make it home in time to whip up a quick something. Are your parents fond of mushrooms? I've been meaning to try out an interesting recipe I found in a very old book I had tucked away in the attic. Not a cookbook, per se, but the dish sounds lovely all the same."

"This is your house, isn't it?" I asked, softly.

"What?" Jackaby turned back to the house and then to me.

"You're looking for her," whispered the shadows just past the bushes that lined the front walk.

"Oh," said Jackaby. He blinked, squinting into the shrubbery. His aura flickered a wistful purple for just a moment.

The girl stood up, slowly. Her hair had not gotten any less messy since I had seen her in the street. Her eyes looked tired. "I haven't gone back in," she said. "Not since that night."

"Mary Horne. She's your mother?" I asked. The child didn't answer. Her aura churned with grief and fear and loneliness. "We'd like to help you find her. Her and a few other people, too. Were you here when it happened? Did you see who took her?"

The girl's lips tightened and her brow furrowed. After a long pause she shook her head. "I was hiding. I went under the bed." The leaves rustled behind her, and she flinched, glancing around nervously.

"What did they sound like?" Jackaby asked.

The girl shrugged and shook her head. "She didn't do anything wrong. She never hurt anybody. She just makes special bundles that help people get better or make their pain go away."

"Spell bags?" Jackaby asked. "Very traditional magic. She sounds like a lovely lady."

The girl wiped her nose with the back of her hand. "She knew she wasn't supposed to keep selling her medicine, but people need it. She was careful. She even went to the fairy lady—the one who helped Mr. Dibb deliver his special vegetables. But it didn't matter. They came anyway. There was a scuffle, and then . . ." Her voice petered out.

"They took her?" I said.

The child's eyes fixed on a scrap of pavement at her feet. "They didn't look under the bed," she mumbled. "I waited. And then I ran."

"I'm so sorry," I said.

"Mary Horne knew Mr. Dibb?" Jackaby asked.

The girl sniffed. "She gave him medicine sometimes. And he found ingredients for her. Mr. Dibb was good at finding ingredients and stuff. He's the one who told her about the fairy lady."

"Who is the fairy lady?" I asked.

The girl shrugged. "She's gone. They took her first. And then they took Mr. Dibb."

"Actually, Mr. Dibb—" Jackaby began, but I put a hand on his arm and shook my head. The child did not need to know the grisly details.

"He's dead, isn't he?" She looked from Jackaby to me, her expression stoic. "I'm not stupid. I heard the policeman talking about a body. They're coming for all of us." Her eyes just stared off into the distance. "One by one."

"We don't know that for sure," I said.

"Do you think that she . . . that they . . ." The girl's voice faltered. Her brows were turned down in a strong glare, but there were tears welling up in her eyes. Her aura raged like a hurricane.

Jackaby and I exchanged a quick glance.

"We'll find her," I said.

"Are . . . are you lying?" she managed.

I took a deep breath. "A lot of those people who have been taken appear to have had . . . certain items they might have needed to deliver in secret—enchanted clothing, exotic vegetables, medicine. If there was one person helping all of them do that, then she might be the connection we're looking for. Do you know if the fairy lady lived near here?"

The girl glanced around again, but ultimately nodded. "Not far."

"Well." I turned to Jackaby. "Dinner's already going to be late. What's one more stop?"

chapter sixteen

The girl took us through back alleys when she could and kept to the shadows when she couldn't as we made our way toward the home of the "fairy lady." She looked over her shoulder at every turn.

"You never did tell us your name," I said.

"Nope," she confirmed, curtly. "I didn't."

"I was only thinking it might make conversation slightly easier."

She glanced back at me and shrugged. "I'm not supposed to give my name out. That's giving away your power, and you should only do that with people you trust."

"Ahh." Jackaby let out a contented sigh. "Great advice.

I love to see parents raising their children with practical knowledge and a realistic view of the world around them. I like your mother more and more, young lady."

"Do you have a nickname or something you would like us to call you instead?" I asked.

The girl shrugged. "Something tough?" she said, after a few more steps. "And scary. Like . . . *Grim Reaper of Souls.* Or *Deadly Nightshade.* Or something like that."

"Those are superb selections," Jackaby said with a sober nod. "Yes. Trust your gut."

"Or take your time," I added with a small cough. "You don't think those ones might be a bit too . . . ostentatious?"

"Nonsense," said Jackaby. "She could go by *Grim* for short. Marvelous name for a young lady. *Grim.* It's sharp, but still unique."

"I don't think—"

"I like it," she said, flatly. "You can call me Grim. That's the house, up there. The one with the green door. Her husband should be there. He's called Mr. Finkin—but nobody's seen the fairy lady for days."

There was a light on in the house ahead, and smoke was coming from the chimney. It was an unassuming building, physically no different from most of the others on the block, but the whole property was surrounded by a bubble of protective charms and hearth energy—not unlike some of the wards Jackaby kept around our place on Augur Lane.

"It definitely has a fairy touch," I said.

Grim hung back behind as I gave the knocker three sharp taps. The door cracked open a few inches and a man's face poked out. He had a graying beard and round spectacles that he peered over to survey the three of us. A storm of emotions swirled around him, none of them particularly happy.

"What do you want?"

"Hello, Mr. Finkin," I said. "Pardon the interruption. We're here to speak with you about your wife."

The door slammed shut. I blinked.

"Why'd you say it like that?" asked Grim.

"Like what?"

"Like you're police or something."

I knocked again.

"Go away," the man yelled through the door.

"Please," I called back. "We only want to help."

"You the authorities?" Mr. Finkin demanded.

I glanced at the kid. "No," I said. "No, we are not the authorities."

The door opened again, just a crack. It was difficult for me to tell if Mr. Finkin had silver streaks running through his hair or if it was just the wisps of anxiety and distrust swirling around his head. A heavy amber fog of secrecy hung on his shoulders like sandbags. He bent under the weight of it.

"What do you know about my Maeve?" he asked.

"Not enough," I said.

"Why do you care so much about her?"

"We . . . don't," I said. "Not about your wife specifically, anyway."

Jackaby shot me a surprised glance, but kept quiet.

"We *would* like to find her, though," I continued, "and return her to you safe and sound. I'm sure she's lovely. Well—actually I'm not sure of that. She could be dreadful. The truth is, we don't know anything about the woman, except that her thread is somehow twisted up with a handful of others, and a friend of ours has recently gotten snagged on the big, messy knot. If we help your wife, we help our friend—and in the process, we help everyone else mixed up in whatever this is."

The man seemed oddly satisfied by my answer. His shoulders relaxed and his aura cooled slightly.

"Were you aware that your wife is not human?" I asked, as gently as I could.

The man's eyes widened, but it was clear that this was not new information. He leaned his head outside and glanced to either side. "Not so loud," he whispered. "What do you know about her?"

"We know that she sold her services to a number of clients, including this young lady's mother."

"To who?" the man asked.

I gestured behind me, only to find that the girl had vanished. "Grim?" I called into the shadows.

"Grim?" said the man.

"It, erm, often seems so," said Jackaby, "but we try not to give up hope. We can help you find your missing wife, right, Miss Rook?"

"Yes," I said. "Probably. Maybe. We'll try."

The man scowled. "Keep yer voices down. I suppose you'd better step inside." He pushed the door open and allowed us to enter.

The man's house smelled like leather, old books, and binding glue. I could sense a fairy aura all around the place, as well as faint traces of elves and goblins and various spirits all colliding—mostly in a cozy nook just off the kitchen. Hovering alongside all of that was the distinct turnip aura we'd been following. It was older here, but still so strong.

"That's where she met with her clients, isn't it?" I said, nodding toward the nook.

The man scowled. "She didn't give anything to anyone who wasn't decent, if that's what you're thinking. She was most particular about that. Only shared her secrets with good folks who would use them to do good things. It isn't right, all the pointless restrictions they've been setting. There's people all across town who *need* things they can only get from magic folk—things that keep them healthy, keep them feeling like themselves. What are they supposed to do?"

"You're preaching to the choir," Jackaby said.

"My Maeve just helps people get their goods to the people who need them. That's all."

There was another bubble of energy around the nook, protective, but not like any charms we used back at Augur Lane. My eyes traced the source of the spell to a fine line running along the floorboards.

"What sort of magic is this?" I asked.

Mr. Finkin opened his mouth, but then shut it again with a shrug. "Sorry," he said. "I couldn't tell you."

Jackaby peeked over my shoulder. "You really couldn't, could you?" he said. "Unless I'm very much mistaken, that's a dome of confidence."

Finkin gave a little smile of confirmation, but didn't add anything.

"That's basically a secret-proofing spell, yes?" I asked. "Anything a person learns inside the dome cannot be repeated outside?"

"Handy bit of magic." Jackaby nodded. "I knew a master chef who used one of these to teach his cooks secret recipes. They could re-create them in his kitchen—but try as they might, they couldn't share the secrets."

"I assume this was for Maeve's protection," I said to Mr. Finkin, "as well as her clients'."

"She just wanted them to know that their secrets were safe with her," Finkin said.

I ran my hand over a sheaf of blank papers on the counter. The material felt sturdier than average stationery, more like artist's paper.

"Don't go touching those," the man said. "Maeve is very

particular about all that. She wouldn't like strangers handling her things."

"Sorry." I took my hand away and peered around the room instead.

There were several watercolors hung up in the house that looked as if they had been painted by the same hand. Soft and fluid, they depicted fantastical landscapes in vibrant hues. One of them, in particular, hummed with quiet urgency, its surface practically rippling to reveal a deeper truth behind it. I leaned in to get a closer look. It appeared to have been painted on the same sort of paper as the ones in the stack behind me. But there was something more. Deeper.

"Those look like the Hills of Elfame," observed Jackaby, following my eyes. "Is that where your wife was from?"

The man nodded. "We put in a travel request months ago, when the Om Caini first opened the list," he said. "But right from the start there was some mess that got the whole program shut down again for weeks."

"Ah. That was probably the dismemberment in Trollsburg," Jackaby said.

I raised a brow.

"If it makes you feel any better, they were able to reattach the gentleman's arm," he said.

Finkin shook his head. "It's just been one delay or cancellation after another since then. Still no approval for us."

"I don't think Alina anticipated just how many people would need processing," Jackaby said.

"Given recent events," I added, "I have a feeling she's not going to be able to expedite the system any time soon."

The image was beautiful. I could see the love that had coursed through her brush. But that wasn't what kept my eyes on the piece. I shook my head and shifted my focus. The aura my eyes were stuck on was beneath the paper—behind the painting entirely. It was stronger there than anywhere else in the house. Behind the painting was a hidden compartment of some sort, and it was thick with that turnip-tinted energy.

"Can you tell us anything about the day she went missing?" Jackaby was asking as I pulled my attention back into the room. "Did she meet with any clients that day? Perhaps she turned someone away and they got upset? Anything like that?"

The man looked pained. "I've tried so hard to recall," he said at last. "I came home like usual, I remember that. Maeve was working on a new painting in the den. It's been weeks since she's felt like making her art. She's been so caught up with—" He hesitated. "But the rest of the evening's a blank. Next thing I remember, the sun had already gone down. Maeve's brushes were all rinsed and set to dry, and we must have eaten dinner, because our dishes were in the sink—but I was all alone. I don't know what happened in between."

"Memory gap." Jackaby shot a glance my way. "Seems to be going around." He picked up a bottle of iridescent ink from the counter, gave it a quick shake, and watched the colors within spin around one another like the rainbow whorls on a soap bubble.

"What did you do when you found that she was gone?" I asked.

"Well, at first I just figured she had gone for a walk," said Finkin. "She's always been a bit mercurial, you know? It's just her way. So I didn't think too much of it. But when she hadn't come back in the morning, I knew something was wrong."

"But you didn't file a report?" I asked.

He bit his lip. "Maeve wouldn't like me to go to the police," he said.

"I can see how that put you in a tricky position," I said. "Maeve's less-than-legal secret must have made it hard to know who to trust. But I can assure you, we are not the police, and so long as she wasn't harming anyone, we're not concerned about any of her so-called contraband."

Jackaby looked up from the swirling ink bottle. "Absolutely. Not interested in this, either. I just think it's pretty."

"We just want to help find your wife and all the others," I continued. "Please tell me, Mr. Finkin—what's behind the painting?"

I did not need the sight to tell that my question made

the man uncomfortable. "It's nothing," he said. "There's an old wall safe, but it's got nothing of any real value in it." My vision flickered. I could tell that the old man was both telling the truth and lying. Before I could press him further, however, there came a loud knock at the front door.

Jackaby started and fumbled the bottle. It slipped out of his hands and shattered on the kitchen floor. He winced. "Drat! So sorry. My fault. I'll tidy this up." He hurried to mop up the liquid with a dish towel as the spilled ink sent waves of magical energy wafting through the room like steam billowing up from a boiling pot.

Finkin looked miserably from the mess to the front door and crossed the room uneasily. He opened the door just enough to peek outside.

"Mr. Finkin," a familiar voice said. "My name is Mr. Kit. This is Mr. Garabrand. We'd like to have a word with you, if you don't mind."

"I—I'm busy," said Mr. Finkin. "I'm sorry, but you'll have to come back some other time." He attempted to pull the door closed, but a polished boot slid into the gap before he could shut it.

"Not very hospitable," said Kit. "Some agents would find that downright suspicious."

"I don't have to let you in," said Mr. Finkin. "I have rights."

"You seem nervous," said Mr. Kit. "Is there something to be nervous about?"

Mr. Finkin let out a little yelp as the door swung suddenly open. I saw Mr. Kit on the front step, his partner standing not far behind him. Kit narrowed his eyes when he spotted me.

"That's enough," Mr. Garabrand said, calmly. He gave us a nod through the open door. "No need to be so rough, Mr. Kit. My apologies, Mr. Finkin. We weren't aware that you were already in communication with representatives from the New Fiddleham Police Department."

I glanced at Mr. Finkin, who looked understandably betrayed.

"Take all the time you need," Garabrand added. "We can always compare notes with Detective Rook and Mr. Jackaby tomorrow."

Finkin's aura fumed.

"We're not representing anyone but ourselves at present," I corrected, pulling my focus back to the agents on the doorstep. "The police have insisted on making that point very clear in the past. We're simply making a few friendly inquiries as concerned neighbors."

"Ah." Garabrand smiled politely. "My mistake."

"You've gone rogue, you mean," Kit mumbled.

"Be nice, Mr. Kit." Garabrand straightened his tie. "The good detective appears to be consistently one step ahead of our investigation. That's commendable. Better than the commanders she typically answers to."

"I make a habit of answering to myself," I said, crossing my arms in front of my chest.

"Disregarding the chain of command," Kit muttered. "Impersonating an officer. Interfering with an ongoing investigation."

"Enough. Get out!" Mr. Finkin demanded. "The lot of you! Out!"

"Nearly finished here," said Jackaby, scooping up bits of inky glass with the saturated dishrag. "I'll just throw this mess out." The whole kitchen was a cloud of magical energy. I could feel my pulse throbbing against my temples.

"Throw it out? You'll do no such thing!" Agent Kit's suspicion hummed like an overtightened piano string as he pushed past Mr. Finkin to get a better look at what Jackaby was doing. "Whatever that is, it's evidence!"

"Hey! This is my house, you brute!" Finkin hollered.

Between the boiling emotions and the radiant magic, I couldn't take it anymore. I felt as if my skull was about to burst.

Squeezing past Agent Garabrand in the doorway, I made my way out into fresh air. I stared up at the sky and gulped several deep breaths until I could breathe evenly again.

"You okay?" Agent Garabrand leaned against the door frame, watching me.

"Grand," I croaked.

He nodded and stood in silence for a few moments. From inside, Jackaby's, Kit's, and Finkin's raised voices overlapped as they each insisted the others honor their priorities.

"If you don't mind my asking, why are you here, Detective?"

"Just following the trail," I said. I had no intention of telling him about Grim. I tried to focus my attention on a cracked flagstone ahead of me rather than the chaos behind, willing the world to stop tilting.

Garabrand took a few slow steps away from the door, drawing even with me on the front porch. "I don't mean *here*." He nodded toward the house. "I mean *here*." He gestured widely at the landscape in front of us. "You're not from New Fiddleham. You and I have that in common. This isn't your town. A year ago you didn't know it even existed, and yet now you're taking risks, running yourself ragged, trying desperately to help people you've never met. Most of them don't even want your help. So . . . *why?*"

My brow crinkled. "Because *somebody* needs to," I said. "People here are scared, and they have every reason to be. They see their neighbors getting hurt—disappearing. Now people are dying. If I have the power to help them—how could I not?"

"Mm. Love that." Garabrand nodded approvingly and

put his hands in the pockets of his coat. "You noticed something in there, didn't you?"

"I—I notice a lot of things," I said.

Garabrand eyed me in silence for a moment. "For someone concerned with the truth, you're awfully hesitant to share it."

"You want the truth?" I said. My head was beginning to feel clearer, but the dull, angry throbbing remained. "The truth is that I don't know you. Frankly, I don't believe you have this city's best interests at heart—and, with all due respect, I don't trust you."

Agent Garabrand didn't respond immediately. He turned his eyes up to the overcast sky and nodded. "Good," he said at last. "That's good. Don't trust anybody, kid. Least of all some cagey old suits from out of town. Trust gets people killed." His aura soured for a moment to an ashy amber color. There was a sadness there, beneath the layers of grit.

"That's not a very reassuring defense," I said.

Garabrand took a deep breath and rubbed the back of his neck with one hand. "I suppose not," he said. "Stay suspicious. It's a good instinct in our line of work. People will let you down."

I waited for him to elaborate, but he just gazed into the night. Thoughts swirled around his head, dark and bitter, like cigar smoke and stale coffee.

"You've had your trust broken," I said.

He looked me in the eyes, and his aura confirmed what I had said. He glanced away again before he answered. "That," he said finally, "is classified."

"Is that why you're so afraid of magic?" I asked. "Tricked by too many monsters?"

"Monsters?" Garabrand allowed himself a chuckle and shook his head. "When I was a little boy, my old man told me all sorts of stories about monsters. His favorite one was the snallygaster. Ever heard of that one?"

I shook my head. I had not.

"A classic," he said. "Scaly lizard with wings and a beak, but also nasty fangs and tentacles. My mother tried to convince me it wasn't real, but Pop took that sorta thing seriously. He even had a tattoo that was supposed to protect him—a seven-pointed star. He said it kept him safe."

"Did it?" I asked.

"I like to think so." He slid up his sleeve, turning his arm over to reveal a faded tattoo of a seven-pointed star of his own. "There's a sort of comfort," he continued, "in knowing that you can counter evil magic with good magic of your own. Power's just power, after all. Potential is just potential. In the right hands, it can be a great boon." He brushed a hand fondly over the old ink lines on his skin.

"Jackaby and I employ a number of similar wards," I said.

"I know." Agent Garabrand pulled his sleeve back down. "You two have a healthy respect for the supernatural. That's good. Been training Agent Kit in there to see it the same way. He'll get there."

From inside came a clatter, followed by Mr. Finkin cursing furiously.

"I caught a snallygaster once," Garabrand said, kicking a bit of gravel off the porch. "A real one. It was my very first year with the bureau. Shrimpy thing, actually. Skittish, but not overly aggressive. Ended up keeping her like a weird parrot for a while. She loved boiled eggs. Used to screech like the devil to warn me when I was in danger. Probably saved my life more than once. Of course, she also tried to take my head off a few times." He smiled fondly at the memory.

"I must admit, I was under the impression that you didn't trust magic," I said.

"Only in the same way I don't trust people." He shrugged. "If anything, I trust *wild* magic to be *wild* more than I trust *civilized* people to be *civil*. People lie. People turn on you." His aura dimmed again, but he rallied. "But you counter the bad with the good. You, Miss Rook, have the power and potential to do a lot of good. Gives me hope. You need hope in this career."

"Well," I said, "now I'm not sure if I'm supposed to stay suspicious or stay hopeful."

Garabrand's mouth twitched up in a smile. "Both. Constantly both."

"I'll take that under advisement," I said.

"Out!" Finkin hollered. Jackaby and Agent Kit finally emerged, the angry old man all but literally kicking them from behind. "And stay out!" He slammed the door the moment they were both clear of the threshold.

"He's hiding something," Agent Kit snarled, dusting himself off. "The old man's hiding something. What did you observe in there?" He jabbed a finger at me, his mustache trembling on his upper lip and his aura a steely cobalt blue.

I considered for a moment. Whatever secrets lay behind Maeve Finkin's painting, I could wait until the agents weren't peering over our shoulders to discover them. "Classified," I said.

Kit flushed with frustration, but Garabrand chuckled. "Fair enough," he said, clapping a hand on his furious partner's shoulder. "Stand down, kid."

"I would love to stay and compare notes," I said to the agents, "but the most daunting leg of our evening lies ahead, I'm afraid—and we're already running late. Mr. Jackaby? Shall we?"

"You have a lead?" Kit demanded.

"Something far more grave," I answered, heavily. "We have a dinner."

chapter seventeen

When I was a young girl, my mother used to take me with her on her trips into London from time to time to try on itchy dresses and have my head patted by total strangers she insisted were dear old friends. Mother had a seemingly endless supply of dear old friends—most of whom we never saw more than once or twice, but whose inclusion in *Burke's Peerage* ensured that they would never be demoted to acquaintances. My favorite part of these trips had always been the journey home. I would fight against sleepy eyes to take it all in. Before our carriage crested the final hill, I would see the faint glow of home reaching up into the dark sky—the light of countless lamps and brightly lit windows, melting together into a warm halo—welcoming me back like an *actual* dear old friend.

As Jackaby and I trudged up the last stretch of sidewalk, I could see a different sort of halo swelling to greet us. It was not the golden glow of the gas lamps—but it was the color of home. My home. That strange, messy old house on Augur Lane meant something to me I might never be able to explain to my parents.

"Before we go in," I said, breaking a silence that had kept us company for the last block, "please don't tell my parents about—well—about any of it."

"Understood," said Jackaby without hesitation. And the curious thing was, he did understand. I could see it in the halo surrounding him, as well as in his eyes.

"You're not going to press me to be honest with them or something? To trust them?"

"You're the new Seer," said Jackaby. "You're a different person than you were when you left them. Your world is not their world, not anymore, and they won't understand. They can't. You love them, of course, but you don't want them to get hurt. It's ironic, really. You're bombarded by everyone else's truth but burdened with keeping your own to yourself." Jackaby's aura darkened from its usual vibrant turquoise to a dark blue-gray.

"When was the last time you spoke to your own family?" I asked.

Jackaby's lips pursed. He trod a few steps before speaking

again. "Anything in particular you'd like me to say when we get inside?"

I shook my head. "No. I don't want you to lie or anything. Just . . . I don't know. Maybe omit all the big facts."

"Don't lie, but also avoid the facts. Got it. Going to be an interesting night, but I've played charades with Chief Nudd and the goblins before. Always up for a challenge."

"I'm sorry," I said. "I don't mean to make things complicated. It's just . . . as far as my parents are aware, I'm still the same bookish little girl reading silly adventure stories in the nook. They still think that I'm pursuing paleontology, but we both know that my only real dinosaur digs both ended in disappointment and disaster."

"Ah, maybe a bunch of dusty, mineralized bones are enough to get your father out of bed in the morning, but the bones you're finding are more pressing by far. And also more fresh. Just today you've found not one but two mutilated corpses, a connection between several missing persons, and all manner of malevolent magical residue. Our work might even prevent total unrest in this city. Or possibly contribute to it. Either way—it's very important."

"Comforting. But really, the last things my parents need to know about are dead bodies and malevolent magic," I said. "They hardly think that I'm mature enough to walk to the market and back without an escort. They want to see me in a nice, stable, respectable household. Maybe, just maybe, if I can convince them that my life is normal and pleasant, they'll go home and let me stay."

"Mm. *Normal.*" Jackaby chewed on the word as we started up the front walk.

"Please," I said.

"I'll give it my solemn best, just this once," he promised.

It was at this moment that the front window burst open and a flurry of feathers and shouts erupted into the still night air.

"Shoo!" my father was yelling. Somewhere behind him, my mother was squawking. A large mallard quacked indignantly and battered my father with its wings and beak.

"Douglas!" I shouted. Duck bill and human face both turned to look at me, then back at each other.

"*Normal* is a somewhat subjective word," said Jackaby.

Several minutes and a cloud of feathers later, I had successfully ushered Douglas back to the safety of the third floor and left Jackaby downstairs to settle my parents. I caught up with Charlie in the hallway on my way back.

"I'm so sorry—" I began.

"Don't be sorry," said Charlie. "It was no trouble."

"Of course it was! Your nerves are like packed fireworks."

"It was fine, really."

"No. It wasn't," I insisted. "And you can *tell* me that it wasn't. I really wish you would. My parents can be exhausting under the best of conditions."

"They were fine," he said. His aura crackled with

pressure. "Mostly fine. I only left them alone for a minute toward the end there. I'm sorry about that. I just had to go check on the potatoes."

"Don't *you* go apologizing, now!" I threw back my head. "Ugh. You're a saint. It's maddening. And sweet. But mostly maddening. Lord, you've been stuck here all day, and I'm only about to make it worse. I've so much to tell you, and none of it is good. And—wait, have you been cooking, too?" The smells coming from the direction of the kitchen were uncharacteristically mouthwatering.

"It's been mostly Jenny," Charlie said. "I suggested a few dishes I thought might go over well, but I would have made a mess of things without her. I made a bit of a mess anyway." He gestured down at his shirt, which was splattered in some dark brown stains. "I feel very uncomfortable taking all the credit, but Jenny thought that it would be better if she waited for a proper introduction before meeting your parents."

"Oh, you're both absolute gems," I said. "I'm so sorry, again, that I left you alone with them all day."

"It's okay," said Charlie. "I can still try to find some time to prepare for the press briefing after dinner. And perhaps I could run a few thoughts past you in the morning?"

"Oh lord." My breath caught in my chest. "I completely forgot." Charlie simply could *not* put himself in front of the public. Not now. It would be marching straight into a massacre.

"Don't worry about it—you have more than enough on your mind," he said, but his aura spun with dull gray coils of disappointment. "Forget I brought it up. I can handle it."

"No—stop it," I said. "Stop pretending everything is okay just to keep from overburdening me."

"I'm not—" he started. I crossed my arms and raised an eyebrow. "Maybe I am. A little," he conceded. "But I'll be fine. Perhaps it's best I don't overthink it anyway."

"Why overthink it when you can rethink it entirely?" I swallowed hard and managed what was probably a rather manic and unreassuring smile. "You should cancel."

His brow furrowed. "Abigail . . ."

"I need to tell you something," I breathed. "It's about your—"

"There you are!" my mother declared, coming around the corner. "They're right here, Daniel! Oh, Abigail, really. You've already kept us waiting all day. You and your gentleman can catch up anytime." The hallway was already feeling exceedingly crowded when my father came around the bend.

"Ah, there the two lovebirds are." He gave me a fatherly wink that did nothing to make the situation any less awkward. "He seems like a very nice young man, by the way. He was telling us that he works as some sort of civil servant. That must be nice."

"Cultural liaison," I said. "It's a very important job. And a respectable one."

"Yes, yes," my mother said. "Of course, he also let slip that he was working as a policeman when the two of you met. Fine work, of course. I'm not one to judge. But much too dangerous an occupation for a gentleman of good standing who might be looking to start a family. And you would not have enjoyed all the drama of being an officer's wife and worrying about his safety all the time."

"No." I looked pointedly at Charlie. "No, I suppose I would not enjoy all that worrying."

"On the other hand, your daughter is more resilient than you might think," said Charlie.

"Perhaps," said my mother. "But still, all the better that you've taken a more reliable position in government. And one more suited to the lifestyle to which our Abigail is accustomed."

"That is more than enough of that conversation," I said. "Shall we go see if Mr. Jackaby would like some help with the table settings?"

"You go ahead," said Charlie. "I was about to change into a fresh shirt." He nodded toward the staircase. "I'll be right down."

"You're not going up to Abigail's room to change?" my mother asked.

"Hmm? Not at all," Charlie said. "I'll be going to my place. I won't be a moment."

"Your place is up the stairs?" My mother's eyes darted to me. "Are you two living under the same roof already?"

"Oh!" Charlie said, his cheeks flushing. He glanced at me, and then back at my parents. "No. No, I meant I was going to go to my . . . place for spare clothes. Here. It's a place that I have here, in this house. In a . . . closet. Where I keep a few clean clothes in case I need to change." How Charlie had ever kept his supernatural identity concealed was beyond me. It was almost adorable, but I was engaged to the world's most atrocious liar.

My mother did not look convinced, but Charlie gave her an awkward nod and scampered up the stairs anyway.

"So," my father said. "What about your new line of work? Your fiancé tells us that it's important, too, but he was rather vague on the details. Something about laws and policies?"

"Oh. Is that what he said? Yes. Yes, that's a lot of it. I've learned quite a bit about laws and policies. But mostly it's about looking out for people. Lots of, erm, research involved."

"Well, you always were a clever study," my father said.

"So you're a secretary?" my mother asked.

"Erm. You could call it that," I hedged. "Although it's a bit more complicated than secretarial work."

"I'm sure you're a great help to your employers." My father's tone was supportive, but his aura flicked in patronizing purple hues.

"I *am*, actually," I said, a tad defensively. "I've been a great help to the entire city. Only the other day, the commissioner personally asked for my help, in fact."

"That's grand, dear," my mother said. "We've always found you to be a tremendously helpful and capable young woman." Her aura disagreed.

"I *am* capable," I muttered.

"That's what I just said." Mother shook her head. "I'm sure you've made yourself indispensable here in New Fiddlesham."

"New Fiddleham," I corrected. The contrast between their words and their meaning was beginning to make me feel seasick.

"You're old enough and mature enough to be making your own decisions," my father added, although his aura was still on the fence about the matter. "It's only that we don't want you to feel as if you *have* to stay here out of some misguided sense of obligation."

"What? Of course I'm staying. And I *do* have obligations here. In fact, I've put off certain obligations for much too long already."

"One could reason," my mother chimed in, "that if you've been able to put off obligations and they've made do without you, then they will continue to make do without you, should you decide to—for example—return home to England. Just an observation."

"Don't pressure her," my father chided. "I'm sure she does fine work. What is it, exactly, that you do, darling?"

I hesitated. *Well, Mum and Dad, since you ask: I have magical eyeballs and I solve mysteries—often violent ones—about mythical creatures for a living.* "I see things," I said aloud. "Things that other people miss."

My parents both looked at me expectantly until it became clear that I didn't intend to add anything else. "That sounds nice," my mother managed.

"It is nice," I said. "And important. And normal." Oh, lord, I was worse than Charlie.

Over my mother's shoulder, I saw the plaster shiver as Jenny slid into the room through the wall of the library. She straightened her opalescent dress and mouthed the word "Now?" with a hopeful expression.

"No!" I blurted. "Not yet."

"Not yet?" Father asked. Mother looked baffled. Both of them turned to look directly at Jenny, then back at me.

"What are you looking at?" my father asked.

Jenny's face was a mask of hurt and disappointment—but it was a face that only I could see. I winced. I was an idiot. Jenny always looked faintly incorporeal, even when she was making herself fully solid for the world. Now that I was the Seer, I could rarely tell when she was invisible to others. "I'm so sorry," I said. Jenny shook her head and drifted up into the ceiling. I would have to make it up to her later. "I'm not looking at anything. I was only saying *not yet* because . . . now isn't the right time to talk about work. Because, well—"

"Dinner is served," Mr. Jackaby announced from the doorway. "Right this way."

I let out a breath. "Yes. Dinner. Shall we?"

Someone—almost certainly Jenny—had taken the time to make Jackaby's laboratory look like a downright presentable dining room. A clean linen cloth had been spread over the burnt and battered old table, fresh candles had been tucked into several spare flasks, and the shelves with the most disturbing contents had been covered by tasteful curtains. There was still a seven-foot-long alligator skeleton hanging over our heads, but Jenny had gone out of her way to tie a cheery yellow bow tie around its neck. On the table were six place settings—although where Jenny and Charlie had managed to secure six unbroken plates and a full set of silverware whose pieces had not been melted down for one of Jackaby's experiments was anyone's guess.

"Who is the sixth?" my father asked.

"The sixth what?" Jackaby said. "Lots of sixths. Sixth king of Rome was called Servius Tullius. Popular chap, but a bit of a classist."

"What?" said my father.

"What?" said Jackaby. "You asked—"

"Is Charlie not back yet?" I said. "I'll just go and check on him. I'll be right down."

Before anyone had time to object, I hurried up the stairs and made my way to the mirror portal, trying not to think about how my definition of "normal" conversation might differ from Jackaby's. I paused before stepping through the glass. This was probably the only moment I would get to explain the whole situation to Charlie before he rushed off into the jaws of the angry public. I tried to decide which piece of bad news to break to him first, and how. No amount of careful phrasing would make the mess any less messy. Ultimately, I steeled my resolve and just stepped through.

The glass was cool, and yielded immediately to my touch. It was like stepping into a wall of silvery pudding—a sensation that never got any less peculiar. The whole world felt like it was tipping forward, and then, abruptly, I felt air on my cheeks and opened my eyes to see Charlie's carpet rushing toward me. My feet stumbled over the edge of the frame as I pitched forward.

"I'm fine!" I called, picking myself up. "I'm getting better at it, I think. Charlie?"

I had seen him mere minutes before, but I dared wonder if his aura would still brighten up at the fresh sight of me. A tiny, miserable voice in the back of my head reminded me that even if it did, it would only be so that I could bring him crashing back down again with wretched news.

"Charlie?" I called again. The apartment was quiet. There was a light on in the front room, and another down the hall in the bedroom, but no sounds.

I walked the length of the hallway and knocked on the bedroom door. My mother, one looking glass and a flight of stairs away, would have been scandalized as I entered my fiancé's bedroom. I could see the stained shirt lying on the foot of the bed and his jacket hung over the back of a chair. The closet door was still open—but Charlie wasn't here.

A tingle ran up my spine and I opened my eyes wider. There was a familiar smoky energy floating all around me. Turnips and turpitude. My blood felt like ice in my veins, and my head swam.

No. Not here.

I clenched my fists, willing my damnable eyes to succeed now in ways they had failed in all those houses I had visited today. I needed to find a trail. A clue. Anything. I needed to find Charlie. *Now.*

The whole room was awash with his aura—brightest of all was his most recent path in from the door. The ghosts of his energy paused before the closet, intensified, and then stopped. I dropped to my hands and knees, scouring the carpet. There was a fine layer of dust—no, ash—right where he had been standing last. My searching fingers clasped onto a scrap of paper as well. Just a corner, no larger than my thumbnail, and singed along one edge. I held it up to the light, but there were no words or symbols on it—it was a blank scrap, but it was all I had.

Charlie was gone.

chapter eighteen

I hit the hallway back in the house on Augur Lane without losing my stride, turning the stumble into a frantic run. I nearly flew down the spiral staircase, then burst into the makeshift dining room out of breath.

"Good lord, Abigail. Decorum." My mother put a hand to her chest.

"Respectfully, stuff decorum, Mother," I said. "Mr. Jackaby, dinner is off. We're going back out."

"What?" My father coughed.

"Uh," Jackaby contributed, thoughtfully.

"It's Charlie," I said. "Same aura as the others. Don't forget your coat."

"You're not going out at this hour!" Mother huffed.

"I wasn't asking for permission, Mother." I spun on my heel and out the door.

My heart was pounding in my ears. I stormed into the office across the hall to root through drawers and upend storage boxes in search of any of Jackaby's collected trinkets that might prove useful.

"Miss Rook?" Jackaby's voice came from the doorway.

"I've got all the usual wards," I said without turning around, "plus a spare vial of holy water. I also packed two dragon's breath charges, just in case we run into some heavy trouble. You've got a jar of finfolk weed in here, by the way, but I can see that it's gone off. It won't be potent enough to do anyone any good. What I really need is something that's good for *finding*. We should visit that medium in town, Little Miss."

"Little Miss went into hiding," Jackaby said. "Her mother, too. A few of the anti-magic hooligans broke all their windows and started a fire."

"Ugh. There's got to be something or someone that can help us find him. What does that do?" I pointed at a large, round drum propped up in the corner.

"That belonged to a Mongolian shaman," answered Jackaby. "They use the drumbeats to induce a sort of trance state for astral projection."

"Does it work?"

"Well, it's a drum, so it makes a *thump-thump* noise pretty reliably," said Jackaby. "I am, however, not a shaman, so I can't help you with the rest."

"Argh!" I punched the desk with a bit more force than I had intended. I rubbed my sore knuckles and tried not to cry and scream all at once.

"Rook." Jackaby's voice was gentle and his brow was heavy. "Stop. Just take a breath. We won't do anyone any good rushing out there without anything to go on."

"What are you talking about? Of course we're rushing out there. It's Charlie!"

"And if he is in danger, then he will need you at your best."

"I am at my best! This is my best! My best isn't good enough, and it never will be, okay? Which is why I need you to stop wasting time and help me." I panted. My hand hurt.

"We've spent the entire day all over town," Jackaby said. "My legs are so sore I can barely stand, and I can't imagine yours are much better. Neither of us has eaten anything all day, and you're shaking."

"I am not shaking," I protested. "I'm just. I'm . . ." I was shaking—my hands, my jaw, and my lungs shook with every breath I drew. The room blurred and I felt hot tears welling up in my eyes. My legs did feel weak, but this was no time to stop.

"You need to tell us what's happening right this instant,"

my mother insisted, pushing her way into the office past Jackaby. My father slid in behind her.

"You want to know what's happening?" I said. "Murder. And kidnappings. And more weird, inexplicable, awful things, pretty much all the time."

My mother gasped.

"And sometimes—when I work very hard and get very lucky—I help put a stop to some of them, at least for a while. *That's* what's happening. And it *is* dangerous. And important. And that sixth plate was for Jenny, who has been nothing but kind to me since I came to New Fiddleham, and she does not deserve to be treated like some lurid secret simply because she's a ghost. Also, now Charlie is missing—and, if possible, I would very much like to prevent him from being"—I took a deep breath—"from being dead, too. Again. I know from experience that he does not wear it as well as Jenny does."

Both of my parents stood agape. I spun away from them and went back to ransacking Jackaby's shelves.

"Did you get too much sun today?" my father finally asked.

"Yes, I'm sure that's it," Jackaby said. "She's had a very long day. As have you two—travel can sure take it out of you, can't it? Why don't we all take dinner in our rooms and call it an evening. I'm sure everything will be clearer after a good night's rest."

With much coaxing, he managed to shuffle them out of the office and up the stairs to their room.

I was in the library, thumbing through a volume on portals, gates, and teleportation when he found me again.

"We'll find him."

"Will we?" I threw a useless book down on the table. "Because that seems entirely dependent on *me*, and frankly I . . . I . . . I can't."

"You will."

"You keep saying that. But what if I don't? What if I *never* get the hang of this? I've had months to adjust, and I couldn't track a common thief. What we need right now more than anything is someone who knows what they're doing. We need the Seer."

Jackaby regarded me, then took a few measured breaths. "We have her. She's right in front of me."

I sagged until I felt the cool wood of the table press against my forehead. "I wish I could give it back," I groaned. The world was spinning, but I just lay facedown in my own messy research and let it spin.

Jackaby said nothing, but he set a plate down on the table and pulled up a chair across from me.

Finally, I dragged myself back up to sitting. "I thought I *wanted* this," I said. "The whole reason I left home was to be independent. I've been beholden to other people my whole life. My parents, my nanny, my teachers. Even when

I ran away, I still wasn't independent. I was following that expedition leader, and then I got here, and I followed *you*."

"No one gets anywhere without following in the footsteps of others," Jackaby said, gently. "There is agency in deciding which ones you follow."

"I've always had someone *else* in charge. I thought all I needed was my chance to call the shots. But now?" I slouched against the back of my chair and closed my eyes, wishing I could drown out the myriad energies floating in my vision. "I finally got my wish—people are treating me like some sort of capable leader—and I'm not. I can't do it." My throat felt tight, and my stomach churned.

Jackaby's hand was warm as he cupped it around mine. I opened my eyes to look at him across the tabletop. His aura was a wash of sympathetic blues.

I sniffed. "Did it feel like this to you?" I asked. "In the beginning?"

He gave me a sideways smile. "In the beginning," he confirmed. "And also in the middle. Less and less often toward the end—but even then, now and again."

I nodded. "That's both reassuring and completely unhelpful."

"Mostly, I felt . . . alone," he admitted. "Because mostly I was. Before Jenny. Before Chief Nudd and Hudson and Douglas. Before *you*. Those were not kind years, in the beginning." He gave my hand a squeeze. "Miss Rook, if there's one thing I've learned doing this work, it's that being a leader is not the same thing as being independent. In fact, they're quite the opposite." He took a deep breath. "Being a good leader doesn't mean *not* letting other people help you. It means being *really good* at letting other people help you. Real leadership is about trust. It's about accepting that others trust you, and trusting them in return. Most of all—*hardest* of all—it's about trusting *yourself*."

He let go of my hand and pushed the plate of food toward me, between my piles of books. "We *will* find him," he said, softly. "Jenny says he picked this meal himself, so consider this his contribution to cracking the case."

Meat pies. Charlie knew that I loved meat pies. He did *not* know that my mother abhorred them, as well as just about any other foods one could buy from a man with a cart on a street corner—which made me smile. And then the tears were back.

"It's very late, Miss Rook. Why don't you finish that off and then try to get some sleep. We can pick it up first thing in the morning."

"You're right," I said. "You go ahead and get some rest. I have a few more books to check first. That is one thing I was honest with my parents about. This job is a lot of research."

Jackaby looked like he wanted to say something else, but he nodded and slipped out.

It must have been several hours later when I sat up

abruptly and three or four books tumbled to the ground at my feet. I blinked and cleared my throat. Someone had wrapped a warm blanket around my shoulders.

The wall quivered, and in another moment, Jenny was in the library beside me. "You're awake," she said. "I heard a noise."

"How long was I down?" I asked, twisting my sore neck left and right experimentally.

"Not long enough," she said. "A few hours. The sun still isn't up yet. You'd have done yourself far better in your own bed, but I had a feeling that it was best to let you get what you could."

"I'm sorry," I said. "About yesterday. I should have introduced you. You've been a good friend, and I've been—well, a mess."

"All true," Jenny agreed. "But that's not the important thing right now. Did you come across anything that might help?"

I shook my head. "I was reading an impressively dry history of fairy abduction narratives—none of which fit our recent disappearances. There was something about people—mostly babies—being stolen or lured to the other side of the veil, but right around then I fell forward into the book. There was a whole ocean of ink and a lot of words. I had to cling to the edge of the paper to keep from being swept away. It all felt real, as usual, but I think it's fair to guess where the dream took over."

"Well, good job hanging on to the paper, anyway," said Jenny. "Better safe than sorry."

A spring went off in my mind, which was still creaking back to life like a rusty windup toy. "Wait," I said. "I *did* hang on to an edge of paper."

"Are you sure? That part sounded very dreamlike."

"A different paper," I said. I shoved the rest of the books off my lap and felt around in my pockets. "Here. This was in Charlie's room. It's covered in the same energy that we found at the other crime scenes."

"It just looks like a regular old piece of paper to me," she said. "Does it mean anything to you?"

I let my shoulders sag. "Nothing helpful." I held the fragment closer to the light of the lamp beside me. "Hang on. Oh! Jenny, I've been a proper fool. It *is* familiar, but I kept fixating on the aura and not the paper itself. The paper is what's familiar. One of the houses Jackaby and I visited last night had reams of the stuff. Thick and sort of textured, just like this. Do you think you could wake Jackaby up without rousing my parents?"

"Of course." Jenny smiled encouragingly. "I can whip over to wake up Miss Lee, as well, and ask her to ready the carriage right away. I'm not fond of haunting our friends at odd hours, but I certainly wouldn't want to be the one to tell her that I let the two of you waste your time walking when her perfectly good horses were champing at the bit to do their part."

"I don't deserve you," I said. "Any of you."

"You're not the only person in town who cares about that boy of yours, sweetie. We'll all do what we can."

In no more than half an hour, Jackaby and I had climbed into the carriage and were barreling into the predawn city.

"What's our plan?" Jackaby asked.

"Mr. Finkin wasn't telling us everything," I said. "If this paper is a match to his wife's supplies, then there's got to be something more in that house to point us toward Charlie. I want to have a look behind that painting. I don't know if he's hiding something back there or if she was, but it's a starting point."

My heart was pumping. The case was everything now.

Perhaps it was the morning air, but the New Fiddleham that rushed past my window felt unseasonably cold. Boarded windows and crude vandalism hissed at us as we zipped past, and the few people I saw seemed distant and rigid. I spotted a workman installing metal bars on the windows of a building—and the driver of a passing coach held reins in one hand and a shotgun in the other. All around us, the denizens of the city went through their motions, opening shops and sweeping leaves from walkways, but there was a weight pressing down on the whole town. It was as if the oil that greased the wheels of New Fiddleham had turned to treacle. My brow creased, and I felt my muscles tightening.

"Finkin wasn't exactly excited to invite us in last time,"

Jackaby said, "and that was before he knew that we were consulting with the police. Any thoughts on winning him over?"

"I'm going to ask nicely," I growled.

"And if that doesn't work?"

"What's the blast radius on dragon's breath?" I asked. "A few feet?"

"Not the most subtle approach." Jackaby bobbed his head as if weighing the value of subtlety over the chance to field-test a new fiery explosive—although it was clear he had already conceded the win to subtlety.

The carriage was slowing. I glanced out the window as we made a turn. "Subtle might not be an option," I said.

"Sure, but best to avoid unwanted attention if possible."

"Too late."

Miss Lee brought the carriage to a full stop, and the scene outside our window was the house we had visited last night, but it was swarming with police officers. I noticed a few from Dupin's team.

An officer I didn't recognize separated from the huddle and came to intercept us as we stepped out of the carriage. I took a deep breath, preparing to bluster our way in with the usual bravado and confidence, none of which I was currently feeling.

"Detective Rook?" The man tipped his cap. "They told me you have the eyes for the weird stuff. How on earth did you get here so fast?"

I glanced at Jackaby and back at the officer. "The horses helped."

"You didn't get the inspector's message, did you?" the man asked. "Someone was sent to fetch you only a few minutes ago."

"Did the inspector find something particularly supernatural about the missing woman?"

"Woman?" The officer shook his head. "It's not the wife. It's the husband."

"Mr. Finkin?" I scowled. "Oh dear. He hasn't gone missing as well, has he?"

"Not *all* of him." The officer swallowed hard. "You should probably have a look for yourselves."

chapter nineteen

Mr. Finkin was in the living room. Except for the parts of him that were in the study.

What surprised me most about his condition was that there wasn't any blood. Compared to the D'Aulaire mansion and poor Dibb's attic, the Finkin house was spotless. The dead man was upright, more or less—but his body was embedded in the wall, his torso bisected by plaster and wallpaper. His head was slumped over his chest, his right arm hanging slack in front of him. His left hand was only half visible, with the rest concealed within the wall, and just one of his knees was sticking out, a little lower down. If I had been shown a photograph of the grim scene, I might have assumed it was a picture of a fully clothed man lying still in some sort of milky liquid.

Neither the man nor the wall looked significantly worse for wear. A few crumbs of plaster littered the floor beneath him, but the structure looked as sound as if it did not have a fully grown man sticking out of it. Mr. Finkin had no visible injuries—no cuts or bruises—just a wall where his back half should be. All around him were the now all-too-familiar turnip-tinted aura and the dark haze of a fresh death.

"He looks like the barrel we saw lodged in that alleyway," Jackaby observed. "Aha!"

"What is it?" I watched as Jackaby bent down and retrieved a blackened piece of rubbish from the floor.

"Another matchstick," he said. "I'm getting a keen eye for these."

"There's a human being embedded in a solid wall, and you're excited about a match?"

"You know what?" Jackaby straightened. "Yes. Yes, I am."

"Is there a reason you've left him in there?" I asked. "It might be easier to examine the entire body once he's dislodged."

"We tried removing him," Inspector Dupin said. "But we can't tell if the wall went through him or he went through the wall. Either way, he doesn't want to budge, and there's a stud running right up the middle of him. I sent a runner to fetch a saw."

I leaned in close, peering at the place where the man's

shoulder merged into the wall. The wall and the man were unmistakably two different things, but there was a strip running along the seam where the distinction blurred. I shivered. Mr. Finkin's aura had gone entirely dark. It was like looking at the hollow imprint of where a living person had been.

"We were here," I breathed. "Just last night."

"So I heard," said Dupin.

"To be clear, though, we had nothing to do with the magical murder part," Jackaby piped up. "We were just interested in the missing wife. Mr. Finkin was completely free of the architecture when we left."

"We would be having a very different conversation if I thought you two had anything to do with it," said Dupin. "The suits already cleared you, anyway. Agent Garabrand says you two left even before they did."

"Were they the ones who discovered the body?" I asked.

"No. We did," Dupin said. "Which makes us look about seven shades of incompetent, unfortunately. Apparently your run-in with them left the agents feeling wary about Mr. Finkin. I found out only this morning that they ordered two of my patrol officers to leave their usual beats and surveil the house all night for suspicious activity. Our report confirms that Finkin was alive when our uniforms arrived and that his door was locked securely from the inside. They saw no one enter or exit, but apparently they dozed off at some point, because one of them noticed the door ajar around four a.m. They approached, announced themselves, and then entered. That's when they found him."

"Did they really doze off?" I asked. "Or can they not remember the time passing? Lapse in memory is beginning to sound like a familiar tune. Finkin had gaps in his memory, too. So did Alina and that tailor's neighbor."

Dupin shrugged. "The slim good news is their account gives us a fairly narrow window for time of death, and it puts you two outside of it. The bad news is whoever—or whatever—slipped past our officers didn't leave us a lot of clues."

"Not to the average eye," said Jackaby. "Miss Rook?"

I tried to make sense of the trails of energies crisscrossing all over the property. "I can see traces everywhere," I said, "but I can't tell if they're coming or going. That aura we keep finding in the homes of those other missing people—it's heavy here. I noticed it last night, too. It's heavier than at any of the other sites."

"Several of the people taken had connections to this house," Jackaby said.

"We can't be sure all of our missing people were taken," Dupin countered. "A lot of nonhumans have simply fled town recently."

"They wouldn't!" I snapped, more loudly than I intended. "They have people they care about."

Dupin raised an eyebrow.

I caught my breath and tried to keep my chin up. "*He* wouldn't."

Dupin stiffened. "Charlie?"

I nodded.

He scowled. "When?"

"Last night."

He pursed his lips. I appreciated that he did not try to offer any empty sympathy or promises of justice that we both knew he couldn't guarantee. "There's a hidden safe," he said, at length. "It was already open when my guys swept the house this morning. But if you'd like to take a look—"

"I would."

The safe behind the painting was completely cleaned out. Faint traces of magic remained, more of that lingering turnip tint. It was so strong here—concentrated and powerful, but weeks old.

I stared at the swirls of muted energy that hung within the compartment. Half a dozen hands had examined the safe before me, and I could see their echoes cluttering the empty safe as well—but as for solid clues, there were none. I sighed and began to turn away from the disappointing sight when I paused. Something caught my eye. A steady, faint trickle—like smoke from a dying candlewick—crept out from the back corner of the safe.

"What's behind this wall?" I asked, staring at the seam from which the energy seeped.

"Kitchen, I think?" said Dupin.

Jackaby, picking up on my suspicions, walked to the end of the hall on the left and glanced around the corner into the kitchen, then retraced his steps and repeated the check from the living room side. "Huh," he said. "Well, that's slick. The dimensions are off."

"Hidden room," I said. "Okay, so how do we get in?"

I felt around the inside of the safe. It was smooth and a little dusty. I rapped on the side walls with my knuckles, and then on the back wall—the latter clunked, shifting slightly at the touch. "There's a panel," I said. "A false back. It won't press inward, though—hang on. There's a bit of string here. Yes! That's done it!"

I pulled out the false back of the safe and peered inside. Beyond the secret panel was a doorknob.

"Careful examination first?" whispered Jackaby. "Or just open the thing?"

I had already turned the knob.

There was a click, and the entire wall, safe and all, shifted outward. We stepped back and let it swing open. Beyond it was a narrow chamber lined with shelves and a plain wooden countertop.

"I still think my matchstick was a valuable discovery," said Jackaby, "but yours is good, too."

The room was not much larger than a walk-in closet. A small pile of packages of varying sizes and wrapped in plain brown paper sat on the floor. The smallest was no bigger than an overstuffed envelope, the largest about as big as a loaf of bread. They appeared to have been dumped there unceremoniously. The counter was stacked with strange compounds in glass vials and half a dozen wire bins containing piles of Mrs. Finkin's special paper. I leaned over to get a closer look. The paper on top of the largest, central pile had been inscribed with a strange symbol in a sort of metallic paint. It was as intricate as lace, asymmetrical yet elegant, like someone had taken a string of especially fine cursive script and rolled it into a perfect circle. It glittered, catching the light as I turned my head this way and that.

Beside the main pile, another wire bin had been marked with a label that read *Market Street*, and inside it were three or four pages, each marked with what appeared to be a very similar arcane symbol. Next to this was another bin marked *St. Pantaloon's*, then another marked *Chandler's Market*, and another and another—each with a label for a different location around New Fiddleham, and each containing a few sheets of the peculiar papers.

"Does it mean anything to you?" I asked.

Jackaby made a face. "It looks vaguely elvish, but there's at least one other language interwoven within it. That mark, there, it's the elven rune for *travel* or *go*. I don't think it's proper writing, though—not a message meant to be understood. It looks more like spell papers. You see them a lot, pasted to archways in homes for good luck or as general wards against evil. They require a spell-crafter to make them, but once they're finished, anyone can put them up. Which would explain why Mrs. Finkin was hiding them. This sort of magic is banned, currently."

"Why would protection charms be banned?" I asked.

"Because New Fiddleham was running out of good excuses to make life more tiresome for the magical community," answered Jackaby glibly.

"Because magic goes wrong," interjected Dupin. "Jackaby's right. Any transferable magic, including spells, charms, and deployable curses, could fall into the hands of someone incapable of controlling the power they unleash. Which is exactly the sort of thing flooding the streets, currently. Kids get their hands on what they think are harmless pranks and then end up turning their friends into animals or making a bully fall in love with a donkey. I'm sure they think it's good fun, until the spell doesn't wear off and they have no way to reverse it. Watching your friend choking because her lungs have suddenly turned into gills has a way of ruining the joke. By the time these incidents get reported to us, whatever back-alley witch they bought the spells from has long since vanished. Some of them don't get reported at all. It's bad enough when magic users abuse their own power, but when they share it with some idiot kid, then anybody can be the cause of the trouble—and the innocent nonhumans are the ones who catch all the blame."

"I don't think Mrs. Finkin was giving her spells away recklessly," I said.

"No, I imagine she was taking top dollar for them," grunted Dupin.

"I mean, these don't have any sort of malevolent energy about them. She *did* share her magic, but her husband insisted that she was very picky about who she took on as a client. She clearly didn't want her work to do harm."

"That's an excellent point," said Dupin, "and I'd corroborate the statement with the witness, if he weren't currently lodged in his own wall in a pretty blatant display of magic having gone wrong. Do you think he might consider that *harm?*"

"Point taken." I picked up a page, turning it this way and that to catch the light. "Still, this doesn't feel wicked. It feels as if it wants to tell me something, to lead me somewhere, if only I could read it."

The page had fairy aura all over it—and the closer I looked at it, the more I was certain that the ink used to inscribe the symbols was a pure, concentrated source of the turnip-tinted aura I'd been sensing. Had Maeve Finkin's spells been the ones leaving their mark on crime scenes all over town? This had to mean something, yet it was inscrutable.

"How would you approach this?" I asked Jackaby. "Back when you had the sight, what would you do? You had those funny stones with the holes in the middle, didn't you? Don't those help you fine-tune what you're seeing or something like that?"

"Scrying stones are unreliable at best." Jackaby shook his head. "Besides, you do your best when you stop fussing about what *I* would do and focus on what Abigail Rook would do."

I scowled. What would Abigail Rook do? She would follow a near stranger into untold dangers and mad misadventures. How about before that? She would run away from home on a whim to go looking for buried monsters. She would sneak pulpy detective stories into her book bag and read about grisly crimes when she was supposed to be studying her grammar lessons.

"Lemon juice," I said.

"Picking up a new aura?" asked Jackaby.

"No," I said. "It's something I read when I was younger. People who want to send secret messages can write them in lemon juice. To the untrained eye, the paper will look blank, but if you know the secret, you can uncover hidden messages by heating the page over a candle until the lemon juice turns brown and the message becomes visible."

"Invisible ink." Jackaby nodded. "That could work as an activator. If certain parts of the spell were intentionally left unfinished, then finishing them with invisible ink could cause the spell to activate only when the final strokes were revealed."

He sounded as if he might have more to say, but I was already in the kitchen, rummaging through drawers until I found a candle and a box of matches.

"I really don't think that's wise," Dupin cautioned as I lit the candle. "If you're correct and unveiling hidden words sets off some secret spell, we have no idea what it might do."

"All the more reason to try to understand it," I said. "Don't worry, Inspector. I won't reveal the whole thing. I'll just take a tiny peek to see if there are any hidden lines. Anything that gets us closer to making sense of what this paper does"—I took a deep breath—"gets us closer to finding Charlie."

I held the paper over the candle as close as I dared, watching the glow illuminate the metallic inscription from below.

"Is that anything?" I asked after a couple of seconds. "I think there's a little dark smudge appearing right—"

My vision went white.

The whole world whooshed around me for a moment, and I felt weightless.

In another instant, the ground rose up and slammed into my back with a shuddering *whump*. I sat up and teetered, blinking. I was back in the hidden room behind the safe, what was left of the paper smoldering in my hands. I tried ineffectively to blow it out, but the flames greedily sped up the remnants of the page until I had to let go and watch the final corners turn to ash as they drifted to the floor. The paper must have been saturated in something flammable to catch that quickly.

Voices were shouting from the other room, and I heard Dupin issue an order for somebody to search the property. Jackaby's face appeared in the open doorway and broke into a relieved smile. "She's here, Inspector! She's fine." He cocked his head at me. "Is she fine?"

"She is," I said, although my head was throbbing. "I think so, anyway."

Dupin came lurching around the corner, letting out a relieved sigh as he saw me. "Glad you're still with us, Detective."

I groaned as appreciatively as I could.

"What exactly just happened?"

Jackaby grinned. "Deployable teleportation spell," he said. "Activated by burning the page. Fascinating to watch. You almost never see transportation magic performed without a dedicated portal—and certainly never on a human being. I mean, crates and cargo, maybe—but even then, I've never heard of a delivery method so streamlined. That sort of spell is too fickle and volatile, prone to error. She must have crafted each paper at the destination point—sort of like training a homing pigeon. Glad you decided to test that one and not one set for a spot across town."

"Mr. Finkin mentioned that she liked to go for walks," I said. "She was going out every night to make more spells."

"The woman must have been an exceptionally accomplished spell-crafter to have perfected the process." Jackaby let his eyes scan the secret room again, nodding with respect.

"Perfected?" Dupin said. "The late Mr. Finkin might argue that it still had a few kinks to work out."

"Indeed," Jackaby concurred. "We're lucky you didn't end up as another human art installation, or halfway across town keeping that barrel company."

"Or a thousand feet up in the air, like poor Mr. Dibb?" I mused.

"Reckless, Rook, very reckless," tutted Jackaby. "But also fascinating to watch. What did it feel like?"

"Like I got picked up by my brains and dropped on my backside." I looked around at the packages on the floor beside me, several of which were significantly flatter following my entrance. Cautiously, I picked one up from under my elbow and tugged off the twine. Within was an old cigar box. I flipped open the top and showed its contents to Jackaby.

"Dwimmerstans," he said.

"Definitely Terwilliger Highcourt's," I said. I opened another package that contained several dried roots. "And this one has Dibb's aura on it. Well, that does answer one big question."

"It does?" Dupin said. "You think we've found our kidnapper? Or at least her lair?"

"What? No." I shook my head and used the counter to pull myself up. "Mrs. Finkin wasn't a kidnapper. And this isn't a lair—it's a post office. Those"—I pointed at the neatly sorted spell pages—"were her shipping labels. Quite literally. Labels that did the shipping for her. These ones in the middle, like the one I used, she must have given these to her clients. Then they could send their goods here without carrying them across town. The other spell labels must be for drop points throughout the city. So she would get the boxes and send them on to their destinations. Very clever, really."

"And very illegal," Dupin said. "She was trafficking illegal contraband throughout the city using dangerous, unstable magic."

"Do you know what that plant is?" Jackaby asked, pointing at the sprout on the ground. Dupin shook his head. "Dwarven moonroot. It makes spicy food easier on the stomach. I have some in my kitchen at home. It sort of tastes like a potato on its own, but with a hint of a tingly aftertaste. No harmful usage. You could eat a bushel."

"So?" said Dupin.

"So," Jackaby said, "kindly stop acting like Mrs. Finkin was selling rifles to street gangs."

"Fine. She illegally trafficked *mostly* harmless contraband throughout the city using dangerous, unstable magic.

Happy? Still doesn't explain where she or her clients disappeared to. Or why her husband got *returned to sender*."

"They used her," I said.

"How's that?" Jackaby asked.

Dupin raised an eyebrow.

"Mrs. Finkin was the first to go missing."

"No, Mrs. Finkin was the most *recent*," Dupin corrected. "The earliest case we have linked to all this is . . . the tailor. Townsend."

"No. *Mr.* Finkin was the most recent—*Mrs.* Finkin has been missing for weeks. Grim said that her mother went to see her weeks ago, but she was already gone. Her husband just didn't file a report because, well . . ." I darted a glance at Dupin. "Because, yes, she was trafficking illegal contraband throughout the city using dangerous, unstable magic—and for some reason he thought the police might make a big fuss about that."

"Okay. So, Mrs. Finkin disappears first," Jackaby said. "And whoever is responsible for snatching her also finds her safe and cleans it out. But they don't find the back room, it seems."

"The safe must have had her ledgers in it," Dupin added. "Or at least communications from her clients—because one by one, they get grabbed, too."

"But they don't just get carried off," I said. "They leave behind Mrs. Finkin's magical aura—because they weren't grabbed, they were *shipped*. I found a fragment of burnt paper in Charlie's room, and Jackaby has found matches at multiple crime scenes."

"So we're looking for someone who's got it out for non-humans," said Jackaby. "Lovely. That narrows it down to about a third of the city. Why do you look so chipper, Rook?"

"Because she's *alive*," I said. "Mrs. Finkin is still alive. She must be, because she's the only one who could have made the spell labels used at each of the crime scenes. She's probably making them under duress. Or possibly she's been mesmerized or mind-controlled, or . . . I don't know. Maybe she *is* behind the whole dastardly plot. The point is—as long as her spell labels are working properly, then that means the other missing people have been taken alive, too. Which means Charlie is still alive!" The last word caught in my throat as a buried part of me finally admitted that I had *not* been sure he was alive until just now. Another part of me got to work fervently refusing to admit that I *still* wasn't completely sure. Just because they needed Maeve Finkin alive didn't mean they needed Charlie. But I had no time for that sort of thinking right now. We were finally making progress.

"So our Big Bad Wolf is making Little Red Riding Hood do his dirty work," said Jackaby. "How do you propose we track down the villain before he snatches his next defenseless grandmother?"

"I don't know where to find the wolf," I said, "but I'm pretty sure we can catch a rat."

"I hate metaphors," said Dupin. "You two do know you can just *say* things, right? I mean, I get that the wolf is the kidnapper. Who's the rat?"

I dusted off my jacket and squared my jaw. "I believe, Inspector, that he's called Squiffy Rick."

chapter twenty

M iss Lee was leaning on the side of the carriage as I
neared. "Detective," she said. "Ahem. You should
know you've got a little guest." She tilted her head meaningfully at the carriage.

"Not *so* little," came a voice from within.

"I like this one," Miss Lee added in a whisper.

I leaned my head into the cabin. Grim was sitting tight
against the corner of the bench with her arms wrapped
around her knees. "He's dead, isn't he?" she said. "Mr.
Finkin?"

By the heavy weight of her aura, I could tell she knew
the answer already.

"Just like Mr. Dibb?"

"He is," I admitted. "But we have reason to believe your mother and many of the others are still very much alive."

She nodded solemnly and wiped her damp cheek with the back of her arm. "You gonna find her?"

"That's the plan," I said. "Come to think of it, I could use some help. You've been making your way on the streets for a little while; you must have picked up a few things. I need to track down a rather unsavory fellow who frequents the Inkling District. He goes by the name of Squiffy Rick. You don't happen to know him, do you?"

She shook her head. "But I know some people there. Not the best people."

"*Not the best people* are exactly the sort of people I need to help me right now," I said.

"Not with all the badges buzzing around," she said.

I glanced behind me. Inspector Dupin had held back to issue a few instructions to his team about cataloging the papers and vials in the Finkins' hidden room before moving the lot to the evidence locker. He was making his way across the front lawn toward us now.

"Our department horses are faster," he said. "We should take my coach."

Miss Lee raised an eyebrow. "Yours might be *faster*, but the Duke here is"—she glanced at the old gray workhorse—"older and more crotchety." She crossed her arms defiantly.

"Touché?" said Dupin.

"With all due respect, Inspector," I said, "riding a police wagon into the parts of town where we need to go will not make our job any easier."

"Fine. We can take yours, but if that old nag dies on the way, it's not my fault."

I could sense Grim's nervousness from behind the curtain as Dupin approached the step.

"Before we go," I said, "why don't you collect one of your men to come along? If we do happen into a dangerous situation, I'm sure we would be grateful for the support. How about Officer Schmitz? I like him, and he already knows a bit about Squiffy Rick."

"Mm. Wise. She might still be working out the visions, but she's already better at this respectful collaboration thing than you ever were." Dupin directed this last toward Jackaby.

"I'm taking avid notes," Jackaby agreed.

Dupin nodded at me and then doubled back toward the house.

"Well now this just feels rude," I said under my breath. "Oh well. Miss Lee? Quick as you can, yes?"

"Understood, Detective." Miss Lee was in the driver's box in a flash, the Duke stomping his hooves impatiently.

I hurried into the carriage with Jackaby close behind. "All right, Grim," I said. "It's just us. Why don't you introduce us to a few of your *not the best* friends."

Sebastian Gobsallow's clothing was more river muck than fabric. The grime even seemed to bleed into his aura, which was otherwise a cheery golden orange. It was hard to tell under all the filth, but he looked to be no more than eight or nine years old.

"How's the mud today, Gobby?" Grim asked the boy as he climbed up the embankment onto solid ground.

"Fifty-seven cents and a silver ring," he answered. "And that's just since sunup. Best stuff's always in the morning. Or after a good rain."

"Gobby found a whole cat's skull once," said Grim.

The boy nodded. "I cleaned it up real nice. I'll show it to you, if you want."

"Another time," I said.

I carefully explained the situation and why we needed to find the man called Squiffy Rick. Gobby listened patiently. "We don't want to get him into any trouble," I concluded. "Frankly, we don't particularly care about the necklace. We just need to ask him a few questions. So, do you know him?"

"Sure. Everybody knows Squiffy," the boy said, shrugging. A wet clump of river clay sloughed off his leg and plopped onto the ground beside him. "I don't know where to find him, though. You could talk to Fish."

"Fish Pishdar," Grim clarified. "He's a big kid from upriver. Really good at card tricks."

"That's the one," said Gobby. "Some of the grown-ups use him when they need a middleman or a shill, on account of he looks so innocent. Pretty sure he and Squiffy done a few jobs together."

"Why do they call him *Fish?*" I asked.

"Because," said Gobby, "he's slippery."

Amir Pishdar was selling newspapers on the corner of Bollinger when we found him. He was all of fifteen or sixteen years old with a bit of a baby face, but his eyes and aura belied a weathered and road-weary soul within.

"Buy my last paper?" he called as we approached. "Lotta hot stories this morning that you don't want to miss. Farmer's prize pig went missing—you won't believe where he turned up. Page five. Steam pumper blew half the wall off a fire station downtown. Page two. And the big doozy: Mayor Spade implicated in a torrid scandal with the queen of the Om Caini. Just five cents to read all about it."

"Those stories are made-up," I said. "You lie beautifully, though. It's almost poetic. You should be proud. Or ashamed? Definitely one of those. Also, that appears to be yesterday's paper."

"The pig one's real," Fish mumbled.

"Is it?" asked Jackaby. "Where did it turn up in the end?"

"On top of a church roof," said Fish.

"Was it okay?" asked Jackaby.

"Nickel to find out," said Fish.

"I've got a dime for you if you help me find out something *else*," I said. "A friend of ours is looking for her missing mother, and we have reason to think a man you know called Squiffy Rick might have some information that we need. Do you have any idea where we could find him?"

"Squiffy? Haven't seen Squiffy in weeks," said Fish. "Could be anywhere."

"That's a lie," I translated for Jackaby. "Which means he's seen the gentleman. And recently, I would wager."

"Okay, okay," Fish said. "Yeah, I might have seen him around, but it isn't like I know where he's staying these days."

"Oh! Lovely," I said. "He *definitely* knows where Squiffy Rick is staying. You're being very helpful so far, Mr. Fish. Please continue."

"Hang on, now!" Fish protested. "How're you doing that? That's not fair!"

"Not remotely," I agreed. "But neither is having your loved ones snatched away from you without any explanation. Now, where can we find Squiffy?"

"Well, the thing about that . . ." Fish tossed the newspaper at us and spun around to bolt into the night.

To his credit, it was a slick bit of maneuvering. Simple, but effective—or at least it would have been had Grim not been standing directly behind him. He skidded to a stop to avoid colliding with her, and in the half a second that he paused, Grim's leg swung up sharply. Fish clutched his groin and toppled over sideways, making a rasping, squeaky sound.

"It's me," said Grim. "I'm the friend who's missing her mother."

"Right," Fish croaked weakly. "And I am suddenly very interested in helping you all with that."

"That's true," I said. "You are."

"Good news," said Jackaby, finally tossing the mess of newspapers aside. "The pig got down okay in the end."

I asked Grim to stay with Miss Lee as we approached the last place Fish had seen Squiffy Rick. It did not take long to find the man himself. His hideaway was the basement of an old textile factory, bottles and pieces of rubbish lining the approach. He was sprawled out on a pile of dusty, moth-eaten fabric, snoring gently, when we arrived. I kicked his boot and he started, grunting.

"Mm? Who's that?"

"Hello, Squiffy Rick," I said. "We're here to talk to you about a necklace."

Squiffy sat up abruptly, rubbing his face.

"I know who you are," he said, eyes darting between us. "I haven't got it," he added. "You can't pin it on me. Never even touched the thing. Technically."

His aura was a kaleidoscope of deceptive facts and

earnest falsehoods. "You're telling the truth," I said. "But nevertheless, you *did* steal it. Or at least you helped someone else steal it."

Squiffy hesitated. "Can't prove that."

"I'm not trying to," I said. "Because, frankly, it doesn't matter. I don't care about the necklace. I *do* care about finding whoever put you up to stealing it."

"Well, I don't care what *you* care about," said Squiffy, puffing up his chest as his eyes darted around, scanning for exit routes. "You're not cops. You can't do anything to me."

Jackaby flipped open his satchel, not taking his eyes off Squiffy. "You're sure about that?"

Squiffy sneered. "I'm not scared of you."

"*I'm* not scared of *geese*," said Jackaby.

"What?" Squiffy's brow wrinkled.

"Now that we're both done lying to each other," Jackaby said, "perhaps we can get on to the facts."

"I'll start," I said. "Your silent partner is a killer."

Squiffy narrowed his eyes.

"That's a fact. Did you know? Three bodies in as many days. Reasonable to expect more to come. That's not to mention all the kidnappings."

"I—I don't know anything about any of that," said Squiffy.

"They've also taken my fiancé," I said.

Squiffy's expression softened. "Charlie?"

I raised an eyebrow.

"Knew your boy back when he was a copper," said Squiffy. "One of the decent ones. Caught me fair and square once, pulling a little confidence job. Made me give the pocket watches back, but instead of booking me, he bought me a hot meal and gave me a good talk about morals."

"Clearly it didn't take," I said.

"Hey—I don't steal from anybody who can't afford it. That's better morals than most of the people who live in fancy houses and look down their noses at me." Squiffy let out a breath. "Look, I didn't know about Charlie, and I don't know about any killing or kidnapping. That's the truth. I didn't want nobody to get hurt." His aura still spun with nervous energy, but he was not lying.

"Where did you get the magic spell paper?" I asked.

"Never saw the guy's face," said Squiffy. "But he said he would pay me good money to pull an easy job. All I had to do was find the most expensive thing I could get close to, paste this funny-looking symbol onto it, and light the paper on fire. Figured it was just to scare the rich, stick up for the working folk, that sorta thing. Like what's-his-name. German fellow with the manifesto. Anyway, the guy gave me ten percent and the piece of paper, then told me to meet him for the rest when the job was done. Said he'd know if I had pulled it off or not."

"Where did he say to meet?" I asked.

"Funny thing," Squiffy said.

"You don't remember?" I said.

Squiffy nodded. "I know that sounds shady, but it's the god's honest truth."

"I know it is," I sighed.

"I got a feeling it was in a sketchy part of town," he added. "But in a town like this one, 'sketchy' don't narrow it down much. Anyway, after I did my part, the whole cabinet just sort of went *poof.* I didn't know it would do that!"

"Would you have gone through with it if you did?"

"I mean. Sure, probably. But I wouldn't have frozen up and let security rough me up like they did. I got out of there before the cops could nab me, though. It all gets sort of hazy from there. Next thing I remember, I'm sitting in an alley and the sun's going down. I can't remember the rendezvous point. At first I figured I'd been conned, but I had a wad of banknotes in my pocket telling me I got paid, so I figured I must have just had one too many pints of celebration."

"Do you know where the necklace was transported?"

"The necklace was transported?" said Squiffy.

"That's what the magic spell was for," Jackaby explained. "Those papers take whatever is touching them back to a predetermined location."

"Huh," said Squiffy. "I suppose that would explain how he would know if I had done it or not. Giant cabinet with priceless jewelry showing up in his front room would be a good marker for a completed job."

"Which means," I said, "the delivery point must have been near the rendezvous."

Squiffy shrugged. "I promise, I'd tell you if I remembered."

"I don't need you to remember everything," I said. "Just tell us where you were when you snapped out of it. We'll find your trail from there."

chapter twenty-one

Squiffy Rick's fragmented memory brought us to a run-down neighborhood a mile or two west of his hideaway. I started picking up on his trail even before we pinpointed the alley where he remembered stopping for a rest. It had been two days, but the man left a distinctive olive drab and mustard aura, laced with residue from the spell he had activated. The path was now weak, and it wove up and down the narrow streets in a seemingly random pattern. Whenever it grew too faint to follow, we simply looked around for the darkest, seediest route—and nine times out of ten it brought us straight back onto the trail. The tenth time proved a little trickier.

"Look. I'm sorry, but I don't remember." Squiffy Rick shrugged, spinning around on his heel. "Lots of good spots around here for a clandestine and legally questionable meeting."

"Maybe we should circle back to that last intersection," said Jackaby. "We could try the path to the left this time?"

"No need," I said, coming to an abrupt stop. My eyes fixed on a wide, ominous building in a weedy lot across the street. "We're here."

The structure was the least enticing sight we had come across all evening. It was three stories of crumbling bricks and climbing ivy. A portion of the roof had collapsed, the door had been boarded up, and most of the windows were broken—but these gloomy details were downright inviting compared to the building's energy. Misery and pain saturated the ground and clung to the walls more densely than the climbing vines. Flickers of movement darted past the window, and a shiver ran up my spine.

"The old hospital?" Squiffy Rick paled. "Nope. Not on your life. That's not it."

"How can you be sure?" I said. "I thought you couldn't remember."

"That place has given me the willies since I was a kid. I'd need to get paid a lot more before I'd set one foot in there." He glanced up at Lydia Lee, still perched atop the carriage. "You grew up here. Tell her."

Lydia nodded in confirmation. "We used to dare each

other to get close enough to touch the front door," she said. "You hear voices on the wind when you get close. Screams."

"Lefty Higgins broke his ankle stumbling over himself to get out of there one time," added Squiffy Rick. "Swore he felt icy hands on his neck. Place is evil."

"Fair to assume that the locals all know to steer clear of here?" I asked.

"Darn right," he replied.

"Then it seems like an ideal spot to hide out if you don't want to be discovered," I said. "We're going in."

"By *we* you mean *you*, right?" Squiffy Rick said. "Because if by *we* you mean *me*, then we are *not*."

Lydia Lee looked uncomfortable as well, but said nothing. From inside the carriage, Grim's eyes peered up at the imposing old building.

"It's fine," I said. "You can go, Mr. Rick. You've been very helpful. Miss Lee, we're just going to have a look inside. Shouldn't be more than a few minutes."

She nodded. "I'll watch the kid. Try not to get eaten by demons or anything."

"I generally do," I agreed.

The air all around the grounds was thick with the residue of spirits—human souls no longer of the corporeal world, yet not fully gone—and from the lower windows poured a silvery, keening aura of anger and shame. The closer we drew to the decrepit building, the more confident I was that we were on the right trail. From out of the second-story windows, I could see the turnip-esque energy of Mrs. Finkin's magic trickling like thick fog.

"This is a hospital?" I said.

"What's left of it," said Jackaby. "The campus used to have three or four buildings, I think, but most of them got demolished after they finished St. Pantaloon's, decades ago. Surprising that this portion of the property hasn't been repurposed yet."

I swallowed. "It might be the ghosts," I whispered. "I imagine they have an adverse effect on prospective developers."

Jackaby looked at me, then back at the building. "Haunted?"

"Thoroughly," I said.

"Well." He clapped his hands together. "That's lucky for us! I mean, *I* won't be able to see them, of course, but you've got a property full of potential witnesses."

"Or potentially angry and confused phantoms, with plenty of rusty medical equipment to throw about if they get out of control."

Jackaby waved a hand. "Most spirits just ignore passersby," he said. "And if they're corporeal enough to hurl scalpels across the room, there's a good chance they're also sentient enough to be helpful. You should at least say hello."

I took a deep breath. The air near the front door was dense with spectral energy. It glistened prettily, like glittering dust motes in a sunbeam. At the sound of the leaves crunching under our feet, the energy seemed to tighten. It pulled itself together, coalescing into the figure of a tall, thin man in a baggy hospital gown.

The apparition did not look as solid as Jenny. The form was like a soap bubble in the shape of a man; only the light catching his contours with hints of silver and gray set him apart from the walls behind him. I was silently grateful for this, as it made positively identifying the color of the stains on his chest more difficult.

The spectral figure seemed to sense my gaze, and turned to face me.

"Hello," I said, through a dry mouth. "We don't mean to be a bother. We're just looking for some people. We think they might be inside. You haven't seen any activity around here recently, have you?"

The man stared at me, the details of his form wavering like smoke in a gentle wind. Slowly, he opened his mouth, and then he opened it farther, and then he let out a piercing scream. I threw my hands over my ears, but the sound was more inside my head than out of it. I glanced over at Jackaby, who was looking around as if trying to pinpoint the sound of an annoying, noisy cricket.

"Can you hear that?" I called over the din.

Jackaby nodded. "It's faint, but it sounds like a bloodcurdling scream. Is it a bloodcurdling scream?"

"I don't know about bloodcurdling," I managed, "but it's doing a number on my eardrums."

The noise tapered off at last, and the image of the ghost blurred for a moment as he swayed unsteadily on a pair of feet that weren't entirely there. Finally, he blinked and looked at me sheepishly. "C-c-can you s-s-see me?" he asked.

I nodded, slowly lowering my hands from my ears.

"Did you hear me m-m-make a noise, just now?"

"Erm. I did notice that, yes," I answered.

"Sorry," he said. "I'm no g-g-good around the living. Ingrid! Ingrid, there's someone who can see us!"

From around the side of the building, the air rippled and condensed into the form of a short woman with a pearl-white apron and a square hat that covered a high bun on her head.

"What are you jabbering on about, Leland—oh!" The ghost looked me up and down. "Well, hello, my dear. You're a spiritual sensitive, are you? That's grand. We haven't had a sensitive in, oh, how long has it been, Leland?"

Leland flickered in and out of translucence uncomfortably.

"Hmph. He's no good with time anyway. Hello, dears. Don't mind Leland's screaming fits. He does that."

"Often?" I asked.

"Every five or six minutes," answered the shimmering lady. "You get used to it after the first few decades. Once he made it a whole half an hour! We were very proud. I have my own small eccentricities, of course, but I haven't had an episode in weeks."

"How's it going?" Jackaby asked behind me. "Everything all right?"

"They seem to be friendly spirits," I reported.

"Oh, aren't we just." Ingrid straightened her apron, which did not actually become any straighter for her efforts, it being only the memory of an apron. "Dr. Brunson always said that I had excellent bedside manner. Although, to be honest, you want to watch out for Henriette. And Charles."

"D-D-Doctor," Leland stammered.

Ingrid's silvery skin paled moon-white. "We don't talk about Dr. Mudgett," she whispered.

"Why don't we talk about Dr. M—" I began to ask.

Ingrid's face contorted, flickering like a wet candlewick, and the air felt suddenly very chilly.

"We do *not* talk about him," I said conclusively. "Understood."

The chill calmed, and Ingrid cleared her throat daintily.

"Ask them if they've seen anybody inside the building," Jackaby prompted. "Any *living* bodies, that is."

I looked back at Leland and Ingrid. "Well?" I said. "Have you?"

"Oh, yes, in fact." Ingrid looked delighted. "It's been very satisfying to see patients on the grounds again. We used to do so much good here. Didn't we, Leland?"

Leland's eyes rolled, his head tilted back, and he let out another chilling scream.

When it was over, with my ears ringing slightly, I assured the very embarrassed-looking specter that it was no bother, and that he had nothing to apologize for. "Happens to the best of us," I said. "The new, erm, patients?" I asked Ingrid. "What do they look like?"

"There was that woman they brought up first. She was a lovely creature. I suspect hysteria," said Ingrid. "But they took her up to the second floor." The ghost said *second floor* as if the words tasted bitter on her tongue.

"What's wrong with the second floor?" I asked.

A faint flicker, like a twitch, shot across Ingrid's face. "Nothing at all," she answered sweetly. "Good works being done all through the hospital. *My* ward is on the first floor, though. Dr. Brunson didn't like for us to disturb the upstairs wards if we didn't need to."

"Naturally," I said. "Who else did you see?"

"Well, there was a gentleman who escorted her upstairs," Ingrid said.

"And what did he look like?" I asked.

"I didn't get a good look at his face," she said. "Had a hood pulled over his head like he had been out in the rain. There have been others, too. I've heard them talking and moving about. Nice to have voices in the place again. Mostly crying, but still—it's nice. I didn't see when the others were brought in. They must have slipped in between my shifts."

"Between your shifts?" I said. "Is there a time you aren't haunting the grounds?"

Ingrid blinked at me. "What a silly question. Of course not, dear. I'm always here. Always."

"Right," I said. "Well, Mr. Jackaby, the second floor seems to be our destination."

"You don't want to go up there," said Ingrid. Her smile faltered, fleeing from her eyes entirely. "There are no visitors allowed on the second floor."

"Ah," I said. "But we're not visitors, exactly."

Ingrid seemed puzzled.

"We're here to help," I said. "We're . . . specialists."

Ingrid bit her lip. "Is the doctor expecting you?"

"Dr. Brunson?" I said. "Erm. Possibly."

"Not Dr. Brunson." She shook her pale head. "Dr. Brunson is in charge of the downstairs ward."

"Right, yes, of course," I said. "The . . . *other* doctor is expecting us."

Ingrid's whole body quivered, and for a moment I saw a flash of a very different face, one with dark, hollow eyes and skin stretched tight against its bones. The ivy curling around the railings to the front entrance withered, and a thin layer of frost crept along the ground, spilling out from beneath Ingrid's feet.

"Problem?" Jackaby whispered. His breath made puffy clouds in front of his face.

"Not *that* doctor!" I squeaked. "No, not the one that we don't talk about. Not him. Different doctor entirely. Our doctor was brought in to, erm, consult. A consulting doctor."

The air crackled with energy like a building thunderstorm, and I felt the hairs on my arm standing on end. Gradually, Ingrid seemed to come back to herself, though, and the hum of unnatural energy slowly faded. The frost crackled on the ground around us, but it stopped expanding.

"Ahem. Pardon me," she said. "I must have a bit of a cough. Come, come. Let me show you inside."

chapter twenty-two

The boarded-up front door of the haunted hospital would have taken a great deal of effort and noise to open, but conveniently, the ghostly figure of Nurse Ingrid led us around the side of the building to an entrance almost entirely obscured by ivy. Someone had already gone to the trouble of removing the boards that had sealed it, and it swung open at my gentle tug. I felt a tingle run up the back of my neck as I crossed the threshold, although it might have just been Leland's spectral form breezing in behind us. Jackaby pulled his coat a little tighter around him.

The interior was only slightly creepier than I had

envisioned. Silvery cobwebs caught the beams of light that cut across the lobby at rakish angles, and every surface was coated in a fine layer of dust and depression. The echoes of anxious nerves and ancient pain drifted through the silent hallways. Bed frames and old mattresses had been left behind in most of the rooms we passed, and the stink of mildew and dust was strong. We followed Ingrid down a long hallway. The farther we walked, the darker the corridor grew. I began to notice that many of the rooms farther back were fitted with sturdy-looking chains bolted directly into the walls.

"That's not unsettling at all," Jackaby murmured.

"Whoever did this," I whispered back, "clearly spent some time converting this hospital wing into their own personal dungeon. We should check with the locals nearby. Maybe someone on the street saw them carrying in all these chains or overheard them being installed."

"The chains?" Ingrid chimed in. "Oh, no, those were always here, dearies. Hospital property."

I blinked. "Why would a hospital need chains?"

"Necessary," she said, matter-of-factly. "For some of the more excitable patients."

I nearly jumped out of my skin as Leland began screaming right behind me. I tried to steady my breathing.

The scream tapered off after a few seconds, and Leland apologized again.

"Here we are." Ingrid paused before a staircase. "The

floor nurse on duty should be able to direct you at the top of the stairs."

"You're not coming?" I asked.

"Well, if you—" Ingrid drifted forward toward the stairs again, but then paused abruptly, as if tugged back by an invisible string. "No. No, I'd better not."

Jackaby nudged my shoulder and gestured at the floor. A line of white powder ran from one end of the step to the other. "Salt," he said. "Classic ethereal ward. Somebody's been here."

"Somebody with a body," I agreed. "And whoever it is, it seems they've been making an effort to keep the resident spirits out of their way."

Jackaby took a careful step over the line, and I followed suit.

There was a wide, circular desk at the top of the stairs, but it did not look as if anyone had used it in the last fifty years. Wind whistled through a broken window behind us. Ahead, there was another hallway, along with heavy clouds of the turnippy transportation aura.

"This way," I whispered.

Jackaby peeked in open doors as we crept forward. "There's a water cup in here, and an apple core that hasn't even rotted yet," he said quietly.

"They were here," I agreed. "Mrs. Finkin's energy runs up and down the hallway. I recognize it from her paintings. I can see traces of a trollish aura in this room. Elven aura there. It doesn't look like most of them ever left their rooms."

"Precision transapparation into a locked room." Jackaby looked impressed.

"And out again, it seems," I said. "There's nobody here. Although there is a human aura mixed in with it all. Someone who moved with Mrs. Finkin up and down the hallways. Oh, it's frustratingly familiar." I followed the human aura into one of the empty rooms and froze. The space was empty, like all the rest, but I could practically see his face in front of me. "Charlie," I whispered.

Jackaby slipped past me and turned the room over, checking for clues under the bare mattress and the single tin cup. There was nothing to find; Charlie was not there. There were no windows to the outside, not from these rooms, and the walls were all padded with old, moth-eaten cloth. It had all the charm of a prison cell with an added soupçon of institutional nightmares. Charlie's aura was so heavy within the tiny room that I could practically breathe him in—but he had left us no further trail to follow.

"Locks on the outside," said Jackaby. "And there are slots in the doors for passing meals to the captives. This place was clearly a functional prison until very recently. But where are the prisoners now? And where are the wardens?"

I took a deep breath. "Gone."

From up the hallway came the faint squeak of a floor-board and a muffled bump.

"Did you hear that?" I whispered. About halfway down the length of the building, the prison cell rooms ended and the hallway opened before a pair of broad double doors—the sound must have come from behind them. For several seconds Jackaby and I strained our ears against the silence. There was a soft shuffling and what might have been a pair of footfalls, but then the hospital was still once again.

Just as I was finally about to break the tension, a loud crack issued from outside.

"What now?" Jackaby muttered. We made our way to the dusty window.

The hospital formed a broad L shape, which meant that from our position in the ward, we had a clear view of the front door. Below us, two figures in matching suits had cut a line across the overgrown lawn to the main entry. Agent Kit had one foot braced against the wall as he tugged with both hands on the weathered boards that sealed the front door. Agent Garabrand had his hands on his hips, peering into windows.

"Them again?" I muttered.

"They must have followed us," Jackaby said. "If they were half as good at tracking missing people as they were at tracking us, this case would be wrapped up already."

"If they're going to let us do all the work, they could at least have the decency to allow us to finish before interrupting."

The plank in Kit's grip pulled free with another sharp crack that echoed through the still hallways beneath us. The air chilled a few degrees.

"He won't approve," Ingrid's nervous voice echoed up from the stairwell at the end of the hall. "Not at all."

"Come on," I said. "Let's see what's behind those doors before they get in our way."

Together we threw open the doors.

On the other side was a wide, open room with tattered chairs stacked against the walls and various pieces of furniture littering the center. None of them looked like they belonged in a hospital. There were wooden crates, an oil painting of a dignified-looking man sitting in a plush chair, a wide cabinet with a broken glass front, and what appeared to have once been a full set of ornamental armor—although the latter had fallen to pieces, polished sword and ornate shield tossed on top like dirty socks on a laundry basket. What there were not were any signs of life.

"There's nobody here," I said. "Just . . . stuff."

"This looks like it was a common room, once," said Jackaby. "Before someone dumped all their broken old furniture in it."

I focused on the clutter and tilted my head. "Not dumped," I said. "Delivered. Look, there—that fancy hand-bag lying on the floor is the most recent to be transported. Maeve Finkin's aura is still pouring off it—in fact, I would wager that was the thump we heard. I do believe *all* of these things got here through Mrs. Finkin's spell labels."

"Are you sure?"

"I'm certain. Look! There, in the case! That has to be the necklace Squiffy Rick stole! Lord, that thing does look like it costs more than a house." I pried open the top of one of the crates. "And this is full of wine bottles. Château Rupin. This is posh stuff."

"And that enormous chandelier over there appears to be fitted with real crystal." Jackaby scowled, surveying the boxes and piles cluttering the room. "Somebody went to a lot of trouble to steal all these things just to leave them piled up in a heap."

"Would you rather the violent criminals be making better use of their magically stolen goods?"

"Frankly, yes, I would," said Jackaby. "Or at least selling them off to some secret bidder or something practical. It doesn't look like any of these things have been given a second glance since they landed."

I gazed around. He was right. There was a fortune in purloined rarities in front of us, and I knew people who treated muddy boots with greater dignity.

"Maybe that's the point," I said. "Squiffy Rick told us he had been instructed to steal the most valuable thing he could get his hands on. Not the necklace specifically—just something expensive. So whoever gave Squiffy the order didn't care *what* he stole or how easy it would be to fence; they only cared that it would be *missed.*"

"Cherry-picking targets to upset the town?" Jackaby nodded. "That fits. It also could explain the high-profile murder of a controversial but very public socialite."

"And why they took Charlie," I said, clenching my fists. "He's the inter-realm liaison. His whole job is to make sure people get along with one another—and he's good at it. Everybody likes Charlie. Humans, paranormals, cops, even the criminals."

"Can't have someone like that running around if you want to make everything awful." Jackaby sighed. "So, if chaos were your end goal—who would be your next target?"

"It could be anyone, I suppose," I said. "Who do you know who stands in the way of this town tearing itself apart?"

"Commissioner Marlowe, maybe?" suggested Jackaby. "Inspector Dupin?"

On the opposite side of the pile of stolen goods, there came a shuffle and the sharp creak of a floorboard. Both of us snapped to attention.

"Or maybe *us?*" I breathed.

"Always a possibility," Jackaby whispered back.

The curtain on the other side of the cache fluttered in the breeze from an open window. "Someone's definitely in here with us," I whispered. Their aura had left a trail from the windowsill. The trail was awash with sharp tones of fear and anger—it was human, and eerily familiar. "We know you're here," I said aloud.

Silence.

I gestured at Jackaby to edge around the left side of the pile while I crept up from the right. He nodded and moved in. Behind us, I could hear the murmur of Agent Kit's voice echoing up the stairwell. The agents had made it inside. Good. They could make themselves useful.

I moved around the expensive mess, my eyes following the aura trail. There was panic and desperation in the energy, but also fury and hatred. As I followed it farther, the sallow tint of fear dominated the trail. They knew they were about to be caught. An elegant armoire stood tall near the edge of the collection, the nervous aura heavy on its doors. I held my breath and clasped the handle. With a tug, the door flew open.

The armoire was empty.

A prickly feeling ran up the back of my neck just a moment before I heard the floorboard creak behind me. I turned my head too late to catch more than a glimpse of a shadowy figure as someone slapped a hand hard on my back, the force sending me toppling forward. I caught myself on my hands and knees, my hair coming undone and tumbling into my face. As I pushed it aside, I caught the scratch of a matchstick and felt a sudden heat on my back.

My thoughts were a blur. In the span of a frantic second, I imagined being transported to some secret dungeon or, worse, spliced fatally into the musty old walls of the hospital.

I threw myself backward, slamming my shoulder blades hard against the cool floor. For good measure, I wobbled back and forth, grinding my back into the tiles to be certain I had smothered the flame.

Fast footsteps echoed across the floor as I sat up, reaching a hand back to rip the piece of paper off my back. The sheet was inscribed with a circle of arcane symbols identical to the ones I had seen in the secret room at the Finkins' home. The burn had eaten most of the bottom left corner, stopping only a hairbreadth from the design. I was a centimeter away from having been stolen. I let out a shaky breath.

An icy gust of wind whipped the curtains into a frenzy, and the heavy double doors slammed shut behind me. I heard Agent Kit yell something from the other side of the door, and then the handle rattled and fists pounded on the wood. Agent Garabrand's voice barked something, but it was hard to make either of them out.

"Rook!" Jackaby called. "Are you all right?"

I nodded, pushing the hair out of my face again and stuffing the spell paper into my pocket. Movement caught my eye; the assailant was making a beeline for the open window.

"Hold it!" I called.

As I ran to intercept, it finally occurred to me where I had seen that energy before. Auras were tricky. They were unique, like fingerprints, which is all well and good—but it wasn't as if I could have picked out even my own fingerprints from a lineup without double-checking. I had seen this aura before, though. I had seen it in the streets of New Fiddleham and I had seen it sitting across from me in my own carriage.

My throat felt tight. "Grim?" I managed.

chapter twenty-three

Grim hung on to the window ledge, both of us locked in a moment that couldn't possibly last. Her aura churned with dissatisfaction and fury. What had she been hoping for? That the spell paper would have whisked me away? That it would have killed me? The temperature in the room continued to plummet, and the glass above her head was slowly frosting into a glittering, opaque white. Behind us, Kit and Garabrand pounded on the door.

"Why?" I asked.

"Stop her!" Jackaby yelled, rushing toward Grim before she could descend. He didn't make it far, skidding to an abrupt halt a few feet away from the window. He looked as if he were trying to force his legs through thick mud. The air hitting my lungs suddenly stung from the biting cold, and the hairs on the back of my neck stood on end. A hazy cloud condensed between Jackaby and the girl—wicked, furious energy crackling off it like lightning. An old man's face coalesced in the center of the mist, like ice forming on a frigid lake. The apparition had a thick, white mustache and eyebrows to match. He did not look happy.

"Can you see this one?" I asked, shakily. Jackaby nodded, his feet frozen in place.

"Good patients," the ghost rumbled, his voice as deep and ominous as rolling thunder, "do not . . . *run* . . . in the hospital."

Beyond the spectral figure, Grim dropped silently out of view.

Jackaby was backing away, very slowly. "Of course not," he said. "Very rude, isn't it? Right there with you. We'll just nip after that patient who just ran off. Got to give her a quick reminder about the hospital code of conduct."

Wind howled, and tattered curtains snapped like cracking whips. From the other side of the heavy double doors, Agent Garabrand's voice yelled a muffled something that might have been "Hang on," but it was hard to make out the syllables.

The ghost hung in the air before us. It had condensed to a fully corporeal form, but the figure was still a little foggy around the edges. The whites of his eyes glowed with unnerving intensity, and it hurt to look at him for too long.

"Dr. Mudgett, I presume?" I managed.

"Good patients," the doctor said, ignoring me, "stay . . . in their rooms." The man's silvery eye twitched, and his nostrils flared. The spattering of stains across his white coat seemed to darken as he glided slowly forward.

"Right you are," Jackaby said, nearly tripping over the slack chain from the chandelier as he backed farther away from the ghost. "And that's why we're here, obviously. We're—what's the word. Hospital people. Helping maintain order. Orderlies. That's the one."

"Lies," growled the ghost, "are a symptom of a corrupt and deviant mind."

"Not lies, exactly," Jackaby hedged.

The doctor's eyes darkened until they were inky pools against the paleness of his skin—his pupils glowed within the shadows like dying matchsticks. A sudden wind whipped his coat around him. "Disorderly behavior," he rumbled. "Violent outbursts. Unrepentant deceit. My professional diagnosis: psychosis. Treatment to begin immediately."

The few window panes around the room that had not already been ruined suddenly shattered inward. The sparkling shards hung in midair, spinning weightlessly as if suspended on invisible strings.

"Treatment?" Jackaby squeaked.

The doctor's pallid mouth tightened. "Bloodletting."

A heavy gust whipped the shards widdershins around the room, and Jackaby and I found ourselves very suddenly in the eye of a glittering storm. I felt a sharp pain on my shoulder and dove into the open armoire as still more blades of jagged glass whipped toward me. A shard of glass as wide as my open palm whistled through the air toward Jackaby, who ducked just in time. He staggered toward cover as a second and then a third shard carved slits in the hem of his coat.

"Now would be a good time for that holy water," Jackaby yelled over the din.

Maneuvering clumsily, I tugged both vials from my pocket, leaned out of the armoire, and threw one of them forcibly toward the malevolent spirit. Almost as soon as it had left my fingers, the slim bottle was whipped into the maelstrom and spun away to be lost uselessly in the mess of dust and glass.

I could see Dr. Mudgett's silvery face plainly. His jaw was clenched and his eyes were like embers. He must have felt my gaze, because his head snapped toward me, and I felt my breath catch in my throat.

"Good patients," he hissed, "do not . . . throw things."

At that moment, the doors across the room exploded open in a spray of splinters. Dr. Mudgett looked up as Agents Garabrand and Kit dropped a low bench that had apparently served as their makeshift battering ram.

"Good patients do not slam doors!" the spectral doctor howled.

"Ghost," Agent Kit barked. He drew his sidearm and aimed it at the furious spirit.

"You think?" Garabrand grunted.

The gun was shaking in Kit's hand, but he stood his ground. "Poltergeist. Aggressive. Threat level: ten."

"Quit naming the damn thing and shoot it!" Garabrand growled, shielding his face with one arm and squinting into the glass storm.

Kit fired two shots, but Dr. Mudgett had vanished into vapor before the second round had left the chamber. Instantly, the maelstrom of glass came crashing down to the floor all around us. The noise was intense, but the silence that followed was somehow more so.

Jackaby poked his head out from behind the suit of armor, and I gingerly stepped out of my armoire, my feet crunching on the tiles. I slid the spare bottle of holy water back into my pocket.

Agent Kit's eyes narrowed as he watched me emerge. "Of course it's you two. It's always you two."

"We like to make an appearance at all the important soirees," I managed, trying not to let my voice sound as frayed as I felt. "Thanks for cutting in on that last dance."

"Were those salt and iron rounds?" Agent Garabrand asked.

"Mm?" Kit glanced at his weapon. "I—I don't know."

A sparkling eddy of dust spun in the air in front of me.

"That sounds like a *no*," grunted Garabrand. "Everybody out. Now!"

Jackaby and the agents hurriedly crossed back through the double doors, but I hesitated. In spite of myself, I darted to the window and peered down. Grim's aura clung to the thick ivy on the side of the building—but the girl had long gone. I checked my pockets and confirmed that I still had the spell paper she had slapped on my back. It was scorched and crumpled, and the tacky adhesive on the back was sticking to itself, but the symbol remained intact. There was no telling where it would have sent me. How on earth was that child mixed up in all this?

"Rook!" Jackaby yelled from the hallway.

I nodded and hurried after them. The chilly breeze had picked up again with a tinkling of shifting glass. I was nearly to the door when the spectral doctor coalesced—directly in front of me.

"Oh, bother," I said. "We really don't need to do this."

"Patient is refractory." The doctor's voice was low and rumbling, his eyebrows locked in an angry glower. "Unyielding to treatment. Irrational. The mind is rotten. Trepanning may prove necessary."

"You know what we might try before poking any holes in my perfectly good skull?" I said. "A nice, refreshing shower. Everyone feels better after a shower. Don't you?"

And with that, I plucked the cork from my last vial of holy water and threw it over the apparition.

The doctor let out a horrific screech—like metal grating against stone. Steam poured off him as he clutched his face. Under his fingers, splotchy streaks and splatters were rapidly melting to vapor. With an inhuman bellow, his eyes glowed white-hot and he vaulted toward me.

I was struck—not by the icy hands of the surgeon, but by a sudden wave of heat. In front of me, the dreadful doctor burst into a ball of orange flame. I threw my hands in front of my face, but the fire extinguished itself almost as quickly as it had appeared.

I blinked as my eyes readjusted to the dimness of a suddenly still and silent hospital ward. The air reeked of rotten eggs and burnt hair.

"Holy water's pretty good against ghosts," said Agent Garabrand from the doorway. He waggled a slim brass tube at me as the smoke faded. "But hellfire's better. Harder to come by, of course. Been saving this canister since Demorest."

"Thank you," I said. "But this isn't over."

"Never is. It'll take at least a few days for the doc to bounce back, though."

I pushed past the agent and hurried down the hallway. "It's not ghosts I'm concerned about—it's the living. We need to go. Fast."

I raced back past the rooms where the stolen prisoners had been kept until so very recently. A pang of anger stabbed my chest as I passed Charlie's room.

"You saw her, right?" Jackaby asked, jogging along beside me.

I nodded. "It was the girl."

"What girl?" Garabrand demanded.

"We call her Grim," Jackaby contributed.

"Mary Horne's daughter," I explained. "She witnessed her mother's abduction. She's been assisting with the investigation—at least I thought she was assisting. She knew about Mrs. Finkin. She was the one who brought us there that night we ran into you two."

"She was there?" said Garabrand. "She was there the same night *Mr.* Finkin ended up in the wall?"

I swallowed, trying to remember if I had seen Grim anywhere after we left that night, but it was as though a sliver of my memory right after we left had been plucked out of my mind.

I sped down the stairs and hit the ground floor of the hospital in a blur, nearly rushing straight through Ingrid, who didn't seem to notice us as she drifted nervously back and forth in the hospital lobby, mumbling.

"Hang on," said Agent Kit.

I ignored him. The clear air hit my lungs like a splash of cold water as we emerged into the night.

"Hold it!" Agent Kit called after me. "Stop!"

"What?" I spun around to face him. "You saw the cells. They were *here*. Charlie was here. I don't know how Horne's daughter features in all this, but she can't have gotten far. If I can catch up with her quickly—"

"Mary Horne doesn't have a daughter," Kit said.

I stared at him, unsure how to respond.

"I do my homework, Detective. I wrote the official reports on all of the victims myself. Horne has no children. If she did, I'd have done a separate write-up on her and we'd have pursued the child ourselves."

"But—she had a room," I stammered. "There was a wee stuffed elephant."

"You can tell when a person's lying," Garabrand said. "If the kid told you she was Horne's daughter, I'm sure she was."

I nodded. That was true. Yes. I would have seen the lie.

"But she *didn't*," said Jackaby, quietly. "She never actually said she was Horne's daughter. *We* said that. The child just didn't deny it."

I felt light-headed.

"Lies of omission," Garabrand grunted. "Simple, but effective."

"No, no, no." I closed my eyes tight and rubbed my temples. I was supposed to be the Seer, but I hadn't seen it. What else had I missed?

"You can still find the trail," Jackaby prompted. "It's not too late."

I drew a deep breath, trying to believe him.

"Is that her?" Agent Garabrand pointed over my shoulder.

I turned my head in time to see a girl with a mess of black hair stepping across the overgrown weeds toward us. Her eyes darted among the four of us. She was anxious, but her anger was stronger than her fear. It boiled around her in brooding reds and blacks. Twenty feet away, she came to a stop, fists clenched.

"Grim?" I hazarded, taking a step closer.

She opened her mouth—and my memory of what happened next is entirely blank.

chapter twenty-four

"Miss Rook!" Jackaby's voice echoed as if caught in a labyrinth of caves. "Miss Rook!" A hand shook my shoulder and the world suddenly snapped back into focus. I was still on the weedy grounds of the haunted hospital. My senses were flooded with a scent like burnt lime.

Agent Kit groaned beside me, rubbing his eyes.

The patch of weeds in front of us where Grim had been standing was notably empty. Dizzily, I lifted my eyes to follow the wispy trail of her aura. It led toward the busy center of town.

"Stop right there!" Agent Garabrand was already at

the far end of the overgrown lot, bounding after the girl. Agent Kit stumbled into action, giving chase behind his partner.

"Come on," Jackaby urged, tugging my arm.

"What was that?" I managed, shaking off the fog and joining the chase.

"No idea," he said. "I have a feeling I'm missing a few minutes. Could have been a hex?"

The haze surrounding me was so familiar, but it didn't feel like witchy magic. It felt earthy and natural. I blinked several times, focusing on Jackaby. The supernatural residue was all over him, as well. "I've definitely seen this magic before," I said. "In fact—I think it's been all over the trail, but I keep forgetting it. It doesn't want to be remembered."

"That sounds about right," Jackaby panted. "Haven't you missed this?"

We skidded between two buildings. I had long since lost sight of Grim, but her trail was more vivid than ever— practically electric with intense crackles of fury and fear. We whipped around another corner, and I just about plowed into Agent Kit, whose own trail had veered left, then right, before doubling back on itself. He had lost the scent.

"They went this way," I called, following the other two auras deeper into the city. I narrowed my eyes and held the twin lines in focus as best I could. I kept atop it for several blocks—I could tell we were getting closer as I spun into another alley just in time to see Agent Garabrand glance up at me, his eyes wide and his aura sparkling with alarm.

Then a glittering flash lit the narrow corridor and Garabrand was gone. Agent Kit barreled past me. "Garabrand?" he yelled. "Garabrand!" It was futile. Both auras came to an abrupt end there, in the alleyway.

"They're gone," I panted. "Transported, like the others. She got him."

Kit cursed and jogged to the end of the alley. I followed, pushing through the cloud of turnippy magic to catch up to him. The far end opened onto the busy Willow Street, a crisscrossing mess of energies as pedestrians and horses and carriages poured up and down the cobbles and in and out of the shops that lined the busy lane.

"Well?" Kit demanded, his eyes darting between street carts and carriages. "Which way did she go?"

I shook my head. "It's too much. I've lost her."

With a frustrated sigh, Kit spun back to us. "Okay. Spill it! What exactly were you two doing poking around at that hospital?" he said. "And don't get cute with me. I know you're up to something. We can't seem to kick over a suspicious-looking rock in this nutty town without the two of you scrambling out from under it."

"We were looking for whoever is behind these kidnappings and killings," I said. "Same as you."

"And I suppose I just have to take your word on that?"

"You do," said Jackaby, "but we don't have to take yours."

Kit scowled. "Is that supposed to mean something?"

"It means I don't trust you, either," said Jackaby. "I'm not so sure we really *are* looking for the same thing. Why don't you tell us what *you* were doing poking around that hospital?"

"I don't have time for this." Kit shook his head. "Agent Garabrand could be in need of backup."

"I can see you're being truthful," I said. "But you're still avoiding the question." I watched the clouds form in his aura. "No lies of omission. Tell me the truth. I'm making you uncomfortable, aren't I? Is it my abilities?"

"Don't try getting inside my head. Your special eyeballs don't scare me—I work with paranormals all the time. Comes with the job. We called in a lady just yesterday to reverse-craft those spells Dupin confiscated from the Finkin house. I supervised her myself, back at the station."

"Yeah, but you didn't like her, either," I said.

Kit clenched his jaw. "Maybe because she smelled bad," he snarled. "I said stay out of my head."

"Why were you at the hospital?" Jackaby asked.

"I'm not the bad guy here," Kit said.

"You truly believe that," I agreed. "But it's still not an answer."

Kit swallowed. "I—I don't remember," he said at last. It was true.

Jackaby and I exchanged glances.

"I found a curious note in my files. It was just an address for the hospital—in my handwriting, but I don't remember writing it. Garabrand didn't know anything about it, either. He agreed to come with me to check it out. When we got there, it all felt eerily familiar."

"Memory loss," I said. "That might have been useful information for you to disclose earlier. Your secrets are getting people killed."

"*My* secrets?" Kit shot back. "You mean like being secretly in league with our prime suspect?"

I winced. "Fair. But perhaps now would be a good time for us to begin trusting each other."

"You want me to *trust* you?" Kit ground his teeth. "You two have been at the scene of every dead body we've uncovered. You've admitted to working with that creepy kid. For all I know, you've led me on this wild-goose chase just to separate me from my partner." He took a deep breath. "I don't trust you. I don't even *like* you. And to be perfectly clear, if I find out you're lying to me, I will not hesitate to put a bullet in you."

"Pretty standard relationship parameters, in my experience," Jackaby interjected. "I think my old contract with the police department used similar phrasing."

"We're here to help," I said.

"Oh?" Kit put his hands on his hips. "Then what now, great and magical detective?"

"Now," I said, "I'm going to go get Charlie."

Kit's brow furrowed. "You worked out where he's been taken?"

"Not in the foggiest," I said. "But I do know how to get there."

Jackaby raised an eyebrow.

Kit's head cocked to one side. "How—"

"Out of curiosity, did she manage to crack it?" I asked him.

"Did *who* manage *what?*"

"You told us that you worked with an outside consultant, one who knew magic," I said. "Did she manage to replicate the Finkin spell?"

"Sure." He shrugged. "Copying the spell was just careful penmanship. It's the precise mixture of the ink that gives it its zing, apparently. She's still working on re-creating the recipe, but we confiscated enough of Finkin's original stock for her to mimic the symbol and try it out a few times."

"And it definitely works?"

"It works. It's not going to help you find the culprit, though. The symbol just brings the paper and whatever's touching it back to where it was written in the first place. We figure whoever has Mrs. Finkin has been forcing her to write new spells at their drop sites. The version we whipped up won't bring you to Charlie; they'll just zip you right back to the police station where they were made."

"Perfect."

"How is that perfect?" Kit demanded, but I had already spun on my heel and made for the carriage.

"Come along. We'll give you a ride."

chapter twenty-five

"Where did you go?" Lydia Lee demanded as we neared the carriage. "You said a few minutes! I've been sitting here getting the heebie-jeebies from this creepy hospital for over an hour!"

"And you said *you* were going to watch the kid," I countered.

Miss Lee straightened her vest self-consciously. "I did watch her. I watched her ignore my instructions and scamper over to try to catch up with you two in the hospital. I'm a driver, not a nanny, all right? I'm not good with children!"

"May be for the best you didn't follow," I said. "It seems

there are a few things young Grim wasn't telling any of us."

Miss Lee glanced over my shoulder. "Who's the starched collar?" she asked.

"Agent Kit is one of the good guys," I answered. "Or at least he thinks he is, which will have to do for now. We're headed for the station house, if you please."

"You're the boss." She gave a little salute and swung herself back up into the driver's box.

I'm the boss, I repeated in my head as I climbed into the carriage.

The trip was tense and silent, save for the rolling of the wheels and the clop of hooves. Agent Kit sat on the bench across from ours, staring moodily out the window. When the carriage finally came to a full stop, he was quick to climb out.

Before following suit, I leaned back against the seat and pulled the slightly burnt paper out of my coat pocket, smoothing it as best I could. It was wrinkled and sticky, but the symbol was still clear. It glimmered like silver in the daylight. When the light caught the lines just right, it was almost as if I was looking through strings of glass—a window into another place. On the other side of that symbol was Charlie.

"They nearly had you," Jackaby said, softly. "Do you think that one is a Maeve Finkin original?"

"I couldn't say," I answered. "It looks the same to me. The ink is definitely a match."

"I could examine it more closely in my office," he said. "Jenny could help. Maybe we could find some indication of where the latest victims are being sent."

"No," I said. "We don't have time to muddle through a lot of science experiments. Whoever is behind this—they know we're hot on their trail. They've already moved their captives once, and they'll do it again. We need to know where their trap is hidden before they have time to dig another new one."

"Their last trap caught Charlie, and he's sharper than your average quarry. They very nearly caught you, too."

"They only caught Charlie because he wasn't ready for them. But we are."

Jackaby tilted his head. "Are we, though?"

"We will be."

"I know that tone of voice," said Jackaby. "That's your bad idea tone of voice."

"The quickest way to get to the bottom of a trap," I said, "is to fall into it."

I hopped down onto the sidewalk.

"Well, at least you've the sense to come here first," Jackaby said, dropping down beside me. "We should be able to assemble a decent bit of backup before mounting our strike."

"I'm afraid backup isn't the objective this trip," I said.

"We'll be proceeding alone?" Jackaby shot me a glance, but then nodded. "Just you and me against unknowable terrors? Very well. We've faced worse. Maybe."

"No, sir. I don't mean just you and me."

"Oh. Well, good. Because that would be beyond reckless, even for us."

"Not *us*," I clarified. I held up the rumpled spell. "Single postage. One package. It's got to be me."

Jackaby looked me in the eyes, and his aura flushed with a dizzying whirlwind of fear and concern and perhaps just a little confused pride. "Miss Rook," he said. "I know I've been a terrible influence, but even *I* wouldn't—"

"I know," I said. I tucked the spell back into my coat. "But it's not about what *you* would do. Isn't that what you've been telling me all this time? It's about what *I* would do." I swallowed. "What I *must*."

Jackaby took a deep breath. "This is a bad idea even by the standards of our usual bad ideas."

"Grim knows we're hunting her. She's going to behave rashly. If we don't act quickly, it could be too late. Charlie could be—" I couldn't finish the sentence.

"Tell me what you need from me."

We mounted the steps into the station house together.

"Abigail!"

I blinked. The cogwheels of my mind skipped several teeth, and my world lurched sideways. There, in the gritty environs of the New Fiddleham Police Department, on the precipice of danger, was the last face I wanted to see—my mother's.

"There she is! There you are! You see, Daniel, I told you we would find her here. The fellow at the desk tried to tell us that you don't work for the police department, but I distinctly remembered that you said you were doing some sort of secretarial work or some such with the New Fiddleham police, so I said to your father—I said: *We'll find her at the station.* Didn't I say so?"

My father looked at me soberly as they drew up in front of us. Something about the expression on his face made me feel as though I were coming downstairs for breakfast after sneaking out through my bedroom window the night before. How much did they know?

"Oh, Abigail," my mother went on. "I am truly concerned about the rumors these . . . quaint people are already spreading about you. That fellow over there with the bushy mustache is under the impression that you walk about on the streets all day looking for common criminals. And his associate seemed to think you were some manner of witchy woman with unnatural abilities. I told them I was quite sure that they were both sorely mistaken, and I scolded them soundly for listening to such preposterous gossip. Grown men, no less."

"How much of it is true?" asked my father.

My mother batted him in the arm. "Don't act like a rube, Daniel. Of course none of it is true."

"There are some strange things in New Fiddleham," my father continued, his gaze fixed on me. "This is not a normal city, is it, Abigail?"

My mother rolled her eyes. "Your father is convinced that he saw a man with antlers earlier. I keep telling him—"

"I *did* see a man with antlers earlier," my father said with a huff. He turned back to me. "How much of what those policemen told us about you is true?"

I opened my mouth, but the words got all caught up in my head before they could find their way down to my throat.

"*Normal* is such a curious word," Jackaby said, breaking the awkward silence. "So subjective. And what city *isn't* a touch abnormal, when you scratch beneath the surface?"

At that moment, the door to the holding cells burst open with a bang, and the image of a towering troll ducked his craggy head under the frame before emerging. His broad boulder of a chest puffed up as he lumbered out into the reception room.

"Rock-Jaw free once more!" the troll bellowed.

My mother made a muffled squeaking sound.

"Shake in fear, tiny, stupid humans! No bars can hold . . ." The hulking figure caught my eye and hesitated, clearing his throat with a gravelly cough.

"That's quite enough of that," I said, sternly. "Behave yourself. And stop yelling at everyone. You're overselling it again."

Rock-Jaw nodded, slouching meekly into his enormous shoulders. "Sorry, Miss Detective Human. Rock-Jaw go. Very quiet." He thudded to the front door, ducked, and squeezed his way out into the city.

I turned back to my parents. My mother's jaw was quivering and her eyes were wide. My father pursed his lips and drew a long breath in through his nose. "So," he said, heavily, "it's all true."

"New Fiddleham is a very special place," I said.

"And you came all the way to America to be . . . a witch?" he asked.

My mother made a burbling noise and gesticulated emphatically with both hands before throwing them up and abandoning her efforts at speech altogether.

"I mean to say," my father went on, "dabbling in the occult is bad enough—and I do not approve—but if you were so dead set on it, what was wrong with proper English witches? We've had witches for ages. Shakespeare wrote about them. I'd wager our lot are better at spells and potions anyway. Americans can't even brew a proper cup of tea."

"I'm *not* a witch," I said. "Although I have met several of them, and on the whole, they tend to be far more reasonable and considerate than the literature would have you believe, English or otherwise."

My mother looked faint.

"Abigail," my father said, "this is all a bit much. We—we only want to know the truth."

"The truth—erm. The truth is—" I hesitated. "The truth is *difficult*. I *will* explain, I promise. I'll explain everything." I swallowed. "Later. But there are things that I really need to attend to first. Mr. Jackaby?"

I ignored my father's startled objections and my mother's incoherent huffs and swept past them and into the corridor. I could hear an officer gently informing them that the area was for authorized personnel only, and willed myself not to glance back as they protested.

"Will you?" asked Jackaby.

I unclenched my jaw. "Will I what?"

"Tell them the truth?"

I took a steadying breath. "Of course I will," I said. "Just as soon as I've settled on which version of it they might be able to handle."

We passed the holding cells and the evidence locker. Agent Kit waved us toward an open interrogation room. "You two. I want full written statements about everything you saw in that hospital."

At the sound of the agent's voice, Dupin poked his head out of his own office. "What is this all about?" he demanded.

"It doesn't concern you," Kit countered, his mustache twitching.

Dupin's nostrils flared. "Really?" he replied through gritted teeth. "This is still *my* department, and I—"

At the same time, Kit started in with, "You truly have no idea what you're—"

I seized the moment to quietly step away. Just up the hall, the evidence officer was looking over a file on her desk.

"Pardon me," I said.

"Oh!" She started and straightened her glasses. "You're that magical detective with the funny eyes," she said. "Right?"

"More or less," I admitted. "The department's been bringing in more and more special contractors, though, haven't they?"

She nodded. "We had to bring in a guy who could speak gnomish and a woman who could read and write magic runes."

"I think I heard about that one," I said. "The magic consultant who came in earlier—she made copies of the spells from that Finkin case, yes?"

"That's right," said the officer.

"Where are they now?"

"The new spell papers? They're in a red folder, locked up in evidence with all the other ones. I can't let you have them, though. Sorry. Dupin made a pretty big deal about it. All of it stays locked up. He said not to trust anybody."

"Good," I said. "Smart. Dangerous stuff, those spells. Keep them locked up tight, the whole lot. In fact, I have one more that needs to get locked up with them." I pulled the scorched paper from my pocket.

"Where'd you get *that*?"

"Other way around. *It* nearly got *me*," I said honestly.

The officer held out a hand for it, but I winced. "Oh, no—sorry. Dupin would rather I deposit it directly. Don't want more people exposed to this stuff than absolutely necessary."

The officer shrugged. "Sure, I guess. You'd know more about this sort of thing than I would. Follow me."

She pushed herself up from her desk and crossed the room, flicking through keys until she found the correct one. The evidence locker looked like any other jail cell, but in place of benches, it housed rows and rows of wire shelves stacked with bins and boxes, each one labeled neatly with an official police tag. The door was no more than a set of sturdy bars with a lock. The officer turned the key, and it swung open.

"Spare evidence tags still just inside the door? Yes, I see them. Lovely." I slipped past the rows of plain brown boxes until I reached the newest additions. It only took me a moment to scan the tags and locate the case marked *Finkin: Kidnappings*.

From the hallway outside, I could hear the bark of Kit's angry voice.

"Mr. Jackaby," I said. "Would you mind?"

"Would he mind what?" asked the officer from the door-way. "If you need help with something—"

"She doesn't need any help," Jackaby assured her. "She

just needs a bit more time." With that, he gave the door a kick, and it slammed shut with a loud clang.

"What are you—" the officer began. "Hey, stop! Those are my keys!"

I wanted to look, but I kept my focus on the task in front of me.

"Whoops," Jackaby was saying. "Looks like they've dropped into my bag by mistake. No worries, I'll have them back out for you in a moment."

I pulled a red folder out of the top of the box. Within it was a stack of notes—ten trial spell sheets. Seven had been successful. Three had failed. I swallowed. There was a single fresh spell page tucked into the folder with the consultant's notes. If it worked the way it was supposed to, it would summon the user right back into this room.

"Here they are," Jackaby continued just outside the door. "Wait, no, that's a rosary. Hold this for me, would you? Monkey's paw. Don't make any wishes! Sorry, Officer. Lots of things to sort through in here. It's deeper than it looks."

I pulled the fresh spell page out of the folder and tucked it gingerly into my jacket pocket. Then I dug through the box until I spotted a stubby candle and a set of matches.

"What the hell is going on here?" demanded Agent Kit, his voice suddenly very close. The officer mumbled something I couldn't hear. "You gave her access to police evidence? Your entire assignment is to *not* let people in there!

Miss Rook! Miss Rook, you will cease what you're doing immediately!"

"So sorry, Agent," I called over my shoulder. "I'm a bit busy just now!"

He snarled. "Turn over those keys at once!"

"It's all a silly mistake, really," I could hear Jackaby telling him with exaggerated friendliness. "Just give me a moment, I'm sure they're in here somewhere."

"Enough! Give me that bag!"

"I wouldn't—"

Outside the door there were several muffled thumps and metallic clangs as Agent Kit turned Jackaby's satchel upside down. The noises kept coming—clanks and thuds and concerning rattles. Something ceramic shattered against the tile floor, a few coins tinkled as they rolled away, and a large bird squawked loudly. There was a fluttering of wing-beats, followed by startled yelps from the officer.

"Huh. How did she get in there?" Jackaby said.

I took a deep breath, trying to ignore the commotion as I smoothed the tacky side of the burnt spell page against my forearm. This had better work. I struck the match.

The door to the evidence locker rattled. Kit shouted something at me, but I tuned him out.

I held my arm over the flame, feeling the heat as it teased the corner of the paper. The material glowed eagerly as the fire caught hold, sparkles of color dancing within the flame.

I was braced for the burn, but not for the hand that roughly grabbed my shoulder. I glanced up into Agent Kit's furious face.

"Oh, no you—"

The world went white. My stomach lurched as my concept of up and down spun into senselessness for several long seconds. I felt a whoosh of cool air wash over me and then the pang of my knees landing, hard, against a cold floor in a dim chamber.

"—don't."

chapter twenty-six

"You're not supposed to be here!" I said hotly, pushing myself up. I blinked as my eyes gradually adjusted to the gloom. The auras of past prisoners swirled around us—like we were underwater in a murky soup.

"Of course I'm not supposed to be here!" Kit growled. "And neither are *you*. We're lucky we both survived the trip without getting ourselves lodged halfway through a wall or in the wrong end of a dairy cow."

"Is there a *right* end of a dairy cow in which you'd like to be lodged?"

Kit ground his teeth and scanned the chamber around us. "Do you even know where *here* is?"

"No," I admitted. "Do you?"

He scowled and shook his head. "A cage," he grunted.

My vision was finally starting to pick up the subtle differences in the shadows all around me. Kit was right; we were definitely inside a cage. The enclosure was only a couple of meters wide on either side, about the same size as a cell back at the station house. Our cell had a single door, and beyond it was a hallway painted a drab green. Other than the two of us, the prison was entirely empty.

"What do you think?" Kit asked. "Some sort of military compound?"

I shrugged. "Could be," I said. "Commissioner Marlowe did mention that there was a facility on the edge of town. An old training camp, I think. Something about nature spirits on federal property. I don't believe it's been in use since the Civil War. Not the worst place to conceal something nefarious."

"You think this is where that kid sent Agent Garabrand? And your boy, Charlie? And all the rest of them?"

I focused on the fuzzy residue of trails until I picked out one familiar aura. "Charlie's been through here, along with a whole torrent of others."

Kit gave the door an experimental push and pull. It rattled, but held firm.

"Hang on," I said. "I think I've got something for that."

I rummaged through my pockets. *Bundle of sage. Loose*

rune stones. Witching knot. No, no, no. When I pulled out the fresh transportation spell, Kit snatched it from out of my hands.

"Hey!" I said.

"Ah-ah-ah!" He jabbed a finger in my direction. "I'm not having any righteous indignation out of you, missy. You *stole* this out of evidence and then got us into this mess. You do not get to just magic yourself out of here and leave me stranded in a prison. I'll be keeping it, thanks. We just need to find a way out—a *real* way, not some unreliable spell—and then we'll bring reinforcements back to sweep the place."

"Fine," I said. "Just mind you don't damage it. That was meant to be my emergency escape hatch. Besides, I don't remember asking you to come along at all."

At last, I found what I was looking for. I pulled the bottle out and gave it a gentle shake.

"What's that?" Kit asked. "Perfume?"

"It's a cleaning solution," I said. "Basically. More or less. Jackaby's been working on it. There's not much left. Hopefully this is enough to do the trick."

"You're going to *clean* our jail cell?"

I leaned down and spritzed the lock until the sprayer ran dry. The mechanism gradually bubbled, layers of metal peeling and flaking away, and after a few moments, a heavy, fizzling glob dropped to the floor with a slap. The air was filled with a smell like pennies and vinegar.

"Cleaning solution?" Kit looked from the ruined lock to me. "For cleaning *what*, exactly?"

"For a *clean* getaway?" I suggested.

Kit rubbed the bridge of his nose, his lips pursed. "I swear to god—"

I gave the door a kick, and it swung open. "After you, Agent."

The hallway beyond the cell was eerily quiet. The ceilings were low and claustrophobic, and I could sense packed earth on the other side of the walls. We appeared to be in some sort of underground bunker. The fear and confusion of the beings who had moved through the narrow passage before us was almost overwhelming. The hall opened onto an office of sorts. Rows of filing cabinets lined the walls, and a pair of desks sat stacked with folders and loose paperwork. I glanced over the stack on the nearest desk. *Taggleburn, Tippets, Townsend.* "What on earth?" I whispered, flipping through files. "Hang on. Townsend is one of our missing people. He's a tailor."

"He's also a gnome," breathed Kit. His aura had abruptly paled to a straw-colored uneasiness.

"You're right. These are profiles of magical beings in New Fiddleham." I tugged open the top drawer of the filing cabinet. There had to be hundreds of dossiers, all labeled in neat, orderly handwriting. "What do you suppose these numbers at the top mean?" I whispered. "*Applegate, Elliot—T7, A4.* They all seem to have them."

"Threat and asset rankings," answered Kit, his voice shaky. "These shouldn't be here."

"Threat and asset?" I said.

"Yes." He shook his head, as if trying to clear away cobwebs. "How much of a ticking time bomb a subject is versus how well they can be controlled and directed. Threat and asset."

"You mean to say that someone has been assessing the citizens of New Fiddleham for their potential to be *weaponized?*"

"Not just *someone*," said Kit. "*Me*. Us. I filled out a lot of this paperwork myself. That's my handwriting there. These are Bureau of Curiosities files. These are supposed to be secure."

I felt my muscles tighten.

"*You're* behind all this?" I took a few steps back, eyeing Kit, but his aura was rippling with genuine confusion.

"*These.*" He gestured at the paperwork. "Not *this*." He waved at the walls around us. "Of course we keep records. We have a record on *you*, too. That shouldn't come as a shock. The entire purpose of the bureau is to keep tabs on supernatural entities active in the United States. Whoever that creepy child of yours is working with, they're using our files to help them target paranormals."

"These records shouldn't exist in the first place." I scowled at Kit. His aura was honest, but there was still something else behind it. "A lot of these people live in secret for a reason. Many of them rely on discretion to simply live their lives."

"The Bureau of Curiosities *is* discreet," said Kit. "Hell, I've helped cover up more supernatural nonsense than you've ever heard of."

"I'm sure that will come as a great comfort to the hundreds of innocent people whose names you handed over like a shopping list. What are *my* numbers?"

"What?"

"My *threat and asset* rankings. How did you score *me?*"

"I don't memorize every file."

"You know very well that I can read your aura."

Kit sighed. "You're a two-eight. Low threat, high asset potential."

My eyes narrowed. *"Low threat?"*

"We meet people who can literally transform into tigers or turn their enemies into livestock," Kit said. "Two is generous."

I ground my teeth. "When we get out of this, I look forward to showing your bureau just how much of a *threat* this *level two* can be."

The trail of auras led out of the office and down another hallway. This time it opened into a chamber lined with glass cases.

Kit leaned down and peered into the nearest one. "Salamanders," he said.

I peeked over his shoulder. The label on the glass read *Urodela Plinius*. "Oh, they have a fascinating energy about them. Look, that one's glowing."

"It's also dangerous," said Kit. "Bureau training covers a lot of creepy-crawlies, and there are salamanders and then there are *salamanders*," Kit said, tapping the glass with his finger. "Ouch—that's hot. Yeah, these guys are definitely supernatural. Salamanders are classified under elementals. Something about living in flames, storing up energy. They're supposed to be mostly harmless—but if they get agitated, they can let all that fire out again, all at once."

"Well, then, I wouldn't rap on the glass again if I were you." I pressed on through the room. The glow of the lamps inside the cages cast eerie shadows along the floor, which bent and twisted, getting lost in the river of residual auras that hung, fading, in the air in front of me.

"None of that explains what they're doing here now," Kit said, following me farther down the chamber. "Or what *any* of this is doing here."

The other cases we passed held creatures I had encountered before—common pixies, brownies, and even a lone, fluttering wisp—as well as several I didn't recognize. In one cage slumbered something that looked like a mongoose, and below that there was a downy-soft jackrabbit with horns like a deer. The wee thing pressed itself against the back wall of its cage, shivering. The largest enclosure took up the entire far wall of the chamber. It had bars rather than glass, and the creature within looked like something between a black bear and a panther. It might have been intimidating, except that it lay on its side, barely breathing as we neared. Its magic was old and earthy, but the poor thing looked exhausted. Its nose twitched as we neared, but it did not open its eyes.

"I'll be damned—they caught one," Kit muttered, following my gaze. "That has to be a glawackus. They're supposed to be uncatchable. Is this whole thing just some sort of supernatural zoo?"

"It sure looks that way," I said. "Someone has been collecting magical creatures, and it appears our zookeeper decided a few of my friends and neighbors would make for interesting attractions." I stepped toward the far door, my eyes narrowing. I could sense them on the other side—human and nonhuman, the trail of auras culminated in that room. "They're here," I whispered. "The missing people are through here."

"If they are, then whoever or whatever took them is probably in there, too," Kit said. "We need to surveil the room before rushing in. Identify threats, locate resources, scout exits, and then make a plan of action."

"Mm-hm, mm-hm," I said. "I hear you, and yet . . ."

I turned the doorknob and threw my shoulder into it,

bursting into the next room—which turned out to be a broad two-story chamber. The walls around me were lined with rows of what appeared to be prison cells, each one little more than a closet of a room with barely space enough for a bunk. Their doors were made of simple iron bars. Above us, a basic catwalk that ran around the perimeter provided access to the upper cells.

Auras spun in and around one another, sharper than ever, and then they separated at the last moment to split off into the barred chambers. My eyes scanned frantically until my breath caught in my throat. There—three cells from the left on the ground floor. I nearly tripped over myself hurrying forward.

Charlie was seated on the edge of his bed. He blinked and swayed as I grabbed hold of the bars.

"Abigail?" he managed. He looked as if he was trying to wake himself up from a deep sleep.

"Charlie," I panted. "I'm here."

Charlie pushed himself up to cross unsteadily to the door. "Where is *here*?"

"Still working on that," I admitted. "Military bunker of some sort? Underground, I think. The term *lair* feels right. Wherever we are, I'm going to get you out of here. Who kidnapped you?"

"I don't know," said Charlie. "Last thing I remember, we were talking—and your parents were there—I . . . I should have told you." He reached a hand out and touched my face.

My chest pounded in my throat. "Told me what?"

"I should have told you that I—I needed you. That I was drowning. And I kept waking up at night remembering being . . . *gone*."

My throat felt tight. Charlie had been dead for two days. I had truly believed that I had suffered the worse trauma for the loss. "You said you didn't have any memories of that."

Charlie's eyes glistened brightly from the shadows of the cell. "Only feelings. Nothing solid," he said. His aura thrummed with purples and reds, throbbing like a sore bruise. The memory haunted him. I bit my lip. How had I not seen it before? "I thought being busy again would give me something else to think about," he went on, "but it's gotten worse. I was waiting for the right time to sit down and talk, but then . . . I don't know. I was somewhere else for a while, I think, and then I was here. It's all foggy. But I needed you. I still need you. I always need you."

"I need you, too," I managed. "I'm *not* fine. I think, perhaps, it's been a rather long time since I was even a little bit fine." Charlie's hand was warm on my cheek. "But we've found each other," I added. "And we'll get out of this."

"What's the plan?" he asked.

"That," I answered, "is an excellent question."

"No plan," Charlie said. "Okay. We'll think of something."

I pulled the vial of Jackaby's cleaning solution out of my pocket and shook it over the lock, but only a single, weak drip hissed against the metal. The door stayed firmly stuck. I cursed under my breath.

"I don't see him," Agent Kit said. He was frantically darting around the room, peering into cells. "Agent Garabrand's not here."

Trying not to imagine Agent Garabrand lodged in a brick wall somewhere, I straightened up and scanned the room as well, searching for signs of any human prisoners. My vision quickly locked on to an aura I recognized in the far cell on the same row as Charlie. I blinked. That couldn't be right. I crossed the floor hastily to peer inside.

A pair of dirty knees dangled over the side of a small cot, and two scowling eyes glared out at me. My mouth hung open. "Grim?"

"I *knew* I should never have trusted you," she growled. "You were working with the bad guys all along!"

"*We're* working with the bad guys?" I said. "No, *you're* working with the bad guys!"

"What?" She threw her hands in the air. "That doesn't even make any sense!"

"Back at the hospital," I said, "you tried to kidnap me!"

"I didn't try to kidnap you, stupid! I tried to *warn* you!" she yelled.

"Wait—if you didn't put the spell on my back, then who did?"

"The *bad* guys!" Grim declared emphatically, as if that cleared everything up.

"I keep telling her . . ." a familiar voice said from the second story of the bunker. Agent Garabrand stood on the catwalk that encircled the room. "We're *not* the bad guys."

chapter twenty-seven

Agent Garabrand's aura flickered with calculating caution, but he remained fundamentally confident. It was a confidence I was rapidly growing to dislike. He had something in his hands. From a distance it looked like a medicine bottle, the sort with brown-tinted glass.

"What's happening, sir?" said Agent Kit.

"The same thing that's always happening," Agent Garabrand answered. "We are doing our job."

"*This* is your job?" I said. "Was kidnapping in the fine print of the contract, or right up front in the perks and benefits?"

Garabrand shook his head and tutted.

Agent Kit's eyes shot between me and his partner. "Mr. Garabrand. I want to know what's going on, and I want to know right now."

"You always do." Garabrand sighed. "This is well above your pay grade." He considered his partner for a moment, one hand running along the railing as he gazed down at us. When he reached the stairway, he paused. "But you're a good agent—one of the best I've trained in a long time. I would have preferred to introduce you to this next level of security more incrementally, but here we are."

"I'm waiting," Kit said.

Garabrand shifted the bottle from one hand to the other and began to make his way down the steps. "Do you know why you were selected for this detail, Agent Kit? Your exemplary record. Sharp, clever, never afraid to wade right into the fray. People just like you have been protecting this country from behind the scenes for generations. Our organization is larger than any government body—older and more significant than any president."

"No, it's not." Kit scowled. "I do my homework. The Bureau of Curiosities was founded in 1861 by special order of Abraham Lincoln."

"That's right." Garabrand chuckled. "Lincoln had one slightly haunted mirror, so he created an entire covert federal agency to look into it. Makes for a good brochure. But who did the leader of the nation trust to investigate paranormal phenomena both in his own home and all across his country? Paper pushers? Flashy charlatans? No. He trusted experts. He trusted people who knew what they were doing, because they had been doing it already. The name *Bureau of Curiosities* came about in 1861, but the organization itself is far older. And like a snake shedding its skin, that title, too, will eventually crumble away. The body beneath will live on—called something else, but steadfast in its purpose. The world has always needed us, carrying out our work in the shadows. It is a thankless, solemn duty, but for those worthy of it, there is no greater honor."

Kit swallowed, his brow knit.

"Sorry," I said, cutting in. "Not to interrupt this lovely bit of propaganda that you've clearly rehearsed with such care, but there's not much honor in kidnapping innocent people and locking them up in prison cells."

"Honor is just ego. I do what's necessary for the greater good."

"It was in the greater good to try to kidnap *me*, then? Back at the hospital?"

"It was," Garabrand confirmed shamelessly. "Would've been better for us all if I'd succeeded, but I didn't account for Dr. Mudgett and his nasty cold snaps. Rookie mistake. Oh, you acted quickly to put it out—full marks for that—but I suspect the specter's chill gave you the time you needed to pull it off. Not fond of flames, the old doc. He blew me clean out of the room before I could put match to paper for a second attempt. The silver lining, of course, was getting to see you perform under pressure. You have proven yourself quite capable, Miss Rook. A nuisance, yes, but a resourceful one. I respect that. I've said as much since I first read your paperwork. You will make an excellent asset."

I rolled my eyes. "Well, that's obviously not happening," I said.

Garabrand smiled and shook his head patronizingly. "I think you'll find any reasons that you have for distrusting us will be easily forgotten in the face of the good you could do with the bureau."

"Is that so?" My fists clenched. "You'd have me do what, exactly? Help you protect the world from magical beings? From where I'm standing, it's increasingly clear that they are the ones who need protection from *you*."

"I understand how things look," Garabrand said, gesturing at the cells with the bottle in his hand. "But you're wrong. You can trust me. What we do—what our organization has done for generations—it isn't as simple as protecting the world from magic. Magic is a *part* of the world that we protect. I have the utmost respect for it."

"You respect it so much, you kidnap it and lock it up in a cage?"

"Yes." Garabrand was without shame or contrition. "Yes, I do. I admit, it may appear blunt and crude—and perhaps it is—but it is also necessary. Good must counteract evil. Wild magic must be tamed and turned toward productive ends. That snallygaster I caught so many years ago—it was an unruly, dangerous thing. My fellow agents would have destroyed it, but under my care it became an unlikely asset and an ally. All of the individuals we've detained have a part to play—whether they see it now or not—just as you have a part to play. What we are doing here is *curating* a world in which magic need not be seen as a threat."

Confidence thrummed off him like a heartbeat, and it was almost mesmerizing—he believed his own words, he really did—and yet, there was a brittle, silver streak running through it all. "You're lying," I said. "To me or to yourself, you're lying. Of course you want magic to be a threat. You *need* it to be a threat. You just want it to be *your* threat."

Garabrand nodded, thoughtfully. "Hmm. I suppose there is a truth to that. I have always preferred the gun that's in my holster to the one that's pointed at my head. But is it really such a bad thing to be made into a threat, Detective? The Bureau of Curiosities turned a rudderless kid like *me* into a force to be reckoned with—just as I'm now doing for Agent Kit—and not unlike how Mr. Jackaby made a veritable weapon out of *you*. Sharpened you up good and keen, didn't he?"

"That's entirely different," I said. "I *chose* this."

"Did you really? You left England thinking you were going to hunt mythical monsters in America? That was your exact plan? No. I didn't think so. But you're *good* at it. They will be good, too." He gestured to the cells. "You've already seen how instrumental powers like Maeve Finkin's can be. The ability to abduct persons of interest without leaving a trace—it's stunning. Witches who can craft deployable hexes? Tailors who can stitch vests as strong as steel and light as feathers? Soldiers with the strength of ogres? These individuals are being given the same opportunity that you and I were—to become a threat, yes, but against the forces of evil."

I rolled my eyes. "You want to force midwives and greengrocers to be your soldiers?"

"What I *really* want," Garabrand answered, "more than fear or trust—is *order*. Establishing order means establishing peace. Threats can be useful to that end. After all, what is a law if not a threat, Miss Rook? You know as well as I do that we cannot make change through empty promises. We make change through fear—real and legitimate fear."

"Spoken like a frightened little boy who got paddled one too many times at primary school," I said. "I'll take hope over fear any day."

Garabrand tutted. "You can't have one without the other, kid. Together, hope and fear can accomplish great things. Yes, hope inspires, but fear is what bands people together. Fear strengthens armies and tightens bonds. Fear accomplishes the things that hope dares only to dream about."

"Oh, for goodness' sake," I snapped. "*You're* the ones causing strife in New Fiddleham. All the new dangerous magic flooding the streets. The spells being passed around freely to petty grifters. *You* gave Squiffy Rick that spell sheet, knowing it would stir up tensions between the human and paranormal populations when he used it. That's why all that stolen property was just abandoned at the hospital. It makes perfect sense now. You didn't need it—you didn't even *want* it—you just needed people to be mad about it. You say you want order, but you need chaos! The faster things got out of hand, the sooner you could put the city under your jurisdiction and seize total control."

Garabrand nodded his head, his eyes frustratingly keen. "You're so close to getting it," he said, encouragingly. "But this is about much more than one little city."

My mouth felt dry. "The veil-gate."

"The veil-gate!" Garabrand snapped his fingers and nodded. He was holding the shiny brown bottle by the neck. It had sort of a spigot head, like a soda siphon, and the liquid inside looked dark and thick. "A major metropolitan city on the coast of these United States sits totally defenseless, Miss Rook, borderless, ripe for an attack. Invasion is not merely possible; it is inevitable. The lid is off the cookie jar. Foreign powers would be fools not to take advantage of our weakness."

"You're being dramatic. We're not about to be invaded."

"We already *were* invaded!" Garabrand burst out, his placid calm shattering for just a moment before he composed himself again. "Or have you forgotten so soon? I've read your file. You were *there*. Do you deny it?"

I pursed my lips.

Garabrand nodded. "Less than a year ago, New Fiddleham became home to the single most significant threat to the stability of our nation since the Civil War. I do not hold Mayor Spade to blame. It's a miracle it ended as well as it did—the world as we know it mere moments away from being torn apart. You all must think yourselves terribly heroic for preventing that cataclysmic disaster. But there are no such things as heroes, Detective Rook, only more disasters. You can survive them, pat yourself on the back for thwarting one or two, or you can get to work preparing for the next one. There remains a very real and imminent threat of invasion through that gate. It could happen at any time and take any form. The diversity of paranormal life in this very city is evidence of that."

"Even if you were right, the people in your cages aren't soldiers," I snapped. "They're not foreign invaders. They're *people*—most of them citizens who have lived here for years. But you know that already. And you don't care."

Garabrand stiffened. "On the contrary, Miss Rook, I care very much. I am neither cruel nor naive. I know very well that paranormals—like all people—can be good or bad. They can be *with* us or *against* us. I do not assume the worst in any of them. Quite the opposite—I am giving them the chance to show us their best. I'm giving them the opportunity to prove which side they're on. Those paranormals who are *with us* will be proud to see their unique abilities become their country's strengths. As for those who are *against* us"—Garabrand cleared his throat meaningfully—"it is our responsibility to do whatever it takes to protect our people."

"Is that what you told Juliette D'Aulaire when you murdered her?" I spat.

Agent Kit's eyes fixed on his partner, but Garabrand did not respond right away.

"It's true, isn't it?" I said. "Even you can't pretend she was an *outsider*. Heck, she might have been your greatest mouthpiece. She spent every day spreading hate and fear for you."

"That wasn't us," Kit blurted from beside me, although his voice had lost its confidence. "We didn't do that. That was *your* friend Alina." He turned, again, to his partner. "Tell her."

Garabrand did not speak. He was watching me intently.

"She confessed," said Kit, his aura churning frantically now.

"She *did*," I agreed. "And she truly believes that she's guilty—but Agent Garabrand doesn't. Isn't that right?"

"You're making a rather bold accusation," Garabrand said, at last.

"You're not denying a rather bold accusation," I said.

"Alina Cane *is* guilty," he finally answered, but his aura spun with the discordant hues of a half truth.

"You're lying," I said. "And all for a tactical advantage. You would kill, kidnap, and frame innocent citizens just to weaponize their powers. I shudder to imagine what you would do with the access the veil-gate would grant you. How would you weaponize an entire *world* full of magic?"

"That's not how the bureau works," said Kit. "We're the good guys." The man's aura was shaking apart as he desperately tried to maintain that conviction.

"The only reason that's not how the bureau works," I corrected him, "is because until now, the bureau hasn't been *able* to work that way. But suddenly a door opens up and the sole obstacle between the kid and the magical sweet shop is a dutiful pack of guard dogs."

"The Om Caini should never have been given control over the crossing," said Garabrand.

"Which is why you had D'Aulaire killed," I said, "and had Alina framed for it."

"No!" Agent Kit blurted. "He crossed some lines, clearly—but we don't go around killing innocent people. If we wanted the veil so badly, we have more than enough agents to just take it without all that nonsense."

"But all that nonsense is necessary," I said. "Your partner knows that. He knows that most of the city would have sided with the Om Caini if a bunch of government thugs had come and kicked them off their sovereign land. The whole of the Annwyn might have sided with the Om Caini. You might have started a war with a hundred enemies at once—and that would have only reinforced the need for Alina to regain control and protect the gate even more fiercely. No, you needed the city to think that it needed *you*. So you caused a bunch of chaos, made daily life dangerous and awful, and then framed your greatest obstacle for a murder she didn't commit."

"Stop saying that," Kit demanded. He turned to Garabrand. "Tell her it isn't true."

"I have the utmost respect for Alina Cane," Agent Garabrand answered, calmly, his eyes locked on me, "but make no mistake—she *did* kill Juliette D'Aulaire. You saw the evidence with your own exceptional eyes, Detective. You just don't want to believe it."

I faltered. His aura was infuriating. Truth and lies wove together in seamless ribbons. His confidence was absolutely ironclad. I tilted my head. He was *too* confident. "You know it's true," I said.

Garabrand nodded. "Finally ready to accept the facts?"

"No, I mean, you *know*. You don't *suspect*. You didn't *infer* it. You said Alina killed that woman—because you *know* that she did. And how would you know . . . unless you were there when it happened?"

Garabrand closed his mouth.

"And I'd wager you *made* it happen." I shook my head. "Ugh. Of course you did—it's what you do. You turn other people into your weapons. When Dr. Mudgett attacked, you let Agent Kit fire the first shots. You got Maeve Finkin to craft the spells that would capture her friends and neighbors. You kidnapped all these people just to use them the same way. So? How did you make Alina do it? Mind control?"

"Hardly," Garabrand answered. "It didn't take much. Your dear, sweet friend is no innocent. She only needed the right provocation, the right circumstances, a moment of confusion at just the right time. It wasn't pretty. She realized what she had done almost at once, even tried to stop the bleeding—made a mess of herself."

"That's horrible," I breathed.

"Our work is not always clean," Garabrand conceded. "Our aims are not accomplished without sacrifices—but the ends do justify the means. I have not committed a single act in the service of our mission that I would not repeat. We *will* control the veil-gate, Miss Rook—because we *must.* The well-being of this nation and of the entire world is at stake."

"Stirring," I said. "But it's over. You're caught."

Garabrand let out a laugh, and his eyebrows rose slightly as he shook his head. "Mr. Kit, if you don't mind."

I turned my head. Kit hesitated for a moment, and I could see his eyes dart from his partner to me. His aura was awash with electric hues of confused integrity. Ultimately, he drew a deep breath and plucked the handcuffs from his belt. "Put your arms behind your back, Miss Rook."

"Seriously?" I said.

Kit took me roughly by the wrist. I tried to pull away, but I heard the click and felt cold metal pressing against my skin. He tugged at my other wrist, pulling both behind my back. "Don't struggle," he grunted. It was not the brusque command but rather the unexpected urgency hiding just beneath his words that made me pause. In the glow of his aura, I could sense strands of desperate, reckless hope. I heard the second shackle click shut, but rather than cuffing my wrist with it, this one he pressed into my palm. I blinked. Along with the cool metal, he had slipped a folded piece of paper into my hand.

"She's secure," he lied, his voice even.

I tried to avoid letting my surprise play across my face. I put on my best look of angry betrayal as my mind spun to reassess the situation. Kit was helping me.

"Well? What now?" I managed. "I suppose you're going to manipulate one of your pawns into killing me, just like you did to D'Aulaire?"

"No, Miss Rook." Garabrand swirled the bottle in his grip as he spoke, letting the unsavory-looking liquid slosh rhythmically against the glass. "I have no intention of killing you. I *like* you. As I said, you will make a valuable asset."

"I won't."

Garabrand smiled like a kindly old grandfather. It made me want to punch him in the throat. "You have a gift, young lady, that you have not begun to use to its full potential. We can still turn your power to the greater good."

Agent Kit was stepping toward his partner, and I could see the tremor of his nerves with each footfall. He was moving into a good position to strike. I just had to keep the scoundrel talking.

"You want my visions? The last person who tried to take this power by force ended up getting vaporized by the universe," I said, "so you might want to rethink your strategy."

"There you go again—so close, and yet so far off the mark. I have no intention of taking anything by force. The bureau has been using strategic applications of magic for far longer than you've been alive. We've gotten very good at it. Nobody need be harmed. With our help, you could finally explore the limits of your skills."

"I'm not interested in becoming one of your laboratory experiments. We saw the animals you have locked up back there. That glawackus looks half-dead. Is that your idea of doing no harm?"

Garabrand's eyes twinkled. "Mmm. Now there's a specimen for you."

Kit was only a few paces away from Garabrand now, moving with almost exaggerated casualness, trying not to give away his imminent double cross. His aura glowed red-hot as he prepared to take on his own partner. I forced myself not to look at him, keeping my eyes firmly on Garabrand.

"Have you ever encountered the North American glawackus?" Garabrand was saying. "No, you wouldn't recall if you had. They mostly stick to the Ozarks, but they've been spotted as far north as the Poconos. Hard to get a good sense of how many exist in the wild. They make anyone who sees them instantly forget."

"Neat trick," I said.

"Isn't it? It's a gland, actually. Near the tear duct. The fluid can be harvested, like snakes being milked for their venom. Through meticulous testing and research, we have developed the means to use an extract of glawackus to erase short-term memories."

He gave the bottle in his hand a waggle, shifting his fingers to the spray mechanism at the top.

"I was just on my way to erase that little girl's memory of this place—of me. She will be released back onto the streets afterward, of course, safe and sound. Free from the burden of any of this knowledge. It's a kindness."

I swallowed, my eyes on the drab liquid, still sloshing within the bottle.

"You won't remember this conversation," he said. "I may have to strip several hours away, just to be safe. I don't like to do more than a day at a time, if I can avoid it. Soon after, you will wake up—and Mr. Kit and I will have rescued you. We'll even rescue your sweet fiancé, while we're at it. Wouldn't you like that? He is a beloved pillar of the community, after all. The whole city will be grateful, but none more than you, I suspect. I will tell you just enough to catch your interest while leaving you curious—thirsty for more. And that is how you will come to work for me. For the bureau. A rewarding and exciting future. Again, a kindness."

Behind him, Kit clenched his fists and bent his knees. His aura was on fire with nerves and determination. He knew as well as I did that he might only get one shot at this.

Garabrand's eyes flicked toward his partner. His aura belied suspicion.

"I—I'll see through your lies," I stammered, trying to keep his attention. "I can see when you're not being truthful."

Garabrand chuckled. "Oh, I make a habit of sticking to the truth, actually. Much easier to keep a story straight that way. I just leave out the bits I don't want people to know. And on the rare occasion when that's not enough, I let Agent Kit here do the talking."

Kit's anger flared and he leapt forward, but Garabrand sidestepped, squeezing the trigger on the siphon mechanism and catching Kit full in the face with a blast of green mist from the bottle.

"Watch closely," whispered Garabrand. "This is like working with hot glass. Got to mold them quickly before they seize up again."

Kit staggered, regaining his balance. His vibrant aura faded almost instantly to a pale, perplexed gray. "Wh-what?" he mumbled. "Where am I? How did I get here?"

Garabrand looked his partner in the eyes. "You were dropped off here, Agent Kit," he said, "by—let's have some fun with it—by a magical talking dolphin."

Kit nodded and sniffed, rubbing his eyes.

"Go ahead, Mr. Kit," Garabrand said, turning back to me. "Tell Miss Rook how you got here."

"I—I was dropped off," Kit said, shaking his head, "by a . . . a talking dolphin. Is that weird? That's weird, right?"

"Very strange, indeed!" Garabrand gave me a wink. "But is it a lie?"

I wanted to throw up. Kit's aura was a firm, honest blue.

"How can you still think that you're on the side of good?" I stammered, backing away slowly. "You just turned your secret weapon on your own partner!"

"Oh, the formula is perfectly safe," he said. "I've already used it on *you* a few times. Do you remember when that meddlesome child ran up to us outside the hospital to tattle on me? Of course you don't. I only erased a minute or two then—and see? You're fine."

I gaped. "That doesn't feel like *bad guy* behavior to you?"

Garabrand shook his head. "I have no qualms about doing what is necessary. Agent Kit, here, was the one about to turn on his own. I know the signs. I've seen them often enough." He sighed. "He's turned traitor seven or eight times now—not that he remembers. Breaks my heart every time. But he means well, and he's got an honest face. In the past, rogue agents had to be stopped through more permanent means. This is a better way. He gets to live, and he gets to continue to serve the cause. I like keeping him around. People trust him." He raised the spray bottle again and pointed it directly toward me. "They'll trust you, too, when you tell them all about how the two of us rescued you and your furry fiancé from—I don't know—goblins? Maybe witches? Some mysterious monster? I still haven't decided. Now, then—close your eyes, if you like."

Just before Garabrand pulled the trigger on the siphon, Grim's voice cried out behind me, "Run, stupid!"

chapter twenty-eight

I ran. Behind me, I heard the hiss of the mist as Garabrand's wicked concoction sprayed the empty air where my face had been.

"Stop her!" he yelled.

Kit looked up, blinking, and then his eyes narrowed on me. His aura pulsed with refound purpose.

This was bad. The unclasped end of the handcuffs slapped heavily against my leg as I bolted across the floor. The paper Kit had pressed into my palm earlier was the transportation spell. I wondered briefly if he had suspected I would end up on my own, in need of an escape plan without his help.

I dove through the door to the menagerie and pulled it shut behind me. The glawackus let out an exhausted grunt as I thudded into the bars of its cage, but it did not raise its head. I swallowed. There was no lock, and the door swung outward, so even if I found a chair or something to block it, there wasn't much I could do to barricade the entry. I was trapped.

I glanced once at the transportation spell before stuffing it in my pocket. No. I wasn't going anywhere without Charlie.

Footsteps were nearing the other side of the door. I looked around frantically, and my eyes settled on the terrariums stacked along the wall. If Garabrand made use of paranormal creatures by imprisoning them, then I could make use of them by setting them free. I gripped the handcuff chain in one hand and swung the heavy shackle toward the nearest cage—the salamanders.

The door burst open just as the terrarium ruptured. Moving as quickly as I could, I reached a hand in past the broken glass and scooped half a dozen squirming amphibians from the back of the pen. It felt like grabbing a handful of warm, wriggling pasta straight from the pot, and even in the short seconds that they were in my grasp, I could feel their heat swell. "Sorry about this," I whispered, and then tossed the creatures toward the door just as Agent Kit shoved his way inside. He held up his hands to defend himself, looking baffled as the projectiles bounced off him and scattered. Two of the wee things clung to his jacket, their skin rapidly beginning to glow red-hot.

Kit yelped as the pain began to register and then yowled again as he singed his fingers trying to pull the creatures off. An open flame with four tiny legs and a tail scurried across the threshold and into the next room, leaving a trail of fire where it touched the wood. Another zipped along the floor past me, narrowly missing setting my skirts ablaze. It was a lucky thing that most of the compound was made of bricks and concrete.

"You're only making things worse," Garabrand said, pushing past the distressed Agent Kit and into the narrow chamber. I retreated, darting back into the records office as he advanced. "You don't appreciate what we're trying to do here. I can *help* you, Miss Rook."

"I'll pass, thanks," I said, toppling a box of files behind me as I fled.

Garabrand growled. "You're acting like a petulant child," he snarled, stepping easily over the mess I'd made. "This knowledge—these secrets?" He gestured at the papers all around us. "Every one of them comes with a price. They are a burden we at the bureau bear so that the people don't have to. The more you know, the more weight you carry. You know too much, Miss Rook, and it's already drowning you. The sooner you stop this nonsense, the sooner you can surrender all that pressure and anxiety back to me."

"Your precious confidential files are a burden?" I asked,

backing into a corner. "Well, good news for you, then. Looks like your burden is getting lighter as we speak."

Garabrand turned his head to follow my gaze. The pile of dossiers stacked on the desk behind him had begun to smolder and smoke, and another box beside the desk was already flickering with a live flame. "No! What have you done?!" He ran to the desk and began slapping at the fire, and I seized the opportunity to make a break for it.

I leapt over the fallen files, raced past Agent Kit, and rushed back into the room with all the cells.

The salamanders had left trails of flame zigzagging all across the bunker. The stairway Garabrand had descended was already burning, and one of the salamanders had made its way onto the catwalk above. Screams pierced the air. The prisoners were crying out for help as the fiery amphibians skittered closer to the doors of their cells.

"You see? This is precisely what I've been trying to explain to you!" Garabrand called from behind me. "Power without control is chaos. It's dangerous. Under my control, those creatures served a greater good. Left to their own devices, they cannot help but cause suffering and pain. Their captivity was not a cruelty, Miss Rook, it was a calculated kindness."

"Well, your arithmetic is lousy," I shot back. "Especially if you think all these prisoners are equal to a handful of salamanders. Their lives and freedom were never yours to sacrifice."

"You would like to lecture me about what's best for these people? I'm not the one who set the building they're in on fire!"

A broad swath of the catwalk above us was now in flames, and the rafters were beginning to catch as well. My eyes stung. Thick clouds of dark smoke had begun to collect on the ceiling, glowing with the fire dancing within them. This was not going to end well.

"You can't save them," Garabrand continued, coldly. "But I can." He flipped open his coat to reveal a set of keys hanging from his belt. "Nobody needs to die today."

"Then do it already!" I cried. "Let them out!"

"Surrender first," he said.

I gaped. "Are you seriously holding their lives ransom?"

"I'm not the villain here, but I'm no fool, either," he said. "You're like me—you *will* take advantage of the situation to gain the upper hand, and I can't have that. I don't blame you for your nature. In fact, I respect you for it. But I need it under my control."

"Fine! You have my word. Just open the cells!"

"Your word's not enough. You've learned secrets far above your clearance, and I need those secrets contained. Submit, and I will save the prisoners. Continue to resist, however, and your fiancé and all his friends go up in smoke. The choice is yours."

Agent Kit had emerged from the menagerie just as his partner was delivering his unsavory ultimatum. The halo around his head blanched with sallow swirls of disillusionment. His eyes met mine, and I wondered just how long he had suspected his own partner. How much of that suspicious instinct survived each mental wipe? I still had the spell paper he had slipped to me—he had given me my escape hatch—my one last ray of hope.

A panicked, white-hot salamander darted between Kit's feet and made straight for the prisoners. A roiling aura of fear was pouring out through the bars as smoke and heat filled the room. Kit spotted the scampering creature and looked up at the yowling cells, a defensive impulse thrumming through his aura. He chased after the salamander, stamping out licks of flame as he ran, attempting to stop it. The frantic thing only dodged and skittered faster, headed right toward Charlie.

I gritted my teeth, turning back to Garabrand. "All right!" I yelled. "I won't run any longer. Do what you need to do, just save them."

Garabrand's mouth turned up in a flicker of a smile. "You're making the right choice. No need to look so cross about it. Hold still, now."

He leveled the sprayer at my face. I tensed. The moment Garabrand's finger twitched, I vaulted forward, ducking under the spray and catching him hard in the gut.

My plan—at least the way I had seen it going in my head—was to plant the transportation spell on Garabrand and send him stumbling backward into the fire that was already hungrily devouring the stairway behind him. I would emerge from the scuffle with his keys in my hands, and before the malevolent agent could take aim at me for a second shot with his memory spray, the spell would catch fire and he would be whooshed away into a securely locked facility in the middle of the police station.

I rather think it was a good plan. *Part* of it even worked.

With one hand, I slapped the spell against his side, and with the other I fumbled to unhook the keychain from his belt. What I had not accounted for was Agent Garabrand *not* stumbling backward—not even a little bit. He glared down at me as I fidgeted with the stubborn key ring, the handcuff hanging off my wrist clanking clumsily against his leg.

"Do you mind?" he growled.

With a shove he pushed me away. He tore the spell from his jacket with his free hand and tossed it into the flames. It fizzed and flared before vanishing into sparkling ash.

I cleared my throat awkwardly as I found my footing. "You're—erm—you're very stable on your feet," I said.

"Wide stance," he said. "You should try it." A cool spray of mist caught me full in the face, and the world went fuzzy.

chapter twenty-nine

My memory, as you might expect, is just a little hazy around this next bit. I remember Agent Garabrand's voice echoing in my skull like it was coming to me from the bottom of a deep well, but I couldn't make out what he was saying. My head throbbed.

The last thing I could recall cleanly was going into an old, creepy hospital. Jackaby had been there—and there had been ghosts. I remembered the ghosts.

I opened my eyes. This was not a hospital. The air was hot and dry; it burned my throat and stung my eyes. I blinked. A monster loomed before me, cloaked in rags. How had that thing gotten in here? How had *I* gotten in here? Where was *here*? I shook my head, trying to see the beast more clearly. There were fangs and horns and wicked claws, but something about it felt all wrong. I focused, straining to see through the haze. All at once, the creature snarled and pounced. I was sure to be torn to shreds—but in a flash, Agent Garabrand was between us.

"Get back!" he called. His voice—like all of the noises in this place—was muffled and distant.

I felt a swell of gratitude as the man bore the brunt of the monster's attack. Claws tore and teeth gnashed—but still, something felt terribly off. The room tipped and I could feel my heartbeat pounding against my temples.

"Come on, Detective," Garabrand was saying urgently. I looked up. The beast lay still on the ground. Garabrand had defeated it—I was sure of that—but *how* had he defeated it? Was it *dead*? The ragged body looked dull and ashen and . . . *wrong*. I shook my head.

"Quickly, now," Garabrand urged. "That monster's venom really did a number on you, but there's no time to dawdle." He held out a set of keys, and I took them numbly. The agent's hands were ashen as well—not gray, exactly—but *wrong*. The keys, on the other hand, glowed like gold in my hands. I had wanted these keys . . . desperately needed them . . . but why?

The world, which had felt muted and dull, suddenly exploded in a spray of colors and noise all around me—acrid smoke, crackling fire, and vibrant auras. My ears were ringing as if I had stuck my head inside a church bell. I struggled to catch my breath.

"Well?" Garabrand was saying. "Are you with me? Can you remember what happened?"

I closed my eyes, trying to recall. "The beast. We tracked it back to its lair. I . . . I got in over my head. It used some sort of poison to try to turn us against each other—but you . . . you saved me."

"That's right." Garabrand nodded.

The air around me was hot and smoky. I glanced around. Agent Kit was across the room, stamping at a flame that danced dangerously close to the bars of a door. Was this a prison? Had the monster set this fire? I heard cries coming from the rows of cells that lined the wall. Had we found the kidnapped victims? The flames crackled all around us.

"Good lord," I breathed. "We need to help them!"

Garabrand caught my shoulder before I could join Agent Kit in the effort. He was holding a brown-tinted bottle filled with a dark liquid. It had a nozzle at the top like a soda siphon and an aura like burnt lime. Some sort of fire repellent? "Glad you're with us again," he said. "But we're not finished here yet."

I glanced back. The beast's body was gone. Had it awoken and fled? Crumbled to ashes? What sort of creature had it been, precisely? Thinking about it hurt, like a splinter in the corner of my mind.

My head throbbed. My arm felt heavy, and I glanced

down to see a cuff shackled around my wrist, the other end dangling loose on a sturdy chain. I opened my fist to look at the set of keys—I had been clutching them so tightly they had left deep imprints in my palm. Garabrand had given these to me. *Wrong.* The room spun slightly, and the ringing in my ears got louder.

Thinking about Agent Garabrand handing me the keys made me feel as if I were trying to look at a painting with my eyes crossed. His hand had been reaching toward mine—his complexion strangely muted—the keys had been glowing golden in his fingers . . . but at the same time, there had been no hand.

"Maybe you should give those back," Garabrand said. "Just until the confusion wears off."

He reached out, but I withdrew before he could take them. "Auras," I mumbled.

"What was that?" said Garabrand.

"When I see auras—what I'm seeing is the truth. That's what Jackaby taught me."

"Yes, fine. I've read your file."

"Your hand, in my memory. It had no aura," I said. "There was no truth to it. Y-you didn't give me these keys, did you?" I scowled. "No. Of course you didn't. I didn't need you to. I took them for myself."

From one of the cells behind me, a child screamed. The high ceiling was rapidly filling with acrid smoke. I rubbed my eyes. Why were we talking about keys?

"You're still confused," said Garabrand, suddenly terse. "Do you remember the beast? The venom?"

I squinted. Garabrand's words were all carefully chosen, but I could see manipulation lurking in the corners of his honesty. He was lying without lying.

The ringing in my ears was finally subsiding as I peeled the illusion away. "The monster never existed. There was no truth to it—no aura to remember." I tried hard to push my thoughts past the fog. It was as if my memories had been painted over, but their auras kept seeping through to the top. "Tell me the truth," I said. "There was no mysterious beast, was there?"

"As I said," Garabrand tried again, "you're confused."

"I *am* confused," I said. "But I'm beginning to think the only monster to blame for that confusion is *you*."

Garabrand pursed his lips and took a deep breath. "This is an unfortunate development," he said. "I had very much hoped you would be of use to our organization—but a fire that can't be controlled needs to be put out."

I expected him to raise the sinister-looking bottle—but he let the thing hang loosely from one hand. With his other, he drew a pistol from his side holster. He took a deep breath. "I take no joy in this, but I'm afraid you've made it necessary." His thumb drew back the hammer. My breath caught in my throat.

And then—in a flash of fangs and claws—a mysterious beast really did tackle Agent Garabrand.

I blinked several times, shaking my head. I looked down at the monster that had attacked me and realized it wasn't a monster at all. Rags turned to soft tufts of brown fur, and soon the "creature" stood up on all fours. It was a massive hound. "Charlie!" I gasped.

Charlie padded away from the fallen agent. When he reached my side, he paused and glanced back, velvety ears pricking up.

Agent Garabrand lay on his stomach and moaned weakly. He shifted, grunted, and pushed himself up with what looked like tremendous effort. There was a tinkling sound like soft chimes playing as he rolled himself over to a seated position. He swayed unsteadily, and a haze like burning lime rose up around him.

What was left of the agent's glass bottle clung to the siphon head in jagged shards or else sparkled across the wet cement. Garabrand's eyes crossed and uncrossed, and his head bobbed up and down.

"Hey!" yelled a voice behind me. I turned. Grim had her face pushed against the bars of a cell door as ash trickled down from the ceiling above her. Agent Kit had removed his jacket and was slapping back flames near her as best he could. Prisoners all along the wall were pressing themselves against the back of their cells to escape the heat.

"You gonna stand around," Grim demanded, "or are you going to get us out of here?"

"Good work." I ruffled the fur on Charlie's head. "Go

get changed." I unlocked the shackle around my wrist as I raced toward the cells. It took me only a moment to identify the correct key and reach the barred doors. Grim burst out the moment hers clicked open.

"We need to work faster," Agent Kit coughed, abandoning his smoldering jacket to the fire.

"I'll get the rest of them out," I said. "You find us an exit."

He nodded and dashed toward the stairs as I continued down the line as quickly as I could. Grim had already raced ahead of me, desperately peering into each enclosure until she found her mother. When she did, she let out a gasp. Fingers reached through the bars to hold on to her tiny hands.

I made my way down the line as quickly as I could, the smoke and heat increasing by the moment. Grim threw her arms around her mother the second the door was open, burying her face in the woman's chest. Their auras wove into each other until it became hard to tell one from the other. There was no question that Mary Horne was the girl's mother.

Agent Kit had been so certain that she couldn't be. But Kit had been certain about a lot of things that turned out to be wrong. I didn't envy him the dizziness of constantly stumbling back and forth between the truth and the manufactured fantasy he was being fed. I shook my head, still feeling a bit blurry around the edges myself.

When she pulled away, Grim wiped her damp face with

the back of her arm and clung to her mother's hand. All around, freed prisoners were staggering out of confinement and into the haze of the burning bunker.

"Now what?" Charlie said as he rejoined me in human form.

"Up here!" called Agent Kit. "There's an exit this way!"

We rushed the prisoners up the stairs, my lungs burning and my eyes watering. My chest felt like it might burst as we finally tumbled into the open. I gulped fresh air, panting heavily. But I couldn't stop yet. As the last of the prisoners escaped to the surface, I took one more deep breath and went back inside for Garabrand. He was still sitting where we had left him, although the ground around him appeared to have dried. His entire aura was saturated with the burnt lime tint of his glawackus extract.

"Mr. Garabrand?" I coughed. "There's a fire. We need to go."

"Mm?" His head lolled to one side as he attempted to focus on my face.

"Come on," I urged. "We need to get out of here."

"Am I going to be late?" he murmured, trying unsuccessfully to stand.

"You're going to be *the late Mr. Garabrand* if we don't get moving. Come on, then, take my hand." I helped him to his feet, glass tinkling to the ground as he stood.

"Can't be late," mumbled Garabrand. "School in the morning. I didn't study."

"Is he going to be all right?" Agent Kit asked as I reemerged.

"Honestly?" I said, letting Garabrand slump down to the ground at the base of a tree. "I have no idea."

Kit ground his teeth, his aura churning. With a sudden pulse of determination, he rushed back into the smoky building.

"What are you doing?" I called after him. "Everyone's already out!"

"Not everyone," Kit called back.

I looked at Charlie, who shrugged.

We watched the doorway where Kit had vanished. Thirty seconds passed, then a minute. Something in the rafters gave out and the roof sagged abruptly. The smoke was now billowing into the sky like a terrible, phantom tower.

As we watched the bunker, the air began to buzz, and a swarm of winged creatures burst through the entry and took to the skies. Brownies, pixies, and a single, glowing wisp shot past us and into the surrounding forest. Soon after came the skittering of paws and claws as more creatures fled the burning building. A jackrabbit with tiny antlers bounded over the threshold, followed by what appeared to be a frantic mongoose, and then, at last, came Agent Kit.

He emerged slowly, dragging something behind him. Charlie and I hastened to help, and together we hauled the barely breathing glawackus out of the bunker.

Once we were far enough back, Kit flopped to the ground next to his moony partner, coughing and wheezing.

"What were all those things?" Agent Garabrand asked, his eyes wide like a schoolboy at a magic show.

"That," I answered coldly, "is classified. All you need to know is that they're safe and free, thanks to Agent Kit."

"That was a very brave thing you did," Charlie told him.

"That's my job," Kit said, but then he shook his head. "At least, I thought it was."

The fire crackled away in front of us. It was a minor miracle that it didn't spread to the surrounding landscape. The walls of the old bunker were thick and sturdy, so the whole thing looked rather like an enormous chimney sticking out of the ground, chuffing away.

From a knotty old tree across the path from where we stood, a slim forest spirit poked its head out to watch the fire burn. I was not yet an expert on the auras of nature spirits, but it seemed to be thoroughly enjoying the spectacle.

chapter thirty

Within the hour, the smoke and commotion had attracted enough attention to summon a healthy crowd of gawking neighbors, a fire brigade, and, finally, the police. When he arrived, Inspector Dupin was more than happy to be the one to personally process Agent Garabrand. It may have taken some of the joy out of the situation for him to find out that the underhanded agent could no longer remember anything about the kidnappings, nor even a single moment of his time in the Bureau of Curiosities, but Dupin cuffed him anyway and loaded him into a police wagon. Garabrand swam in and out of lucidity, but for the most part he seemed to believe he was roughly nine years old. He didn't appear to be as bothered about the handcuffs or the accusations of kidnapping and murder as he did about making sure the inspector did not tell his mother.

Officers were dispatched to provide escorts to the newly freed prisoners. A few of them seemed grateful for protection and a carriage ride back to their worried loved ones. Many declined, however, preferring not to have anything to do with men in badges, and opting instead to find their own way home.

The crowd finally thinned as the last of the fire was contained. I found Commissioner Marlowe had made a personal appearance to survey the wreckage.

"Miss Rook," he said.

"Commissioner." I nodded.

He looked out over the steaming ruins of the military compound. "You do know that it's possible to work a case without destroying a building, right?"

"I like to be thorough."

He shook his head with a sigh, then nodded toward Agent Kit. "Should he be in lockup?" Kit sat slouched against a mossy stump, looking defeated.

"I don't believe so," I said. "He wants to help make things right."

"Well, he can start by giving me the grand tour and the full story. You can come, too, and fill in any blanks."

Marlowe snapped his fingers and gestured to Kit, who

pushed himself up. I followed the two of them back over the sooty threshold and into what was left of the old barracks. The cells where Charlie and the rest of the prisoners had been held were all black with smoke damage, and the roof overhead had crumbled away, allowing the early-morning light to trickle through the ashy air.

Agent Kit did his best to explain everything as he walked the commissioner through the wreckage. His story began with a rather unlikely talking dolphin, but it picked up strong after his uncomfortable realization that Agent Garabrand had been erasing his memory. He had suspected foul play for some time, and had taken to leaving himself notes and subtle clues in his own reports, even omitting details to keep Garabrand from pursuing victims' families. It was almost certainly this practice that had kept Grim out of Garabrand's sights for so long—right up until the girl had risked it all trying to warn me. Kit's recollection was full of holes, but he had gradually left himself all the pieces of the puzzle.

I did what I could to complete the narrative where Kit could not. My own memory was still knitting itself back together—and in the end, we sorted out the story as best we could.

When we were done, Marlowe left us alone to go find a couple of officers to sift through the ashes and collect any evidence that hadn't been incinerated.

The battered cages and terrariums lay where Kit had

upended them as he was rescuing the supernatural creatures. I wondered briefly what had become of the hulking glawackus, but I was finding it harder and harder to form a clear picture of the beast in my mind. Around the corner, I found Agent Kit shuffling through debris alone in what was left of the records room.

"I can't say I was terribly sad to see all of those files go up in smoke," I told him. "People have a right to their privacy."

Kit nodded, solemnly. "I helped fill out a lot of these files. We had dossiers on all sorts of people in town—paranormals, civil leaders, political figures. An individual of ill intent could do a lot of damage with that kind of information. I trusted the bureau to keep it out of the wrong hands. I had no idea that our hands *were* the wrong hands."

"For the best that it's all gone, then."

"Not all of it," he said. His aura weighed heavily on his shoulders, and he nodded to a soot-blackened metal box in front of him. He flipped it open with an ash-gray hand. "Lockbox survived the blaze. I got it open a few minutes ago. I'm guessing it was the stuff that even I wasn't supposed to see. It's got all of Garabrand's notes on something called *Operation Aperture*."

"His plans for securing the veil-gate?"

"I always knew that was the end goal." Kit sighed. "It made sense. I just didn't bother asking about *how* we were getting there."

"Does it mention the kidnappings?" I asked.

"Documentation would go a long way toward neatly closing this case."

"More than that," he confirmed. "Garabrand might not be able to remember much right now, but this box is about the most damning confession you could ask for. I think it might also be the exoneration your friend needs." He pulled a set of papers out and passed them to me.

"Alina?"

Kit nodded. "She got a heavy dose of that spray and then he fed her some false memory about needing to defend herself. Apparently she resisted the first few times. Her instincts weren't as violent as he expected—but he kept at it until he got the result he needed. The bastard wrote it all down. The outburst only lasted a few moments before your girl snapped out of it and her own natural instincts kicked in. But a few moments was enough. Alina Cane spent the last few seconds of D'Aulaire's life trying desperately to save her. She couldn't stop the bleeding. Sounds like she was pretty distraught. Garabrand had to dose her again before he sent her stumbling home."

I let my eyes pore over the document. It was just as Kit said—although the cold, apathetic record of the horrible ordeal made my stomach turn.

"I was supposed to be catching monsters," breathed Kit. "Turns out I was one of them."

"You're not a monster," I said, tucking the papers carefully back into the box. I sighed. "I think convincing ourselves that we're on the side of good—or that our enemies are bad—is what lets the real monsters come out. Life would be a lot easier if things were black and white, but we *all* have the potential to do wicked, terrible things. Garabrand was absolute in his convictions. That was the problem. He never questioned himself."

"I liked that about him," Kit admitted. "I question myself all the time. It was nice that Garabrand had answers."

We stood in silence for a moment.

"He was the one who recruited me," Kit said at last. "I liked having somebody see something in me—not that I ever understood what it was. Now I know he just needed someone with rotten judgment and a moral compass that never pointed due north."

"I don't think that's true," I said.

He raised an eyebrow at me.

"Garabrand erased your memory loads of times. He planted thoughts in your mind, manipulated you to trust him, twisted your perception to keep you loyal to the bureau. You had every reason to keep following his lead, but you kept turning against him. You knew in your heart what he was doing was wrong. It sounds to me as though your moral compass was working just fine."

Kit considered this. His aura remained cloudy, but it gradually lightened a few shades. "Maybe," he conceded. "Still, I have no idea what I'm supposed to do next. I can't go back to the Bureau of Curiosities, obviously. And it turns out that my résumé for the past few years basically just reads *evil henchman*."

"You saved those animals," I said. "At considerable risk to your own life. Nobody told you to do that. That doesn't sound like an evil henchman to me."

He shrugged. "They didn't deserve to die."

"Do you know what they were?" I asked. "Their species and abilities?"

"Most of them," he said. "Basic bureau training."

"Hmm." I leaned back against the wall and gazed up through the burnt-out roof at the sky. A pair of birds flitted from branch to branch above us. "I happen to know that Dupin's Paranormal Division is short-staffed," I said. "For that matter, the city doesn't have anyone remotely qualified to manage supernatural animal control. It would be a dangerous job. Foolhardy, even. But the person who stepped up would be in a position to do a lot of good. Especially if it was someone with a working knowledge of the supernatural and a solid moral compass—the sort of person who would want to protect the innocent, even if the innocent were wild and strange."

Kit was quiet. His aura spun with a kaleidoscope of sallow doubts, glimmering hope, and bitter gray regrets. At length, he heaved a sigh and nodded. "I'll think about it."

We made our way out of the debris, whereupon I found that Miss Lee had arrived with the carriage. "You're certainly a welcome sight," I said. "Did Mr. Jackaby send you to fetch me?" I asked.

Miss Lee rolled her eyes. "I saw a parade of emergency vehicles heading toward an enormous column of smoke," she said. "I just assumed you would be at the end of it."

"Rude," I said. "But not wrong, obviously."

"I got your sweetheart tucked in the back already," she added. "Sounds like you two had a long night. He's ready to go home as soon as you are."

"Home sounds lovely," I said. "Thank you, Miss Lee."

Charlie glanced up as I climbed into the carriage. He had dark circles under his eyes, and he looked as if he hadn't slept properly in days, but his whole heart glowed like a bonfire when he saw my face, and his lips spread into a wide smile. I slid into the seat beside him, and he wrapped his arms around me for the first time in days.

"That was frightfully rude of you to rescue *me* down there," I said, melting into his warmth, "right when I was supposed to be rescuing *you*. How did you get out of your cell, anyway? You never said."

"Coaxed a salamander into the lock," he answered. "Melted the mechanism."

"Mmm. That's okay, then." I leaned my head on his shoulder. "I freed the salamanders, so I still get credit." The carriage trundled into motion, and soon we were rolling down a winding road. "Are you all right?" I asked.

He took a deep breath. "No," he finally answered, truthfully. "I'm exhausted. I'm overwhelmed. Very soon, I'm going to need to confront a lot of people who seem like they would be just as happy to see me dead. And even sooner"—he made a show of shivering in mock horror—"I'm going to need to face your parents again."

I smiled in spite of myself and he gave me a squeeze. "Fair," I said. I rested a hand against his chest, feeling his lungs rise and fall. "I like that."

"Me meeting with your parents?" he asked.

"You being honest with me. Even if everything you're being honest about is wretched."

Charlie nodded and brushed his hand through my hair. "I like being honest with you," he said. "What about you? Are you all right?"

I considered. "I . . . I think I am, actually," I said, surprising myself to realize that, for once, it was true. I had taken on a real case and solved it without needing Jackaby by my side at the end. The stress and turmoil would flood over me again soon enough—but for now, I had Charlie back. For the first time in weeks, we were alone, just the two of us. For this fleeting moment, there were no mysteries, no politics—just a gentle carriage ride through the quiet, misty morning streets of New Fiddleham.

chapter thirty-one

The ride home with Charlie was as peaceful and pleasant as the subsequent conversation with my parents was not.

"So you lied to us?" My mother's aura was less angry than it was hurt, which somehow made the whole thing even worse. My father stood just behind her with his arms crossed. I had sent Charlie upstairs without me, but this long-overdue conversation was something I needed to face on my own.

"Yes," I said. "I did lie to you. And I'm sorry. I should have told you about my work and about Charlie and everything. But to be perfectly frank—why *would* I?"

"Wh-why?" she stammered.

"Because we are your parents!" my father said.

"No, that's the reason I *wouldn't*," I said. "I spent my entire childhood pretending to be the daughter you wanted me to be—or else getting scolded and scorned for being anything else. You made it abundantly clear that being myself was second to being acceptable."

"Abigail," my father said. "That's hardly fair."

"I couldn't agree more," I said. "If you want me to trust you, then you don't simply get to demand it. You need to show me that I can—that I'm safe to be open with you. This place might not be as posh and polished as our house in Portsmouth, but Mr. Jackaby has always made it clear that I could be myself under this roof—in fact, he rather insists on it—and Jenny has been nothing but supportive from the start. We've seen one another at our worst, and instead of turning away from all that, we've been there to catch each other when we needed it most. And Charlie . . . Charlie doesn't just accept me as I am, he *loves* me for it. He *believes* in me in ways that lift me up and make me believe in myself."

My mother looked as if she were about to cry. "*I* love you," she breathed. And her aura glowed rose red with trembling sincerity. "I've always loved you."

"I know, Mother," I said, losing steam. "I love you, too. But I think you love the version of me that you could stuff into Sunday school dresses and bribe with lollies. It's not enough to love the person I *was*. I need to know you're open to loving me *now*—and loving whoever I'm going to be."

The room was awkwardly silent for a few moments.

"When you were only a toddler," my father finally said, "you couldn't say *pudding* properly."

My mother laughed and cried in one wet burst.

"You remember that, Bea?" He chuckled. "You would say *poob-bie*, just like that, with your tiny lips flapping. It almost broke my heart when you learned to say *pudding* properly. But do you know what you learned to say that very same year? *Iguanodon*. I was so proud. By third year, you were the only one in your class who could identify an *archaeopteryx*. I will always miss my baby girl reaching for a bowl, yelling *poob-bie*! But not nearly as much as I am excited to see what she does next."

My eyes felt watery, and my throat tightened up.

My father put his hands on my shoulders and kissed my head. "We've always been proud of you, Abisaurus," he said, his aura swelling to agree. "I might not understand this world you've made for yourself. It seems a bit rubbish, if we're insisting on being perfectly frank—but if it's your world, then I still want to be a part of it."

My mother sniffled and nodded. "We *both* do."

"Don't get me wrong," my father continued. "We have enjoyed reading about our young lady in the periodicals, but I for one would rather get a direct post from time to time. And if she insists on falling for some strange, foreign chap she met in the States—well, I might not understand *him*, either, but I don't want my baby to get married without her father walking her down the aisle."

I raised an eyebrow. "Did this just turn into you giving us your blessing?"

He shrugged. "No boy will *ever* be good enough for my sweet girl. You could tie the knot with a crown prince and you would still be marrying beneath yourself." He gave my chin a gentle nudge with his knuckle. "But from what I saw the other night, you could do a lot worse than Charlie Barker. I like how he bristles and stands up for you." He shot me a wink and lowered his voice. "Even against your mother, the daft fool. Anyway, you can't go waiting for *me* to fall in love with him. That's *your* job."

"He's no Tommy Bellows . . ." my mother put in.

"Tommy Bellows is an absolute onion," I said.

My mother held up her hand and continued. ". . . but I must agree that he seems like a decent lad. And he makes you happy—which matters more than silly titles." I could tell that last statement pained her, but I chose to appreciate it all the more. "We won't force you to come home," she said, "if this is what you want."

"We just don't want to lose you," my father added, gently.

"I don't want to lose you, either," I said. "I promise I'll write. And you'll be the first to know when we've settled on a date for the wedding."

"We could stay until then," my mother said. "If you'd like."

"Oh." The relief I had been feeling suddenly tightened into a knot again. "Really? You don't think it's a bit . . . uncomfortable up in the spare room?"

"Oh, good lord—we won't be staying *here* another night," she blurted out.

"There's an odor in that room," my father said.

"And strange lights at night," my mother added.

"And a horrifying china doll in the corner. I keep turning her to face the wall, but every morning she ends up pointed toward us again." My father shuddered involuntarily.

"We've already booked a room at a nice inn near the shore," she concluded. "Only temporary, until we can make proper plans to . . . to go home."

My mother suddenly lurched forward and wrapped me up in a hug. I tensed at first. She had always been tender in her own way, but she had never been one for affectionate embraces. Her breath caught in little hiccuping bursts. I returned her embrace, leaning into the hug.

"I always want you to be honest with me," she managed, sniffing.

"It's all right, Mother," I said. "I just needed to feel safe before I could be open." I blinked, raising my head. A spark of an idea was flickering to life in my mind.

My mother straightened, wiping her eyes. "Mm? What is it?"

I gave her a kiss on the cheek. "I love you. We'll talk more about—well, everything—soon, I promise. But I've just had a thought and I've got to go."

I found Jackaby tying sprigs of sage into tidy little bundles as I burst into his study. "How large can a dome of confidence be?" I asked without preamble.

"Sorry. What?"

"A dome of confidence. We discovered one when we were investigating the Finkins' house. They protect people from sharing secrets outside of a magic circle, right? So how large can the circle be?"

Jackaby shrugged. "They can get pretty large. A room could be encircled. Even a whole house, although a dome that big would take more time and effort to secure it. It would all depend on how many enchanters you could devote to the task at once."

"Could a dome encircle an entire city?"

Jackaby's brow slowly creased as he considered the question. "Why?"

Mayor Spade steepled his fingers at the head of the wide oak table. "I'm not sure I understand," he said.

Sunlight poured in through the tall windows of the conference room in city hall. Commissioner Marlowe sat beside the mayor, scowling in thought. Farther down the table, Charlie and Jackaby perched on the chairs to either side of me.

"Those Humans First people insist that the problem is paranormals living in secret among us," I explained, "but if the paranormal community is ever going to live openly, they first need to know that they are safe and that their neighbors support them. We can't force people to trust one another, but we *can* come at it from the opposite direction. We have to create a situation that lets people know that they *will* be safe if and when they decide to live openly."

"And that's what this dome thing would do?"

I nodded. "By creating a citywide dome of confidence, we could turn New Fiddleham into a sort of magical sanctuary. Everyone within our borders would be part of a shared confidence, and the identities of our most vulnerable citizens would no longer be shared with anyone outside our city limits, including unscrupulous federal organizations. Someone like Garabrand could sneak in and fill out all the assessments he liked—but the documents would turn to gibberish as soon as they moved outside of our border."

"People would still have free will," Charlie said. "It wouldn't force anyone to love their neighbors or anything like that. It would just mean that supernatural citizens would have one less thing to worry about, and that might encourage more of us to show our true colors without shame or fear."

"Supernatural folk showing their colors has not exactly done wonders for the city thus far," Spade said. "Seems like every time one of them does, it's a whole new problem."

"Only because we've made being part of a magical community a crime," Jackaby snapped. "But if we take all of the stigma and terror out of it—just allow magic to coexist with the mundane—then gradually the paranormal becomes the normal. Neighbors could finally get to know their neighbors."

"And that's a good thing?" Spade countered.

"Maybe," I said. "It would be a grand experiment."

Marlowe pursed his lips. "Would the spell be dangerous?"

I turned to Jackaby. "I don't believe so," he said. "I asked around among the occult community. Apparently the worst that happens when this sort of spell falls apart is that it stops working. I couldn't find any known instances of supernatural side effects or snapbacks. It appears to be a fairly low-level enchantment—we would just be performing it on a much larger scale."

"There are more than enough capable magic users in New Fiddleham to do it," Charlie volunteered, "and many of them have even more experienced family members across the veil who would be willing to assist with the process. After it is set up, it would require routine maintenance, but we've asked the experts, and it all sounds feasible."

The mayor nodded soberly. "I just don't know."

"Don't look at me," grunted Marlowe.

"It's not our job to know," I said. "This is *our* city—*all* of ours. Not one group's or another's. We will need to put it to a vote and let the people decide."

Nearly two months passed before all the necessary paperwork had been filed, the ballots had all been drawn up, and the announcements had been made. Factions within the Humans First campaign seemed to be at odds about whether they were for or against the proposal, and I ran into at least three contradictory flyers in one walk. There was an electric crackle in the air, the unspoken portent of an upcoming crossroads—but in spite of this swelling energy, the chaos and conflict in streets seemed, for the moment, to have ebbed. There were the occasional flare-ups of scuffles in line for the ballot boxes, but even the crowds gathering in front of city hall seemed oddly muted as they awaited the results. New Fiddleham was holding its breath.

"They're completing the tally now," Marlowe said, stepping out to meet us on the city hall balcony. "Shouldn't be much longer."

I nodded.

"I met with the widow Finkin yesterday," he added solemnly, gripping the railing and looking out over the street. "She was granted a special exemption to scatter her late husband's ashes on the other side of the veil. Said he would've wanted to make it over eventually."

"That's a kind gesture," I said.

"It's not much, given what she's been through." He shrugged. "Speaking of going it alone, where's that mentor of yours?"

"Jackaby promised Jenny he would stay with her so that they could hear the news together. If the motion passes and people grow more accustomed to the supernatural, then a ghost appearing in public would become a much more viable option—if she wanted to." Even thinking about it had made it harder for Jenny to maintain her form at all, but I didn't feel the need to share that detail. "I told them that I would bring word, one way or another, as soon as I knew."

"How about Charlie?"

"He wanted to be here," I said, "but his sister needs him more than I do right now. I insisted."

"Alina? Really?" Marlowe glanced my way. "She doesn't strike me as the type to need anyone. Seemed perfectly composed at her acquittal. Leadership suits her. Charlie, too."

I smiled and shook my head. "I'm learning that being a good leader isn't about *not* needing help," I said. "It's about being there for others, and letting them be there for you, too."

Marlowe nodded, turning his eyes back out over the city. We stood in silence for a while.

In the streets below us, men and women milled about, many carrying handwritten signs extolling the virtues or the perils of the dome of confidence. Rock-Jaw the not-actually-a-troll was occupying a large swath of sidewalk, wearing a huge sandwich board in favor of the initiative.

"Are you going to be upset," Marlowe asked, "if the city *doesn't* want to turn itself into a magical sanctuary?"

"At least the paranormal community would know where it stands," I answered. I glanced up at him. "What about you? Do *you* want the proposal to pass?"

Marlowe took a deep breath and scratched the stubble on his chin. "If it does," he said, "New Fiddleham will never be the same."

"I don't think that was ever an option."

"Fair," he grunted.

I watched him for a moment. "You're not fond of magic."

"I'm not fond of *messy*," he corrected. He looked over the railing for a moment at the crowds gathered in the street below. "I saw the numbers in that lockbox you uncovered. If the Bureau of Curiosities' estimates are even close to accurate, this city is hiding a lot more magic than any of us realized. We've barely been keeping up with just a fraction of what's out there. Can you imagine what it will be like if this place suddenly becomes a supernatural safe haven? If all of those secrets start tumbling out into the open?"

There was noise from behind the broad double doors, and he straightened. It sounded as if the ballot committee was preparing to emerge.

"I don't hate paranormals," he added, more quietly.

"They're part of this city as much as anyone else is. I just know that we're tugging at the lid of one hell of a Pandora's box, that's all."

The doors swung wide and Mayor Spade stood before us, holding a single piece of paper in his hands. From the harrowed look on his face and the anxious waves pouring off his aura, it was clear that the vote had been very close—but it was also clear just which way it had landed in the end. New Fiddleham was about to get a lot more interesting.

"Here we go," mouthed Mayor Spade as he made his way toward the podium in the town square.

Marlowe drew a long, slow breath.

"Don't forget what was in the bottom of that box Pandora opened," I whispered.

He raised an eyebrow.

"*Hope*," I said. "Let's keep an eye out for that one when the lid comes off, shall we?"

ACKNOWLEDGMENTS

A decade ago, I had a silly idea for a story about a detective who could see magical creatures. As with all the wildest ideas I've concocted, I came up with this one to make my wife smile. (You would come up with wild ideas too, if she was your wife. It's a very good smile.) The only reason the silly idea grew into a complete story—and that story into a novel and that novel into a series—is that this brilliant, razor-sharp woman (whom I constantly want to impress) kept asking me the same question: *What happens next?*

None of my novels would exist without Katrina. This book in particular would not exist without Katrina. She was quite insistent that it must, and so it does. I would give that woman the whole wide world if I could, but I trust that she will settle for New Fiddleham . . . and for an answer: *This. This is what happens next.* I hope it makes you smile.

READ ABIGAIL ROOK'S ADVENTURES

AS JACKABY'S ASSISTANT IN

the Jackaby series: